THE CHRONICLES OF EARTH

ALSO BY CL JARVIS

The Edinburgh Doctrines series

The Doctrines of Fire

A Treatise of Air

The Chronicles of Earth

THE CHRONICLES OF EARTH
THE EDINBURGH DOCTRINES
BOOK THREE

CL JARVIS

PEWTER LYNX PRESS

First published in 2024 by Pewter Lynx Press

ISBN 978-1-7392644-7-5

To OD and PT.
For showing my words could have power.

PROLOGUE
EDINBURGH—7TH OF MARCH 1785

The murmurs quelled as Dr Joseph Black approached the lectern at the front of the university library. Though dressed in his customary black, the chemistry professor had swapped his wool coat for a more fashionable and fitting double-breasted linen frockcoat. His sleeve cuffs were crisper, wider and more pronounced than his usual lecturing garb.

For a moment, the only sound that could be heard was the crinkling of papers in his hand. Fifty members of the Royal Society in Edinburgh collectively held their breath.

Behind Black, the oil lamps fluttered and sighed.

* * *

Two hours earlier, Black and William Cullen were engaged in a furious row, one that caused Black's servants to flee to the cellars and George Stephens—convalescing in his professor's upstairs guest bedchamber—to cover his ears in the cowardly hope he wouldn't hear what was going on and thus the argument would cease to exist.

"Your friend will die if you do this, Joe." The Professor of the Practice of Physic's West coast burr cracked and splintered.

"No, he won't."

"You can't say that with such assurance."

"He's too valuable to be killed." Black's baritone voice rose half an octave. "They need him as a bargaining chip."

Cullen's fist pounded the dining room table.

"You are recklessly endangering another man's life, and a retaliatory murder is exactly the kind of spiteful act our enemy will perform."

"James would say the risk is worth taking." Black's voice was forceful. "You know that as well as I do."

"That doesn't mean you should. How would you cope with his death on your hands?"

"Enough, William!" Another smack on the table, loud enough to rattle china and silverware. "I am going to do it. Precisely because James is my friend and his life is in danger. He would do the same if our situations were reversed."

George wondered if he should get out of bed, stumble downstairs, and try to intervene. He wasn't sure his legs—or heart—could manage it. His shoulder injury remained a dull, aching throb.

There was a terrible silence, even worse than the shouting. George burrowed further under the blanket.

"Do you intend to stop me?" Black asked with chilling coldness.

Was George imagining the scent of phlogiston building up in the room? A metallic taste under his tongue? He must be. The two physicians were too far away for any phlogiston they generated to reach him. If it did, it meant everything in the dining room was close to incineration.

Another awful, drawn-out silence.

"No, Joe." Cullen's voice was equally cold. "I shan't try to stop you."

George hated himself for his cowardice: acting like a scared infant, hiding in here. He needed—belatedly—to be brave. He swung his legs onto the floor. Keeping upright was a challenge. Dizziness plagued him, and grey swirls persisted across his vision as he stumbled into the corridor. He half slumped, half crawled down the stairs, clutching onto the walls for support. Too risky using the barristers: he could easily topple over them in his current state.

Until this point, it had never occurred to him that his beloved professors could use their powers against each other in anger.

"I'll come with you to the Royal Society..." George said as he crashed through the dining room doorway. He moved too fast and dizziness almost claimed him. But he felt two arms steady and haul him up.

"I'll come with you to the Royal Society as protection." George tried again, since he'd rushed so fast to get the words out the first time he doubted he'd been heard. "I'm considerably better than I was two hours ago, and I'll be even stronger in two hours' time." He wasn't sure if Black or Cullen was the one holding him up, the grey swirls were too frenetic, and he didn't want to look too closely at the arguing professors.

"Hmm, we'll feed you some broth and see how you're doing in a few hours," Cullen said, his voice arriving from afar. "If you promise to rest until then."

* * *

Sitting near the back of the library clutching his arm, George watched his former teacher ascend to the lectern amidst polite applause. The fifty gentlemen present were too tense to make much noise. George felt the tension too, but despite everything that had happened over the past few days it was mixed with excitement: it had been years since he heard Black deliver oration.

If Black shared the audience's apprehension he did not show it. His posture and manner were the same cool elegance of the chemistry lecture hall. George dared not look at Cullen, lest he see more proof of the earlier argument. Black placed his papers on the lectern then stepped off to the side, so the audience had a full view of his graceful form.

"Good evening, gentlemen." Black began. His voice was deep and low, flowing to the back of the room like evening tide rushing across the sand dunes. "It gives me great pleasure to read this scientific paper on behalf of my friend Dr James Hutton, who cannot be here tonight, concerning the system of the Earth, its duration and stability."

His dark eyebrows rose as punctuation. A single idle twirl of his reading spectacles in his hand signalled his dive into the meat of the lecture. "The purpose of this dissertation is to form some estimate with regard to the time this Earth has existed. The result of our present enquiry is that we find no vestige of a beginning, and no prospect of an end..."

By then, forty-eight hours had passed since Hutton was kidnapped.

I

ONE WEEK EARLIER

The house George and Black approached was nestled below Salisbury Crags on the modest slopes of John's Hill: a small colony taking root outside the protective barrier of the Flodden Wall, where few Edinburgh citizens dared venture.

It wasn't clear what prompted its owner, Dr James Hutton, to situate himself aloof on the town's outskirts, since his gregariousness drove him into town most evenings for one gathering or another.

They arrived for dinner just ahead of the sunset, which relieved George. It meant the city was moving out of winter, and he could begin thinking about spring. Summer itself was a terrifying thought, but spring was comforting.

Black knocked on the door.

"That yourself, Joseph?" called someone inside.

"The very same," Black replied, opening the door and stepping through.

Hutton was waiting in the hallway—perhaps he'd seen the pair ascend the hill—and rushed forward to greet them. He was a man of unremarkable appearance: balding, with tufts of short sandy hair. His customary rust-brown suit existed in a state between rumpled and dishevelled. During the early stages of their acquaintance, George assumed Hutton only owned one suit—he was always dressed so—but after overhearing a chance remark about tailors he realised Hutton owned several identical suits.

"The guid Mr Stephens," Hutton enthused, not letting go of George's hand. "How are you doing, sir?" He was inches away from George, who couldn't avoid Hutton's usual odour of musty linen, soil, and sweat.

"Never better," George managed. As if realising he was too close, Hutton took a gigantic step backwards, clapping his hands.

"Well, that's excellent. Please, we'll go directly to the parlour."

Hutton disappeared into the recess of the house, humming a tune George couldn't place.

Hutton's formal rooms all sat disused for years on end, acting as storage space for Hutton's rocks, chemical jars and piecemeal laboratory equipment. The dining room was the only downstairs space that saw visitors, and there was barely enough space amidst the clutter for the furniture. Half the table remained strewn with tea-stained maps of the Highlands.

"Sit yourself, George, please." Hutton waved to the portion of the table laid out for dinner. He sat at a right angle to the chair back, hooking his elbow over and crossing his legs. "So, dear boy, what news?"

While an attentive listener, Hutton never made eye contact—preferring to fix his gaze a little to the left of the speaker. His facial expressions were often exaggerated and unnatural: as if a stranger to humanity observed man's common emotional reactions, decided such displays were to his liking, and added his own creative flourishes.

"Your studies, your studies," Hutton was saying, tapping

his finger on the table. "I'm sure Dr Black would have upbraided you if things weren't to his satisfaction."

"No doubt he would," George agreed. "My final examination for the medical doctorate takes place next month."

Hutton gave his interpretation of a delighted look. "Oh, very good indeed, George! You are studying in London after?"

George sighed. He foolishly hoped he would avoid a retread of this conversation tonight, but of course Hutton had trained as a doctor—after training as a lawyer—and would feel invested in his medical future.

"I'm not yet sure," George said. It was the same answer he'd given for months, only the meaning behind the words sometimes altered from 'I'm too confused and stressed to answer' to 'I highly doubt it.'

Hutton, who took the same interest in human emotions as he did geology or chemistry, leaned so far back he appeared in danger of falling out of the chair. "Really? Is money an issue for you, George? You know you need only ask and I'm happy to assist."

"No, no—it's not the money," George protested, annoyed Hutton was so direct and generous. "It's just..."

"Well, you need only ask and we can arrange employment for you at my chemical manufacturing works."

As far as George recalled, Hutton owned a successful sal ammoniac factory a few streets from his house. He'd established it several decades ago, and since then had provided the steady income Hutton needed to live on St John's Hill without having to work a day more.

"That is very generous of you, Dr Hutton." Most affluent men would make that kind of gesture out of politeness for a nobody like George, though Hutton had an embarrassing habit of sincerity. "I will certainly consider the matter."

"Well, my partner Davie is heading to Birmingham in ten days. He handles the works' operation and trivial matters such as securing pay. So let me know before next Monday and I can arrange the introduction. Otherwise, we can talk when he's back in October."

Most of George's tuition fees had been covered by his summer work for the Earl of Hopetoun. Unfortunately, the Earl passed away last winter following an illness. And with it, George's primary source of income. He had a bit of money, but it wouldn't last until October.

Black cleared his throat. Hutton flashed his friend a guilty look.

"How's your phlogiston-wielding coming along?" Hutton enquired, recognising the signal to change the subject.

Here was territory George could navigate smoothly. In response, he held out his hand and flicked his pinkie finger against his palm. In front of the beaming Hutton, a small crimson flame danced in George's hand.

"Oh, excellent!" Hutton enthused. As far as George could tell, Hutton had no interest or ability in phlogiston-wielding himself, but it never dampened his enthusiasm watching the displays of others. George closed his fist and extinguished the flame.

"Mr Stephens' proculopathy skills are exceptional," Black commented as he dislodged an empty distillation flask from one of the dining table's chairs and seated himself. "He is a natural. We calculated he could wordlessly communicate with William and I over fifty metres, didn't we?"

"I think it was closer to forty-five," George answered, trying to suppress his immodestly pleased expression. Hutton's eyes widened.

"Is that so? You mustn't squander this talent, George."

George supposed his blush was visible enough for even Hutton to recognise, because he abruptly looked towards Black, who nodded.

"I don't want to detain you gentlemen from tonight's

experiment," Hutton said, signalling to a servant poised near the parlour door. "I'm rather excited, truth be told."

Excitement wasn't the emotion George felt.

Several days ago at a tavern gathering, Hutton and Black began pondering agricultural improvements. The two philosophers began wondering what alternate food sources could bolster the British economy, given belligerent rumblings from France raised the spectre of war. Black found it curious that the British population had never taken to consumption of snails like their French counterparts, despite a voracious appetite for oysters and clams.

"Think how much the North British economy would save harvesting snails to feed the populace instead of growing wheat," Black had enthused. "I'll have to show the numbers to Adam, but we could be on the cusp of a remarkable innovation."

Immediately enamoured with the idea, Hutton sent his cook and gardener to collect enough snails to serve as a testing dish. Since George was sitting on the other side of Hutton while this conversation occurred, the two friends invited him to join them in sampling the results.

A smell like burnt tar was seeping into in the room, George assumed it came from Hutton's kitchen.

"Say Joseph, did Her Highness Princess Dashkova reply to your letter regarding the consumption of snails on the Continent?" Hutton asked, frowning.

Black shook his head. "Her last letter indicated she was travelling between Italy and Prague, so I imagine it delayed her response."

"That's a shame. I would have found her culinary suggestions helpful." Hutton sighed. "As it was, I instructed the cook to stew the snails. I asked him to avoid seasoning the dish too heavily, since we need a sense of their true taste."

Hutton's manservant entered the parlour with a flicker of

trepidation in his eyes. He set the silver platter in the middle of the table and retreated.

"Well," Black said brightly. "Let's commence."

The dish in front of George was of indeterminable darkness, and smelled like a sweating midden heap. Lumps floated in the grey-brown juices, parting its oily sheen. Neither Hutton nor Black seemed daunted by the snail stew's uncomely appearance, depositing the solids and liquid onto their plates. It seemed churlish to object to the presentation.

Gritting his teeth, George brought a spoon to his mouth.

As expected, the snails required considerable chewing. However, George found every chomp unleashed more slimy juices into his mouth, and the snails' taste was a close approximation to their smell.

Both Black and Hutton appeared intent on their meals, neither one expressing any disgust or hesitation. This was his first dinner at Hutton's house, and George knew his host would be upset, possibly offended, if he complained about the dish. Perhaps like oysters, snails were better swallowed whole. George gulped down his first snail and reached for the more.

In between chews and swallows, Black and Hutton watched each other. Hutton spooned some of the liquid into his mouth. Now braced for the awfulness of each mouthful, George stared at the pile of snails in the middle of the table, which seemed un-dented despite an eternity of swallowing.

Black leaned forward in his chair and coughed delicately. "Doctor..." Black began, in tones he reserved for consulting other physicians on the state of his patients. "Do you not think these snails taste a little...well...queer?" He ventured.

"Queer?! Damn queer!" exclaimed Hutton, throwing down his fork and shoving himself away from the table. He emptied his glass and grimaced. "Take 'em away," he gestured to his manservant, circling the room.

As quickly as he could, George extracted the half-chewed forlorn specimen from his mouth and returned it to his dish.

"George! You hated them too? Why didn't you say something?" Hutton asked. Beside him, Black was coughing into his napkin.

"I didn't want to be rude," George sheepishly admitted. There was a lingering aftertaste in his mouth.

Hutton threw back his head and hooted. "What a trio of gentleman idiots we are! Too polite to admit we're eating shit for fear of giving offence. Slimy fuckers!"

"More sherry might be called for," Black remarked, wiping his mouth with a napkin.

Once they'd washed the worst of the taste from their mouths by drink and potato and apple pie—the cook no doubt predicting the need for palate cleansers—the conversation turned to Hutton's pet geology project.

"Are you sure it's ready to present to the Royal Society?" Black asked carefully.

"Undoubtably!" Hutton seemed relieved they were finally discussing this. "I've prepared the paper, now it's just a case of reviewing the composition."

"Did you time how long it will take to read?" The Society usually allowed thirty minutes for each scientific reading.

"Yes, there's a natural break halfway through—the whole dissertation will fit nicely across two meetings." This seemed satisfactory to Black.

"I am very excited to hear your theory," George said truthfully. Rumours of Hutton's grand theory had circulated convivial gatherings as long as he'd lived in Edinburgh. Hutton must have tinkered with it for most of his adult life.

"Are you familiar with the geological concepts?"

"I'm afraid I've only heard allusions to its significance. It concerns the accurate age of Earth, does it not?"

Hutton and Black chuckled.

"Correct. The theologians devoted much time to calculating the age of the Earth from references in the Bible."

"Yes," George said, aware of the generalities, if not the specifics. "The Most Reverend Ussher calculated the Earth is nearly six thousand years old; created in 4,000 B.C."

"Well," Black continued. "Dr Hutton's new estimation for the age of the Earth diverges from the agreed doctrine, by a not inconsiderable amount." In the corner, Hutton covered his hand with his mouth.

"Really?" George asked. "Did I hear some theologians' chronologies differ by a few hundred years?"

"Dr Hutton has calculated the Earth is millions of years old, if not older still."

"Oh," George tried to line up the zeroes in such a number within his head, but found he hadn't the mental muscles to do so. "That is quite a divergence, then."

"Yes, the Earth is older than man can possibly comprehend!" cried Hutton, thumping the table and jolting to his feet. "Can't put a number on it, George."

George's first instinct was to laugh at the absurdity of the difference between Hutton's proposed age and that of the theologians. The years Earth existed was greater than the number of stars in the sky, or pieces of sand on a beach? His mind couldn't wrap around such numbers.

"Are you sure?" was all George could say.

Hutton laughed. "Absolutely, so. Our friend Dr Black would call my reasoning 'elegant'...not sure I'd use such language myself."

"How...how did you deduce that?" Could Hutton possibly prove such a wild claim?

"Ah..." Hutton wagged a finger. "I don't want to spoil the surprise, much as I wish to share it with you, George. You'll hear it when the rest of Edinburgh does, at the March Royal Society meeting."

"Other gentlemen have been very curious about the content of Dr Hutton's papers," Black said delicately. "He wishes to avoid getting embroiled in debates before laid out his full argument."

To George that sounded more like an excuse than an explanation, but it wasn't his place to point that out.

"I imagine the paper will generate much..." He stumbled, because he wasn't sure how to phrase this question diplomatically. Hutton's idea skirted perilously close to blasphemy—at least to his untrained ears. The local clergy he'd met through Black and Cullen's philosophical gatherings were on the whole an open-minded bunch...but the average Scotch minister wasn't known for his open-mindedness to church doctrine challenges. He cringed to think what his village preacher would make of such talk.

"Controversy?" Black looked amused at George's discomfort. "Without question. But the audience can choose to believe or disbelieve what Dr Hutton says as they see fit. No harm done."

"I'm terribly sorry for dragging you into tonight's experiment," Hutton told George as he accompanied his guest to the door some time later. "Poor hospitality on my part."

"No, I forgive you," said George. The sherry Hutton brought out certainly helped mask the aftertaste, though he feared the snails would cause further disruption in his stomach and didn't want to be in Hutton's home when it happened. "I appreciate the invitation."

"At least it proved for the best your wife didn't join us tonight," Hutton remarked. "Pass on my compliments to Mrs Stephens—I'll arrange a dinner that is more conducive to the fairer sex next month."

"I'm sure Phoebe will be delighted to receive such an invitation," George said, stepping through the front door. "Until the next time, Dr Hutton."

"Of course, of course," Hutton insisted. "Safe passage, George. I fear I'll be up all night shitting—I pray the same fate doesn't befall you too."

2

Crossing the Cowgate with one hand on stomach, George used the journey home to reflect on the good choices and fortunes that had befallen him in recent times.

His wedding banns were read six months ago, and it still surprised George to hear others refer to a Mrs Stephens, and remember he didn't have to retire to a dusty, squalid lodgings room alone. His personal circumstances were on an extraordinary upswing.

In the most astounding twist of fate, George's future wife was suggested to him by none other than Andrew Duncan.

In his third year at Edinburgh, the inevitable happened and George was trapped in a corner with Dr Duncan at a dinner party.

"Mr Stephens! I'm so pleased to see you, for you came into my mind the other day..."

George cast around desperately, but suddenly no one else in the crowded room could meet his eye. Sensing his drifting attention, Duncan's hand clawed at his sleeve.

"...Mr Crown and I were seeking mutual relief in my closet

during the Beggar's Benison last week. I confess it was taking us a while, so we got to talking..."

It took every fibre of George's being to act like he was engaged with this conversation, for it filled him with raw terror at the thought Duncan might raise his voice if he thought he couldn't hear.

"He told me his niece was having trouble finding a suitor in St Andrews, so he was urging his widowed sister-in-law to bring her through to Edinburgh. That's when I thought of you."

The red dining room walls seemed to mock him. "You thought of me as you...were...?"

"Precisely!" Duncan beamed. "The Crown's family fortunes slipped when his brother died, but they tend farmland just north of St Andrews. The wench is, by all accounts, charming but subdued. Seemed like you'd be an ideal match for her, my boy!"

Dr Duncan's wife was a baby-faced woman with a tumble of blonde hair and a laugh like a bleating goat. The entire Edinburgh society recognised her obnoxious laugh, because she deployed it frequently. He could hear it right now in a neighbouring room.

"How can she seem so jovial?" George had asked his friend Thomas Fulhame one evening over oysters. "Does her husband's behaviour not humiliate her?"

Thomas shrugged. "Rumour has it she's modelled for the Beggars."

This should have shocked George more than it did. As it was, he just shook his head.

George would have been too horrified to return to his dinner party conversation with Duncan again, but Black asked him the next day what he'd spoken to Duncan about.

"Dr Black, sensibility prevents me from repeating Dr

Duncan's vulgar ramblings," George replied, swallowing his irritation that his mentor would see the situation and not intervene to protect him. "Some matter about coat closets and marrying me off to someone's niece..."

"The Crown girl?" Black asked. "Andrew mentioned her when we spoke the other week." He regarded George for a moment. "George, that isn't a bad suggestion of Dr Duncan. In fact, I think it might be a very suitable match based on what I know of Miss Phoebe."

George remained sceptical.

Black shrugged. "Well, I can tell Andrew you're willing to meet with the girl and her family when she arrives in Edinburgh. If it's apparent that the match is unsuitable, then no harm's incurred from a single meeting."

"If you're willing to speak with Dr Duncan..." George allowed. "But he said Crown and he..."

"...And he's only the girl's uncle," Black finished with a sly smile. "If he was her father, I wouldn't be counselling you in this direction."

With every reason to dread the first invitation to the Crown's dinner party, George felt he was heading to his execution. Yet almost as soon as he was welcomed into the home, George felt he'd stepped into a dream. He exchanged formulaic pleasantries with Phoebe from across the table, telling her mother about his medical studies and work with the Earl of Hopetoun studying copper seams on his country lands.

Black and Cullen's tutoring paid off, and it astounded George when the family invited him back for afternoon tea.

Despite knowing he was under close observation, it surprised George how relaxed he felt around the girl, and that her family seemed satisfied by Duncan and Black's estimation he would make a successful physician. Within a few months, they brokered an engagement.

* * *

Phoebe smiled when George entered their apartment.

"So? Do we have a new national cuisine to look forward to?" she asked, setting her sewing on the table.

"Regrettably not," George admitted. "Though I wouldn't put it past the two to stumble upon another potential delicacy the next time they meet."

Phoebe drew closer. He could smell the faintest traces of her rosewater perfume.

"Did you tell the professors you'd received a letter from Dr Hunter?"

George wracked his brains for a convincing response.

Seeing him struggle, Phoebe sighed delicately.

"You've sat on that letter a whole week. I imagine with every day that passes, the more hesitant you will get. They'll be delighted to hear it arrived, won't they?"

George hadn't expected Dr William Hunter to offer him a place in his famous London anatomy school. He let Cullen compose the letter of introduction because the old professor kept insisting. To George it didn't matter that the two men had decades of friendship behind them, because why would the most renown anatomist in London accept George Stephens as a student?

"It isn't as if Dr Hunter is expecting an immediate response. I think he'd prefer I consider his offer carefully."

Except that George was pretty sure he knew what his response would be, and worried that too fast a rejection would come across as rude.

"Will you compose your reply to Dr Hunter this week?" Phoebe asked. His wife hadn't pushed him to articulate his decision out loud, but she surely sensed which way his inclination fell. "If you really don't want to talk to Drs Black and Cullen beforehand about your worries."

Cullen's pre-matrimonal counsel involved the warning that wives had the tricky habit of asking questions that weren't really questions.

Cullen had taken one afternoon to entrust him with all the advice he could think of regarding women and marital relations. George's heart nearly burst with gratitude upon receiving so much shared wisdom, before he noticed Mrs Anna Cullen at the other end of the room, shaking over her watercolours with laughter. After that, he was just confused.

"Um, I'll see if I have time tomorrow after reading the avian wingspan treatise Dr Monro recommended I review," George replied.

Phoebe's hands rested on her hips. She had a very pleasing waist.

"My dear, it would make sense to pen Dr Hunter's letter before losing yourself in the treatise."

The other warning Cullen delivered was that it was the curse of man to either marry a woman prone to wild unreasonableness, or one who was unflinchingly sensible.

"I thought you would prefer to remain near your mother," George blurted. "Given your concerns about her health this past winter."

Phoebe tilted her head with incredulity.

"George, there's not much I can do for my mother if our circumstances remain as embarrassing as hers. Declining fortunes is exhausting." She sighed and threw up her hands.

Ever since the engagement became a reality, George had to deal with his fellow students making jocular remarks about hen-pecked husbands, cuckoldry and basket-making. George historically struggled with making decisions about his education, and wasn't sure how to make decisions on behalf of a wife, too. Usually, Phoebe's sensibility made the process easy, but moving to London was the first serious decision he had to make on behalf of them both.

"Alright," George fumbled. "I'll see what time I return from the Infirmary and if I can squeeze in some letter-writing after. The treatise is an integral part of my dissertation, of course."

3

Repressing a curse, George leapt aside to avoid getting run over by a clique of Classics students barrelling the opposite way across the largest college yard.

There wasn't any point in glowering or tutting in their wake: that trio never paid attention to where they were going, and never apologised if they bumped into you. At least he didn't end up in a puddle or twisting his ankle.

The ringleader of that trio reminded George a little of James: his first year lodgings chum, who died in a phlogiston-related accident. It was the pale complexion that did it, because otherwise there was scant commonality.

George often wondered if—had he lived—James would've grown out of his insufferable behaviour. His other lodgings chum Edward proved to be more tolerable once George got to know him—insecurities lay behind the arrogant brusqueness —and George sometimes imagined James would have calmed down once he got settled into his studies.

Skirting the quadrangle, George made a beeline for the new anatomy theatre, an octagonal building sticking out of the Old Library wing. He was relieved there was no sign of

Black at this hour. The chemistry professor would be settled into his laboratory on the other side of these buildings by now anyway, but George held a scrap of paranoia that Black would catch him at his most vulnerable. He promised his mentor he'd practice his aethereal manipulations the other week, and Black would no doubt want a progress report. George didn't want to admit he'd not done more than a cursory practice in his wynd, because he got too jumpy about other residents of the land stumbling across him, practicing an art that was not widely known.

Black and Cullen tried to dispel his fears of discovery in their own ways. "People's eyes deceive them into seeing all sorts of things," Cullen had scoffed. "You can bet they'll think you're throwing a candle if they see anything at all."

He should probably ask Black if he could make use of his Nicholson Street back garden for the exercise, but they thought he'd been practising consistently at home, so it would sting to admit he'd lied about phlogiston-wielding practice for...goodness, months? No, more than months now.

He pushed this repetitive fretting aside at the stairway into the anatomy theatre. The circular rows of benches towered above the dissecting table, so steep and narrow a person in the back row could lean forward and drop a penny onto the table. Fortunately, the amber wood panelling and extensive windows made the room airy instead of oppressive.

Scratch that: the large and looming form of Dr Sandy 'Secundus' Monro was already occupying the space. Before he made out anything the Professor of Anatomy anything said, George recognised a stern admonishment was underway.

George's constitution—already fragile—threatened to snap at the sight of his cowed peer, who he recognised from clinical practice. He was ready to beat a hasty retreat and come back later, when Monro glanced up and made momentary eye contact.

"I may be generous inside the classroom, but know Providence doesn't grant extensions in other areas of life. If you're not ready...well, it doesn't matter..."

Monro took his time wrapping up the admonishment, sending the student away with firm instructions to return in five days. His tone brokered no disagreement: either the student would return on time, or he'd better hop on the next ship to the Bahamas and abandon all thoughts of a medical career.

George studiously avoided eye contact with his departing comrade. The anatomy professor hummed to himself for a couple of seconds to dispel the worst of his humours, before turning his attention to the next disappointment of the day.

"Ah, Mr Stephens. Take a seat."

George dropped onto the front row bench and tried to straighten his back.

"Now...your dissertation." Monro perched on the railing in what was probably an attempt to seem casual and thus reassuring. Then he clasped his hands in front of him and regarded George impassively. The entire effect was of Monro preparing the deliver a sobering prognosis on George's loved one. "Tell me, how do you think you did?"

George gulped. He dropped eye contact. "I'm sorry professor, I know you said..."

"I don't want excuses." Monro held up his hand. "I want you to tell how you think you did."

"I know I rushed the anatomical sketches," George said, staring at his twitching figures. "Then right after I handed you the final draft I read DiGiorgio's treatise on avian wing structure, so I realised I was wrong in saying claims of a lower axial spur were unsubstantiated. And I know I should have cited Ardley and made a mess of describing Hunter's early experimental work..."

Monro let him blabber on like this for a tortuous length of

time, an unreadable expression on his face. When George finally stumbled to a halt, his professor continued to study him for what felt like hours, if it was only a few heartbeats.

"This brings us to the heart of the problem, Mr Stephens," he said, hoisting one leg further onto the bench. "Because I would actually rate your dissertation as broadly competent."

George gaped. In his first year at Edinburgh, such a remark from the eminent Dr Monro junior would have sent him crying, but he'd come to recognise 'broadly competent' was resounding praise by academic standards.

"It has some flaws, obviously," Monro continued, never being one to leave a compliment unmolested. "To be expected with inexperience and an incomplete grasp of the current scientific literature. There are more grammatical errors than one would find in a Royal Society paper, for instance. But those things can be rectified by time, and I try not to get bogged down in the cosmetic details."

Should George be thanking his professor at this point? He wasn't sure, so held his tongue.

"Having supervised your dissection of the goose and swan's wings, I can attest your anatomical ability is substantially higher than I would expect from a medical student. You completed the dissections in half the time most can, and your notes were very astute."

'Astute' was one of the highest virtues Monro seemed to espouse. George nodded and murmured.

"That said, the most overwhelming weakness in your dissertation, as you demonstrated for me again today..." George tensed. "Is confidence."

Here Monro paused, and George assumed he expected a response.

"I'm sorry, professor?"

"You undervalue yourself, George. You undercut and walk back your insights at every turn. Hunter's early work is riddled with errors and the mistakes in his conclusions are obvious, but you shied away from admitting this. Similarly, DiGiorgio is a crank, and his studies—such as they are—shouldn't be taken as seriously as the others. Where your observations differ from the literature, and where they lend themselves to alternative conclusions, you should go ahead and state that, assured in the accuracy of your reasoning."

George didn't want to look Monro in the face, but he was scared of missing something from his professor's body language, so he peered out of the corner of his eyes.

"Patients trust physicians with their lives, and a physician without confidence in his training undermines the sanctity of the profession and endangers innocent lives. There is a difference between arrogance and confidence," Monro added, as if anticipating George's protestation. "And you shouldn't be ashamed of exhibiting the latter."

"But what if I'm wrong?"

"Physicians are often wrong, Mr Stephens. But we make educated guesses, and trust our instincts. I don't yet see that trust in your instincts, and it is something I need before I consider you worthy of a medical degree. Do you intend to stay in Edinburgh to practice?"

"...I, um, am not yet sure, professor."

Monro gave another grim nod. Another unpleasant diagnosis made. "Edinburgh is not short of talented physicians, Mr Stephens. These days, most major cities can boast Edinburgh physicians serving them. It is no longer enough to be an Edinburgh medical graduate to succeed, because talented alumni dwell everywhere. Without confidence, you will struggle to make a livelihood for yourself. It has happened to several colleagues of yours, has it not?"

George nodded. Thomas and his wife Elizabeth had returned to Dublin, ostensibly because Thomas' mother needed him, but his friend had graduated last year and only attended a handful of patients in the city. His older friend Edward—who came from noble stock and exuded charm—was practising in the Aberdeen countryside in between bouts of gentlemanly leisure, but notably he wasn't practising in Aberdeen.

"Unfortunate business," Monro sighed. "Many of my former students are making a satisfactory living here as tutors and grinders. Some have retrained as lawyers. But you won't find those paths fulfilling if you genuinely desire to become a physician. Which, I presume, is what you want?"

"Yes I do, professor." George knew he should project confidence with this response, no matter how misplaced it gelt. His first few years at Edinburgh were hardscrabble due to a lack of funds, with a constant nagging worry about coins in his purse had how long they'd last. It was tiring. He didn't want a lifetime of that exhaustion if he could help it.

"Good." Monro stood and stretched. He probably didn't believe George, but cajoling students was tiring work. "Whatever you do, work at it with all your heart. I look forward to a lively and *confident* oral defence of your dissertation next week. You'll receive confirmation of time and location by Friday."

$$4$$

The first warning of trouble came from Dr Monro. He approached Black in the chemistry laboratory, which was unusual enough for him to suspect something was amiss.

Monro edged into the room, waving a handful of papers without explaining himself. The man was never one for silences, so Black knew there was something serious going on. Monro got within a few metres of Black, then stopped.

"I received a letter from a former student residing in London," Monro began, using silent proculopathic communication after establishing they were alone. *"He told me Lord Ross passed away last week after an unfortunate riding accident."*

It took Black a heartbeat to recall who Lord Ross was, and why there was any significance to his passing. The youthful noble who encouraged John Brown to perform dark chymistry experiments on his students hadn't had cause to trouble him in years: not since Brown was neutralised as a threat and Ross' dark chymistry grimoire burned.

"How does he know this?" Black asked, moving closer automatically, even though no one could hear their conversation.

For a few years after the Brown affair, it seemed Elliott Ross was no longer a problem. With no access to his uncle's grimoire, he left Edinburgh for London, trading dark chemistry power for more conventional political influence. None of Black and Cullen's London correspondents had any concern: Ross slipped back into his former bachelor distractions of art, hunting and society gatherings. Black disdained the man for his duplicity—Ross tried to manipulate him on several occasions—but as the saying went: out of sight, out of mind.

"Frank was called to inspect the body, since he happened to be a guest on the country estate where the party was staying. In his letter, he tells me the cause of death was a broken neck— common enough when thrown from a horse."

Monro blinked and shook his head. Black knew sustained proculopathy—even at short range—gave his colleague a headache. But he appeared determined not to breathe a word aloud.

"Your friend thinks the death is suspicious?"

"Reading between the lines of his note...yes. He notes Ross was separated from the party and his body discovered later that day. No one witnessed the tragic accident."

No doubt Monro brought this to his colleague's attention with a twinge of conscience, because the anatomy professor was the first person Ross approached with oblique dark chymistry questions. Only after Monro rebuffed him did Ross settle on Brown as a surrogate for his experiments: melding dark chymistry sigils to phlogiston-wielding. Those experiments killed several students who volunteered to receive sigils, thinking their idol Dr Brown knew how to keep them safe. Instead, the sigils trapped phlogiston in their bodies until it reached lethal concentrations. The symptoms of phlogiston poisoning—elevated temperatures, delirium—were similar enough to ordinary fever that the deaths almost escaped notice. Almost.

"Thanks for calling, Alexander," Black said. "I'll what I can do with the business."

Monro nodded, satisfied his message had been received.

That was the worst part of having Monro as a colleague. Although they disliked each other personally, both recognised they made excellent professional colleagues. Black and Monro never had an issue conducting faculty business together or communicating with each other over business matters.

"We'll talk some more shortly, I imagine," Monro gathered up his papers. "Take care of yourself, Joseph."

Elliott Ross was too young to recall the dark chymists at the height of their power, when no one in Edinburgh dared go against their interests. The Ross family as a whole were bit-players in their schemes. Excluding Ross and Brown, there hadn't been a serious dark chymistry resurgence since the destruction of their library decades ago. Unlike phlogiston-wielding, dark chymistry had always been a precarious art— knowledge mistrustfully guarded by its practitioners, and families refusing to share their secrets. Once the library went, so did much of the crucial knowledge outsiders needed to practice it.

The subsequent generation of dark chymistry families were born after the Union: the humiliating loss of Scottish autonomy to the English didn't burn their psyche like it burned their fathers'. They didn't mind journeying to Kensington Palace and playing courtly games in London, if that's what it took to gain wealth and status. Dark chymistry outgrew its usefulness to them. Having their wives trade diamonds was a simpler route to power than reconstructing the intricate dark chymistry grimoires of their fathers.

Ross was the only Edinburgh noble of that generation to show an interest in dark chymistry, and manipulate Brown into doing his bidding. That was a demonstration of rare skill. This also made him something of a loose thread.

When Monro left the laboratory, he closed Black's door and made a point of checking the latch shut behind him.

The mail coaches moved quickly between London and Edinburgh, Black noted. If Monro received the letter today—and no doubt Monro came directly here to warn him—it meant that anyone travelling the same route, departing at the same time as Lord Ross was pronounced dead, could already be within the city walls.

* * *

Black made his way up Infirmary Street, the tapping of his physician's cane on the cobbles his only accompaniment. It was a route he'd walked a hundred times, at all hours of the day. The hour wasn't unduly late: once he got home from Cullen's he hoped to leaf through a book in front of the fire before calling it a night. There was no reason for him to be overly cautious—or unnecessarily distracted—on this particular road.

As the road curved towards Nicolson Street, Black turned his face towards the sky. He felt the first spit of rain on his uncovered hand and wondered how much water the charcoal heavens held tonight.

Then he paused. There was a presence nearby. Black ran his tongue across the roof of his mouth, but it wasn't phlogiston he sensed.

A scent.

Or a memory.

Both.

Then the presence behind him spoke.

The physiological layers of remembrance reacted at different rates. Black's body responded with visceral immediacy by accelerating his pulse: flaring repulsion, terror, pain, corrosive rage. Then came the flitting memories, scorched down to nothing in his mind's eye by the wear of time: of blades and fists, desperate struggles in the dark and the sleepless nights that followed. The identity and Christian name of the man provoking these reactions were the final things Black summoned.

"Good evening, Joseph."

It was a majestic voice. The intervening decades had only deepened and burnished it. The same warm flashes of Scots accent washed over the listener like a glass of fine whiskey through the blood on a biting, wintery night.

That was…until you understood who owned the voice.

"Good evening." Every syllable came out of Black's throat tense, coiled. "Reverend."

Black turned to the wynd where the voice originated from, halting when he was in profile to the speaker. They were several metres from the closest street lamp; all he could see was the figure resting against the wall, arms folded.

"Looking well, I see," the speaker continued, not moving from shadows.

"Is Paris no longer to your liking?" Black asked. He kept his hands hanging loose by his sides.

"Ach, not long ago I heard murmurings of what was fermenting in the mind of your friend, Dr Hutton. Didn't want to hear the full story second-hand."

It's been twenty years, Black warned himself. You knew what he was capable of then. You don't know what he's capable of now.

He focussed on relaxing his body. Sensing every twitch in his nervous system, doing little more than feeling the phlogiston and aether as it flowed and pooled inside him, like two fingers poised on his violin strings.

"There's nothing I wish to say to you, Reverend."

The figure in the shadows gave a peal of laughter.

"Oh, Joseph—if only that were true."

Black's arm was already moving. The micro-contraction and pulsing of chest and arm muscles drew phlogiston and aether through his nervous system towards his finger tips.

Phlogiston, the flammable energy inherent in all objects, discharged from wielders as a crimson fire, regenerated within the nervous system. Aether, the substance imbibing all creatures with life force. The former came from deep within Black's body and was easy to wield; the latter floated below his skin but was harder to marshal. By the time his fingers flicked towards the wynd, Black knew this combination of phlogiston and aether would shoot from his hand yellow-white, branching like lightning.

Black could wield many hues of phlogiston: from crimson flames to an invisible propulsive force. This yellow-white light came from another spectrum, another octave, one he couldn't access in error under duress or reflex.

Yellow-white phlogiston fire was for killing.

There was a blinding flash as Black's strike exploded against the wall, but almost as soon as he closed his eyes to shield himself from the glare, Black knew he'd paid the price for those seconds of hesitation.

The wynd was empty.

5

So much for his plan to call on the professors and announce the belated arrival of Hunter's letter. In the parlour, Black appeared shaken: fidgeting where he usually attained perfect composure.

"I hesitated, William," he was saying as George sat down. "I swore if he returned I would kill him on sight, and I hesitated for all of five seconds."

George almost missed the chair. He'd survived several American battlefields where he experienced similar moments spent debating whether to take a life. In the heat of war, after the first few times it got easier. But for Black to decide so rapidly to take a life was shocking.

"Who is this, Dr Black?" he asked.

"Reverend Malcolm Holm," sighed Black. "William and I first made our acquaintance of him in 1748."

"A dark chymist?" George knew the two professors had usurped the circle of dark chymists who controlled the city in those days, and destroyed the grimoires they used to conduct their sigil-based system. He knew most of the chymists came from the upper echelons of Edinburgh society—he wasn't aware the clergy was involved.

"A fanatic first, a dark chymist second," Cullen interrupted, pushing a cup of tea into George's hands. "Some among their ranks were drawn to dark chymistry to concentrate their hold on power—men like Holm were more intent on keeping the old order and smothering new ideas. He thought we were bringing in a new age of atheism and feared the Kirk losing its power over the masses."

"But he's not spent the last thirty years in Scotland?" This was the first time George had heard his name mentioned.

"No, he fled to Paris once the dark chymists collapsed. He kept quiet since then, though rumours reached us he never disavowed his beliefs."

"So what has brought him back to Edinburgh?" George asked.

"Dr Hutton, if I understand Joe correctly."

"It appears so," Black said. "I'm sorry, William. I made this more difficult for us."

"Don't apologise," Cullen said at the same time George asked, "How so?"

Black's gaze wandered towards the fire. "Holm knows he's not getting another five seconds in front of me. He'll either avoid confronting us directly, or use human barricades."

"Can we wield phlogiston?" George tried to get his mind around a person capable of causing such distress in the usually unflappable Joseph Black.

Cullen shrugged. "Holm was convinced of our inferiority right until the moment Joe defeated him. He may or may not wish to play us at our own game—he could acquire the necessary tools on the continent, though if he has, my sources don't know who assisted. He may still have some knowledge from the grimoires, though if he had much I think he would have attacked us first."

"We need to find him," Black insisted. "George, you wouldn't know, but Holm carried out a lot of the dirty work on behalf of the dark chymists. These men wouldn't trust their secrets to hired street thugs, so they used one of their own. Holm enjoyed what he did—he saw himself as a Crusader."

Black and Cullen had once told him the dark chymists murdered those they considered obstacles and threats, the victim often murdered behind locked doors in places they believed impenetrable. Holm must have been the one carrying out those murders.

George could tell by the shape of this conversation what the problem was. "How can we find him?"

"Exactly," Cullen replied. "Someone is sheltering him. He could be boarding in the filthiest Dalkeith tavern, or on a feather down bed in the Lawnmarket. This isn't a coarse fool like Bruno parading up and down the High Street. Holm knows how to avoid detection."

"What's he planning, then?" A vision of Hutton laughing as he departed on his daily walk around Arthur's Seat came to George's mind. Dread seized him.

"If he has demands, he'll make sure we receive them," Black mused. "It's when he doesn't have demands and simply desires a person dead we should be afraid."

George wondered if Black was trying to reassure himself more than objectively present the facts.

"Fortunately," noted Cullen, "there's a few avenues of enquiry we can pursue in smoke out the rat."

* * *

After George passed on his regards and departed for the Infirmary, Cullen beckoned Black closer.

"Alice told me they pulled a dead body out of Robertson

Close this morning—she overheard gossip at the coffeehouse," Cullen said. "Throat cut. No one of particular status."

Robertson Close intersected Infirmary Street.

Black nodded grimly. "Just someone in the wrong place at the wrong time."

* * *

Inside the Nicolson Tavern, George scanned the familiar corners. At a small table in an adjourning room, he made eye contact with a hatchet-faced figure, who seemed for all intents to be scowling at the world around him.

After a second, the seated figure raised his hand with the slowness of a mudslide. Once raised, the hand was momentarily swallowed in a blaze of yellow flames.

George smiled and nodded. The severe expression on Adam Smith's face finally rearranged into a smile.

"Well met, young Stephens," he croaked, as George joined him at the table.

"As always," George replied courteously, signalling to the tavern keeper for his usual ale.

He wasn't quite truthful with his greeting. For the first two and half years George attended Black's Oyster Club gatherings, Smith ignored him. Eight months ago, Smith's behaviour reversed, perhaps deciding George was going to stick around, and he thawed towards the young interlocutor.

Their recent breakthrough came when he decided talking to George—if the two of them were alone—was preferable to talking to himself.

Smith grumbled and fussed with his drink as they awaited the rest of the scholars. George reflected again that with his hooked nose, steely eyes and sombre attire, Smith looked more like a Kirk minister than most ministers. Black seemed to have a way of warming his otherwise chilly friend, because Smith never adopted the pessimistic outlook of his ministerial doppelgängers.

"I heard Dr Hutton's snails proved disagreeable dinner companions," Smith commented, when it became clear the two of them would be stuck together for several more minutes. "It's a shame. I came up with several good petition drafts to bring before Pitt's office to promote their large-scale cultivation."

"Drs Hutton and Black were disappointed too."

"I think the worst meal I ever ate was when I poured ink over my fried pigeon by mistake," Smith said, scratching his wrists. "It tasted horrible."

"Gentlemen." Black and Hutton entered the room and began disengaging from their coats.

Which was just as well, because Smith's anecdote left George with a lot to ponder. Spilling the contents of an inkwell on your dinner was a confusing accident to befall anyone, but Smith's use of the verb 'poured' suggested a measure of deliberation or intent to the act. Did Smith even have a writing desk in his dining room? Was his inkstand a similar shape or appearance to his dinner table sauce boats?

"It's rather loud in here," Smith commented. "Very distracting." Behind them, a group of revellers launched into song.

"We can explore alternative meeting places," conceded Cullen, slipping in behind George on the heels of two lords. "Adam is right: this pokey room isn't conducive to our growing band."

"Princess Dashkova's letter arrived," Black said, sitting down. "She told me the Parisians sauté their snails in copious butter and garlic."

"Hmm, so they don't stew them?" Hutton asked. Seeing Black shake his head, he rubbed his neck. "That sounds quite appealing, actually. Not that I want to risk another experiment—my chamberpot won't withstand a second such onslaught."

The club meeting followed its usual course: a semi-moderated discussion for the first hour, then by the time the alcohol had set in, smaller conversations broke out.

George wasn't in the mood for scholarly discussion: he was still ruminating on the letter burning a hole into his writing desk and the appearance of this Reverend Holm, who'd thrown all his plans into chaos. Nor was he much up to the task of convivial discussion, since one glass of claret needed to last him the evening.

With a playful grin, Hutton leaned over and whispered something in Black's ear.

What happened next shook George to his core, turning his whole understanding of the world on its head.

Black *sniggered*.

George sat there dumbfounded. His whole conception of Dr Joseph Black, professor of chemistry, was that Black was a man who did not snigger, giggle, snort or otherwise let out uncontrolled displays of mirth. As he was so cruelly disabused of this notion, George became angry at Black for withholding such vital information from him.

Then Hutton was distracted by someone else, and the conversation flowed off in different directions, leaving George to his shock.

On his other side, Cullen and Smith retread a familiar argument, possibly because they weren't in the mood for a more intellectually challenging debate.

"The continued existence of unscrupulous institutions charging for degrees is a stain upon our national reputation, Adam. I can't believe you're willing to 'let the market' take care of them—the damage they've already done is self-evident."

Smith chuckled, swirling his wine around his glass. "The

government asked for my opinion on diploma mills like St Andrews...and I gave it. Moral repugnance is not the same as societal harm."

Cullen was not be dissuaded. "Were you not paying attention to the business with 'Doctor' John Brown? St Andrews should never have given him that medical degree. You claimed individuals and institutions can differentiate between a paid-for degree and one earned through personal industry, but Brown clearly could not. He thought it would get him an academic appointment."

The old professor appeared genuinely vexed, though Smith was treating the exchange as good-natured bickering and refusing to be baited.

"Well, in the long run, the problem resolved itself, did it not? Last time I checked, Bruno's fortunes were severely decreased, to the point where he was no longer attempting to prove the validity of his theories through experimentation. I would never place my trust in the market for an immediate self-correction...but it'll happen with a lick of patience."

George didn't necessarily agree with the eminent philosopher's assessment of the situation...unless by 'market forces,' Smith meant 'George Stephen's fists.'

"No thanks to you," Cullen complained, returning to his cups. "His first action after recovering from our rout of his headquarters was bribing a nurse so he could secret treat an Infirmary patient using Brunonian principles. I can't believe he thought he'd get away with it! If Andrew Duncan didn't go out for his blood, Bruno would have regained all his former confidence."

This was the second lesson George learned about Andrew Duncan during his time in Edinburgh. Never let Duncan talk to you at a party, and never (ever) treat one of his patients without first securing permission. Brown paid a heavy price for underestimating Duncan, and was lucky to avoid criminal charges for patient-tampering.

"What did Sandy Monro say about your dissertation draft, George?" Cullen asked, changing the subject.

George started to explain, but as soon as Smith realised his argument was over and turned his attention across the table, Cullen shushed him.

"It's too loud in here, lad. Call on me tomorrow and let's discuss it then."

"What was it you said to Dr Black earlier that he found so amusing?" George asked Hutton on their way to a sedan chair. He hoped his voice carried no hint of the betrayal he felt wrought by the two men several hours earlier.

"Eh?" For a moment, Hutton seemed lost. "Oh, you mean that remark about horseshoes? Can hardly remember how I put it—I didn't think it was all that funny, myself. Have a pleasant evening. You're able to see yourself home safely, George?"

It was a strange question coming from a man who apparently knew he'd attracted the attention of a lethal dark chymist. But George knew well enough by now that academics in Edinburgh were never fearful of their life until the past point they needed to be.

"Of course. And you too, Dr Hutton."

* * *

They didn't have to wait long for Holm's demands. George was at Cullen's receiving feedback on his preliminary dissertation draft, head a little worse for wear from last night's conviviality, when Cullen's wife, Anna, and their housekeeper Alice appeared in his study, pale-faced.

"A Mrs Kitty Holm is at the door," the housekeeper, Alice, whispered.

Cullen and George froze. Alice shot Cullen a pleading look.

"His second wife?" Cullen asked to himself. He rubbed his hands together and chewed his lip. "Very well. Show her in. George—don't take your eyes off her hands."

He didn't need to impress the danger; George's heart was already pounding, as if an enemy detachment had been reported on the horizon. Cullen beckoned his wife over, whispering a few additional instructions before she glided from the room.

The woman ushered in to the study was younger than George expected, and more elegant than most minister's wives. Her bustle was wider than the current mode, and the material a good deal thicker than the clinging chiffon woman her age seemed to enjoy. She had a petite, doll-like face, with round eyes and a pointy chin. However, the severity of her expression suggested she was ready to reprimand the world for its carelessness.

It had begun as a pleasant, bright morning, but suddenly the room was sweltering and oppressive.

"Can I offer you tea?" Anna asked with stiff politeness.

"Goodness," retorted Kitty, rearranging herself on the sofa. "Given the brutish behaviour Dr Black showed my husband just the other day, I shudder to think what poisons Dr Cullen will dispense to a helpless lady."

Anna's eyes narrowed to slits. "Poison your tea, my lady? Why, that would ruin the flavour of a rather fine bergamot blend." She grabbed a teacup from Alice's tray and waved it under Kitty's nose, showing it was free from residue, then poured a stream of tea into four cups.

With a sniff of satisfaction, Kitty picked up her cup and rested it on her lap.

Mrs Cullen shot George an equally fiery look, daring him to accuse her of similar poor hostess form. George hurried to pick up his teacup. The tea scalded his lips and tongue, but there were no ill effects beyond that.

"What is your business, Mrs Holm? Where is your husband?"

"I couldn't say," Kitty replied, scraping her spoon against the cup. "I'm staying with my sister in the Lawnmarket. The good Reverend does not want to endanger me, so I'm happy to remain ignorant in that regard."

"Then this is purely a social call?" Cullen asked sceptically.

"Dr Hutton must withdraw his paper from the Royal Society, burn all copies and offer a public retraction of his misguided theory." Kitty drew her lips together. "That would be an acceptable start."

"I see," Cullen said.

"To avoid unpleasant misunderstandings, it would be best all this was carried out before Dr Hutton is scheduled to present his paper on the seventh of March."

"How unpleasant are these misunderstandings likely to be?" George asked. He couldn't think up a particularly witty way to say this.

Kitty sipped her tea. "Quite, I fear. My husband and I agree the consequences of Hutton's heretical views receiving wider circulation would be terrible."

"Have you also conveyed this sentiment to Dr Hutton directly?"

Kitty looked amused. "I understand you and Dr Black have a familiarity with my husband that the good Dr Hutton does not. I believe the subtleties of the situation might be lost upon the man."

The impact of a threat is rather diminished when you have to repeat yourself, George mused grimly. From the set of Cullen's mouth, it was clear took this seriously.

"Well, I can save you the trouble of waiting for a response. Dr Hutton has the right to present his theory to the scientific community, which he will do shortly. If Malcolm Holm dislikes the theories, he doesn't have to listen to them. There will be no retraction."

Kitty set down her teacup with a sigh. Her disappointment was a touch theatrical—she must have known Cullen wouldn't cave.

"It is incorrect to say that free speech is unfettered in the country, Dr Cullen. Dangerous, libellous allegations are reined in all the time."

"But who is Dr Hutton committing libel against?"

"God." Kitty rose. On reflex, George and Cullen rose too. "I will take my leave, gentleman. There is nothing more to be gained from my being here."

"You are aware of what became of Reverend Holm's first wife?" Cullen asked, a dark edge creeping into his voice.

Kitty's expression barely flickered.

"You think so little of me to assume I would be ignorant? Of course I know. And if I suffered a similar weakness? Why, I'd deserve the same fate."

Once satisfied Kitty was through the front door, Anna swept back into the room. She picked up the teacup belonging to Kitty and dashed it against the hearth.

"William advised me against using our best china set in case she meddled with it somehow," she explained as George stood blinking at her. "Better safe than sorry."

6

It was possible the universe didn't want George to receive his medical degree.

He stopped by the university library first thing in the morning in the hopes of tracking down Ardley's papers, but a yawning librarian told him someone already borrowed that volume and no, he didn't know when it'd be returned. George wanted to stay and argue, or stalk through the library to flush out the culprit, but then he'd be late for clinical rotations at the Royal Infirmary.

As it was, he arrived precisely on time, which brought him to the attention of Dr Gregory. Taking his promptness personally, Gregory singled George out over the next hour for intense questioning.

"Tell me, Stephens, if this patient came to you complaining of febrile fever, what would your prescription be?"

"Um..."

The patient in question looked up at George with damp eyes, nervously licking her lips.

"How much would you bleed her?" Gregory persisted,

prompting a look of alarm from the old woman. Like most citizens of Edinburgh, patients in the teaching wards hated being bled, particularly by inept medical students. They came to the free ward because they had no other option.

Not that Phoebe meant to send him out the door in a distracted mood, but she'd haggled with their landlord over rent that morning and needed to warn him about the state of their household coffers. "I think we can make your savings stretch a bit longer, but I'm not sure we'll have enough for next month's rent."

George had kissed the top of her head and promised things wouldn't get that bad, and he had a plan for getting more money.

Once the clinical rotation finished, George slipped past the scowling Gregory and returned to the College. He needed to avoid Monro at all costs, but George's safe route across the Yards was blocked by the University Provost, tutting in his billowing academic robes at errant students and swooping in to break up gatherings, like a malicious crow.

As George ran for cover towards Black's chemistry class-room, he saw the cause of the Provost's heavy-handedness: a knot of gold-buttoned, high-heeled aristocrats strolling towards their waiting sedan chairs on Nicholson Street.

Weren't the Town Council elections taking place next month? It seemed the horse-trading in the run-up to the crucial board meeting took place earlier and earlier. Or maybe this year there were more seats turning over. The Town Council had the final say in faculty appointments, funding and all the other things professors complained about. Cullen tended to mutter Thomas Paine quotes whenever they came up. Black was usually more sanguine, insisting they were reasonable men to negotiate with. George prayed he'd never be forced into an encounter with them.

At least in Black's classroom, he'd feel safe from the university politics and the turmoil of his final exams.

If it meant he could remain in Scotland, George had decided he should accept Hutton's offer. It wasn't the course he imagined he'd go on, but the thought brought him less stress than contemplating a move to London and eventually struggle to launch his own private practice somewhere.

But he hadn't told Phoebe of his intentions, and he worried that news of his acceptance to Hutton would reach her before he had the chance to tell her himself. Which would lead to an argument he didn't want to have.

This was why he wanted to run the matter by Black— confess to him that Dr Hunter's letter was sitting on his desk at home, and that he'd changed his mind about accepting the offer. Black wasn't a friend of the anatomist the way Cullen was, so George hoped he'd be more objective. There was even a chance—albeit an unlikely one—that Black would mention Hutton's job offer as a natural progression of the conversation.

Except George found the professor already occupied with a visitor.

It was Hutton, of all people.

His bearings momentarily knocked, George froze in the middle of the room. Neither party paid him any attention. Black was frowning and looking increasingly concerned.

That was understandable. Word of Mrs Holm's visit to Cullen had spread. The only person it didn't seem to agitate was—as predicted—Hutton himself.

"You fret too much, Joseph," Hutton insisted. "If the Reverend Holm wanted to cause me harm, he's had ample opportunity to do so over the preceding days. If tomorrow is as charming as today, of course I will head out on my usual walk."

Black reacted with no more than a shrug and returned to his distillation.

"Did you come to see me, George?" he asked, deciding to take a break from persuading Hutton of anything.

"Um, I had a question..." Seeing Black's grave face and Hutton's unashamed curiosity, George's courage deserted him. "But it's not urgent."

"As you can see, it's not the best of time, George. If it can wait I would greatly appreciate it. The Lord Provost just called on me *again* to ask for my opinion on the Town Council candidates. I don't understand why he couldn't write a letter." Black ignored—or perhaps didn't notice—George's surprised reaction to this revelation. Black hadn't been consulted on previous Town Council nominees, and it clearly wasn't a welcome development.

Hutton smiled encouragingly at George. What if he'd forgotten about the generous job offer, or regretted making it?

"It's nice weather this week, isn't it George?" Hutton said. From any other man this would be a passive-aggressive response to Black's insistence he not venture on any more walks. In Hutton's case, it was a sincere observation.

"*It might make sense, Dr Black...*" George affected a nonchalance to his proculopathic tone. "*...If I too took a walk tomorrow morning around Arthur's Seat. Just to keep an eye on Dr Hutton for peace of mind.*"

Phoebe would have more to say about his unfinished letter to Dr Hunter, or his prevaricating ideas, if he stayed home for any length of time. He was also struck by a wave of nerves whenever he thought about approaching Hutton regarding the job offer. One thing was for sure: if he had an opportunity to raise the matter without Black in the vicinity to peer disapprovingly, he would take it.

Black hummed. It was an expression of modest disapproval, though Hutton might assume he was focussed wholly on the slow progress of his ether distillation.

"I suspect Dr Hutton is too stubborn to stay home, even if you demand it. Monitoring him in the relative safety of Holyrood Park won't be a problem, I promise. Besides," George continued to plead. *"Letting him have this walk tomorrow might make him more cooperative on other matters."*

He could feel the chemistry professor relenting; a withdrawal of mental pressure and lightening of his posture.

"Yes," agreed Black silently, stealing a glance at Hutton, now wholly occupied with reading the bottle labels on Black's shelf. *"That sounds like a sensible precaution."*

* * *

There was an emptiness in the valley between Arthur's Seat and Salisbury Crags that put George to mind of the desolate Highlands, despite walking scant miles from Edinburgh.

Grasses slapped against George's ankles as he traced his slow arch up the interior of the Crags. Down below, a few hundred metres ahead, strode Hutton, oblivious to his observer. Hutton would only have to turn around to spy George, for on this disappointing grey but dry day, there was no one else here.

George could hardly believe he this opportunity opened up, especially given the danger Hutton faced. It wasn't really defiance on the geologist's part: Black told him Hutton became very agitated when his routine was disrupted, and objected strongly to changing it.

Then the valley was consumed by the roar of a gunshot. Under reflex, George dropped to the ground as the echoes rung out on all sides. As soon as he landed he knew he hadn't been shot, so crawled half upright to look over the grassland.

Hutton still stood, looking around in confusion. A knot

of shadows hurried from the nearest end of the valley towards Hutton.

He didn't need to be closer to recognise these men had no good intentions. George began hurtling down the slope to intercept them, sliding on the wet, uneven ground. He cursed himself for following Hutton at such a distance. He was well out of phlogiston firing range.

Instead of fleeing, Hutton remained still and straight-backed as the men closed in on him. As George bumped and stumbled, he tried to see who held the pistol, but he had to focus on his feet for fear he'd twist an ankle.

"Hey!" George yelled, momentum carrying him down the last incline. The men—two of whom grabbed an unresisting Hutton's arms—turned to see who interrupted them. Up close, they were mean rascals with harsh faces. None of them looked familiar—but they didn't need to.

George skidded to a halt and raised his hand. He took a breath and tried to decide which man to strike first. The one closest to Hutton? The one reaching into his waistband? The one moving towards him?

As he tried to focus, another image intruded into George's head. It was his former lodger James Campbell, dying in Black's bedchamber. Like him, James thought he was fighting for his life in a staged duel. He tried to fire phlogiston at his opponent, but collapsed with horrific internal bleeding instead.

Until this moment, George thought himself a competent —if under-practised—wielder of phlogiston. He'd drilled with Black and Cullen until the act was instinct, until all fears of self-injury seemed erased.

But every time he'd practiced, Black or Cullen were with him, tutoring and sharpening his technique, but also ready to step in and diffuse a deadly phlogiston build up at a moment's notice. George was alone on the hillside, and as soon as he remembered he was alone, he paused.

His brief hesitation was enough for the second ruffian on the left to pull a pistol from his waistband.

This time, George knew he'd been shot as soon as the bang filled his ear. He felt his right shoulder flail with the impact. Not waiting for him to react, the nearest ruffian's fist was already descending.

Pain consumed George's body: jaw, shoulder and knees as he collided with the ground. A kick to his stomach send him onto his belly devoid of air.

Desperately trying to regain control of his extremes, George struggled up with the aid of one hand. His right arm flopped under him.

Hutton stood frozen, his jaw tense, eyes never leaving George. George didn't think cried out, but he was no longer sure of anything.

"This a friend of yours?" jeered a second ruffian with the pistol. Gunpowder smoke stung George's eyes. The click of the pistol cocking froze him too.

For the first time, George made and sustained eye contact with Hutton. Hutton's skin was paler than marble, his whole body trembled, and he appeared in danger of passing out. George almost tasted Hutton's panic: knowing his answer could result in the trigger being pulled.

George wanted to plead with Hutton, but he couldn't do anything more than groan. His friend's face blurred out of focus.

"This is a stranger to me," Hutton whispered. The ringing in George's ears almost drowned him out. "He can't be more than a boy."

"Ha!" was all the ruffian replied.

George wanted to yell at Hutton for betraying him, for

refusing to plead for his life, when he saw the ruffian lower his pistol.

"Lucky for him."

A blow to the back of head sent waves of grey washing over George's vision.

By the time the grey and the black abated, George lay alone on the Crags, soaked by soft rainfall and indescribable pain.

Hutton and his attackers were nowhere to be seen.

7

George found himself in the second-worst location he could wake up in.

"Ahhh, George, can you hear me?"

The skeleton above him swung idly, the flickers of beeswax candles in the gloom making it seem half-alive.

Monro's large periwigged head came into view.

"There's still a good dose of laudanum in your system, so don't exert yourself."

Pain drenched George's right arm, but he felt it in the abstract, at a distance from his body.

"The second worst what?" Monro asked.

George didn't realise he spoke aloud.

"The second worst location to awaken in," he managed. His voice slurred and didn't sound like it belonged to him, but the words he heard matched what he'd been trying to communicate. He was shivering slightly.

"I see," Monro remarked. "What is worse than waking up on my dissecting table?"

"I think...waking up in Dr Duncan's coat closet."

Monro let out a bark of laughter. "Perhaps," he agreed.

It occurred to George that he was conversing with Monro like the situation was normal, but he had no idea why he was in Monro's old anatomy theatre. Expanding class sizes had caused Monro to abandon the basement anatomy theatre, previously occupied by his father, for the new octagonal construction. It had been years since classes were taught here: Monro currently used the basement to store skeletons and dusty wax casts of blood vessels.

Natural light never made it to the basement, so George swam completely unmoored from the passing of time. He could have been out cold for weeks, or minutes.

He recalled collapsing in the bracken below the Crags with a gunshot wound but, perhaps because of the sedatives Monro administered, he couldn't discern how that memory linked to his current predicament.

Seeing his strained frowns, Monro moved to the foot of the table. "I promised Joseph and William I'd send a note when you recovered consciousness, which I dispatched it a few minutes ago when you started moving and muttering. I imagine they will be here shortly."

"Thank you...but..." That wasn't what George hoped to hear. "I mean, professor....how...?"

"I see." Monro began busying himself tidying the surgical tools and scraps of blood-soaked cloth piled at George's feet. "Well, you stumbled into the Yards with a gunshot wound, collapsing before anyone could get anything pertinent out of you. You'd gone into shock and sustained considerable blood loss by that point. The good news is the bullet passed straight through your tissue, and as long as the wound heals cleanly—which I have no doubt it will—you should retain most of the functions in that arm."

Yes, I had been shot, George reflected. The laudanum was making it hard to connect all his thoughts together.

"You saved my life," he realised, though the words came out more confused than appreciative.

"I did that too," Monro replied.

"I hope I didn't....inconvenience you." George dimly worried he'd interrupted Monro's class time.

"Quite the contrary." Monro looked up. "My students found the operation most instructive."

Drugs and surprising revelations made a shaky combination. "Your students?" George asked.

"Oh yes," Monro continued. "I was the first medical professor to reach you in the Yards—very fortunate for you. Given the condition you were in, I thought it best to operate immediately. Since no one knew what befell you, I decided the basement would be the most discrete location. That said, I thought my brightest students would benefit from witnessing the operation. Your grapeshot wound was one of the most beautiful I've seen—very clean entry, textbook tissue damage, only simple suturing required. They enjoyed the spectacle very much."

George's cheeks and eyes tingled.

"Will you permit me to enquire as to what happened?" Monro switched to proculopathy, glancing around the space.

"A group of men attacked Dr Hutton..." Wait, George thought to himself, Hutton got attacked? *"On Salisbury Crags. They shot me and...I don't know what they did to him."* George now was sniffling, and hating himself for doing so, but his emotions seemed puppeteered by someone else. *"I tried to stop them professor, and...I failed."*

"I see." There wasn't a lot of reaction in Monro's features: as a physician and surgeon he no doubt heard all sorts of desperate confessions from wretches on the brink of departing this world. "Well, I've heard no word of Dr Hutton's demise. No doubt Joseph and William will be better informed."

George was trying to haul himself under control when Monro stopped moving.

"I think that's Joseph now."

George wasn't in a position to move about, his arm still hurt and the rest of his body felt cumbersome to move. There were light footfalls, before he felt Black slip a cool hand into his own.

"George?" Black's face rose into view, and George found his emotions reeling off again.

"Professor...I'm so sorry..."

8

At ten o'clock the next morning Black departed his house, instructing the servants to accommodate Mrs Phoebe Stephens if she arrived before he returned. No doubt she'd seek assurance her husband was recovering under his supervision. George was either still asleep in the upstairs guest chamber when he left, or pretending to be.

Waiting outside the Tron Kirk, Black was surprised to see Cullen emerge from Mint Close with Mrs Cullen on his arm.

"Is this a good idea?" Black enquired once the couple reached him.

"Yes," Anna Cullen answered, tapping her husband's elbow. "To avoid any questions of impropriety when meeting an unaccompanied woman."

Word that Mrs Holm wished to meet them came an hour after news of Hutton's kidnapping reached his ears via Monro and a garbled, feverish George Stephens. The wait hadn't been pleasant.

"Indeed," Black agreed, his voice tinctured with irony. "As we negotiate the release of a hostage, kidnapped by the wife of a man I intend to slay on sight, we better not lose sight of impropriety towards the fairer sex."

"I'm sure Dr Hutton is safe and well," Cullen replied, aware Black's sharp tone belied anxiety about his friend. "And more to the point, we need a third set of eyes."

That they did. While Anna Cullen acted in some ways as if proculopathy and phlogiston-wielding was beneath her, Black couldn't fault her ability to act in concert with her husband.

Despite the clamour in St Giles square, Kitty Holm was not difficult to spot. She stood next to a squat man in a bright red jacket with navy cuffs and gold buttons, a few curls of his wig peeking out underneath his bicorne hat.

"This is my brother-in-law, Balfour," Kitty explained. "Captain of the Town Guard."

The captain grunted and tightened the grip on his sword pommel.

Well, Black thought, that's a clear enough warning.

The captain's other hand rested on a walking cane.

"Left knee injury by the looks of it," Cullen's voice noted with clinical efficacy. *"Probably shipped back from the colonies to recuperate—given an easy Town Guard post to occupy his time."*

"I'm not fighting him in the middle of the street, William," Black snapped. *"We're practically standing inside the guard house."*

"Calm down Joe, I know that," William protested. *"But it's useful information for later, is it not?"*

"Mrs Holm," Black said instead, bowing to the woman. "Unless you have information pertaining to the whereabouts of Dr Hutton, this rendezvous will be very brief indeed."

"Dr Black, your charm with the ladies is everything I expected," replied Kitty. With a snap of her wrist she extended her fan. "I thought the subjects of North Britain had better social airs."

"After Paris, I fear Edinburgh society will disappoint you," Black said. "Where's Dr Hutton?"

"A loyal wife does not intrude upon their particulars of her husband's affairs," sniffed Kitty. "But I can assure you he is well cared for. Alas, Dr Hutton appears reticent on the whereabouts of his heretical papers, claiming he did *not* in fact entrust their keeping to his closest friends."

"As you said, knowing too much of another man's business is rude."

"The Royal Society's next meeting tomorrow afternoon, correct? That will give you ample time to collect Dr Hutton's papers to bring them to me here at midday. It goes without saying that Dr Hutton will stay in our care until after the meeting date, lest his friends act against his best interest. After that he will issue a public retraction and lay his blasphemous inquiries to rest."

Kitty slid her arm into the crook of the captain's elbow, but paused as they turned to depart.

"Dr Black? Don't try anything too intelligent over the next few days. You are a smart man, but you're not that smart."

"What should be done?" Cullen asked, eyeing Black once they were alone again. "You know Hutton's sentiments best, Joe." They came to a halt outside South Gray's Close.

"He is, I'm afraid, rather steadfast when it came to his theory," Black said. "His worst nightmare is being forced to capitulate like Comte de Buffon."

The Comte was the last man to make a stab at estimating the Earth's age, some forty years previous. Though Hutton considered the Parisian's deviation from biblical chronology laughably timid and theoretically unsubstantiated, there was enough outcries of heresy to prompt a hasty retraction. The Comte ceased all enquiry into geology after that.

"Unless a massive stroke of Providence blesses us, we won't have time to rescue Hutton before tomorrow's meeting."

"Indeed," Black said, unclenching his jaw. "I rather think that was Holm's plan."

"Do you know where Hutton's papers are?" Cullen asked, lowering his voice to a whisper. "Or what proofs he's devised?"

"He didn't tell me their location," Black said. "But I know what he intends for first part of his presentation, because James gave me a copy of it to review."

"You have that in your possession?" Cullen's frown solidified, sensing the general outline of unfolding events and disliking its appearance.

"Yes." Black tapped his breast pocket. Four sheets of neatly folded paper traced a barely visible outline in the fabric. It was unlikely that even if Mrs Holm noticed Black's pocket she'd realise what it contained.

"I didn't know James gave you a copy of his paper," Cullen said slowly. Anna tightened her grip on her husband's elbow, sensing the change in his mood as clearly as Black could.

"He wanted me to check the grammar and flow of his intended speech. I would have returned it yesterday." Black refused to break eye contact. "I've not assisted him in any other way with the paper's composition or content."

Cullen looked like he was debating whether to ask the obvious question—why am I just hearing about this now—deciding against it on the obvious grounds Black withheld the information until their conversation with Mrs Holm and her brother-in-law was complete.

Black could see the storm rolling in. There was no use fighting it, but he could delay its arrival. "I have business to attend to, but let's regroup tomorrow morning to discuss our plan of action. Holm will know by noon that we aren't intending to cooperate."

Cullen sucked air over his teeth. Anna squeezed his arm in warning.

"And any movement from us before then will tip our hand," Black pointed out, anticipating this reaction and trying to nip it in the bud. "So we better move with economy."

"Indeed."

Halfway down the Canongate past the churchyard, Black ducked through a close. As soon as he left the bustle of the Canongate he felt a measure of his stress lifting as the imposing rough stone home of Adam Smith rose into view. Like the man himself, the building's exterior was well-fortified.

Quickening his pace, Black approached the boxy dwelling and rapped on thick wooden door.

He found Smith in his upstairs parlour of Panmure House, sitting at the desk with his back to the hearth. The room had the pleasant aroma of old books, which liberally covered the walls and surfaces.

"We need to find out where Hutton is being held, Adam," Black said, knowing he didn't need to waste time on pointless pleasantries.

Smith raised both his hands to the heavens. "Without question, Joe. But we have precious little to go on."

Black leaned on the table.

"We know that Holm's main connection to Edinburgh comes from his wife, Kitty MacBride."

"That's who he married?" Smith frowned. "I would not have predicted that."

Black filled his friend in on the pertinent details from his encounter with the current Mrs Holm.

Where Hutton was light-hearted and whimsical, Smith

possessed all of Cullen's worst brooding tempers, with none of the physician's charisma. Yet his thought processes existed in such flawless concert to Black's that working with him felt like a kind of proculopathy. Between the light and dark of Hutton and Smith, Black decided, he had all the friendship he needed.

"It's a starting point," Black continued. "Based on what properties the MacBrides hold, and other family or business connections that converge with dark chymist sympathies."

Smith chuckled. "A fair contest of wits, this will be. I can tell you the MacBrides own numerous properties in the Lothians, and their familial interests overlap with a number of the old chymist order. As do most nobles in this fair city."

Black said nothing.

"That said..." Smith's eyes crinkled. "Through consideration of multiple influencing factors, I imagine a reasonable deduction can be made as to where they'd keep a hostage of Holm's. Not too far from Edinburgh, but not so close we'd stumble upon him. Defensibility, ease of transportation, proximity to other locations whose import we don't yet appreciate."

"If anyone can tease out those threads, it's you," Black said.

"Best immerse myself in some land tax rolls, then," Smith remarked, a verbal shooing away of his friend. "We'll reconvene at the Oyster Club tomorrow after the Royal Society meeting." Unlike Cullen, Smith seemed to accept what Black would do next, without needing to state it out loud.

"Ah yes," Black sighed. "That was the other thing I needed to tell you about..."

9

"I don't wish to belabour the point," George said, every word dipped in as much sarcasm as he could muster. "But I notice we are congregating in a brothel."

Black blinked. "Yet the sign above the door says 'Victualler'. And when I went inside to inquire about meeting spaces the other day, they offered astonishingly reasonable rates for the use of this room one night a month for the rest of the year."

"Yes. Because it's. A. Brothel."

Black sighed. "I don't think you understand how uncommon two pounds for a room of this size is in Edinburgh, George. The floor is clean. The room has decent lighting and isn't too noisy. They are most generous in providing us with drinks."

"Because it's a brothel." George repeated. Phoebe would eviscerate him when she learned about this. He was still on edge, floating in pain and exhaustion.

When he arrived ten minutes later, Smith appeared agitated. He didn't spare a moment to congratulate Black on the successful paper reading.

"There are at least five properties Hutton could reasonably be held at," Smith explained, pulling up a chair. "He'd need to be guarded to prevent his escape, so that requires multiple people housed on or about the estate; a sizeable dwelling that's not so sizeable it can't be secured."

"And you can't narrow it down further?" Black asked. He didn't question Smith's decision-making process.

"Not from tax rolls—it's not just about money and geographic location," Smith groused.

Other gentlemen were filing into the room. Most came direct from the Royal Society meeting. A few patted Black on the shoulder as they squeezed past.

"What specific information are you missing?" Black asked. His attention remained on Smith.

George nervously glanced around to see how the Oyster Club members were reacting to the new venue—nary a snicker—and to Black's reading of Hutton's paper—muted.

"The behaviour of the late Lord Ross splintered the remaining dark chymist families. Some were repulsed by his experimentation with Brown, others wanted to cling to his lordship's coat tails for protection. Who knows what this then means for Holm, strutting back into the city he terrorised?"

Black bit his lip.

"When he first taunted me, I wondered what drove him back to Edinburgh after all these years. Hutton's blasphemous theories are an excuse, but not the whole story. His preference was always slitting the throats of multiple birds with one knife, to adapt the popular metaphor."

A rouged serving girl finally caught Smith's attention long enough to get a drink order from him. She winked at him, but the philosopher didn't notice.

"That's even more of a muddle," Smith sighed. "How do you expect me to sort out this mess? Do you even know how the Argyles reacted to news of Holm's return?"

Through very circumspect whispers, George had learned the Argyles were once the prominent dark chymistry family. Their patriarch was found dead on the day the dark chymist's library was reputably destroyed. George didn't dare ask Cullen and Black what occurred.

"Afraid not."

"Well, knowing if the MacBrides are supported by the Argyles is one factor. The second is what motivates the MacBrides. Whether they care about revenge, survival or consolidating power."

"Rather abstract, is it not?" George snapped. "How would that influence which of their properties they're hiding Hutton in?"

"You'd be surprised," Smith replied. "Well, if you read the latest edition of my treatise you wouldn't of course, but..."

"Don't worry, Adam," Black interrupted. "We'll get as much information to you as we can before Saturday. Do you think you can make a quick deduction once you have that information?"

"We'll see, won't we?" Smith's crabbiness got the better of him, and he turned to his companions on the left.

Black took a long drink from his sherry.

Given their blistering argument earlier in the day, George wasn't sure Cullen would turn up at the Oyster Club. As it happened, Cullen arrived late enough for it to be an obvious snub, and didn't immediately acknowledge Black or Smith.

Cautiously lowering himself into the seat beside him, George wasn't sure if he should mention Black's reading. If Cullen noticed anything untoward about their location, he didn't remark upon it.

It seemed bizarre no one but George recognised they were in a house of ill repute, but though the attendees were brilliant men, they often demonstrated a certain obliviousness to their surroundings. He'd heard a few sympathetic mutterings about Hutton's ailment—that he'd vanish right before reading his paper with a claim of ill health struck no one as suspicious.

Cullen broke the awkward silence by nodding at George's arm. "How's the shoulder holding up?"

"As long as I keep it still, it's fine." George's arm was still bound up and strapped to him, and he enjoyed a wide berth from everyone as a result. "It looks like Mr Smith hasn't had much luck in his search for Dr Hutton."

Cullen took the news grimly. "I'm not surprised. Much credit to Adam—there's not a sharper mind in Britain—but it appears Holm has more tricks up his sleeve than we appreciated."

"Hmm?"

"After our unpleasant rendezvous with Mrs Holm yesterday, the good Mrs Cullen and myself launched our own enquiries. On the one hand, there's fortunately not many people in Edinburgh now for whom the name Malcolm Holm means anything, save for old fogeys like myself. But unfortunately, that makes the man nigh-impossible to track. Are you acquainted with Mrs Margaret Monro-MacDonald?"

"...I can't say I am, professor."

"Sorry, I thought you might have come across her—she's the older sister of Dr Monro. A very insightful lady." From the way Cullen delivered this assessment George knew this was high praise. "She apparently saw Holm walking atop Calton Hill with John Playfair a week or so ago, engrossed in conversation. That's not good at all," Cullen muttered.

"If I'm supposed to know who Playfair is, please accept my apologies because I don't." Sometimes George thought Cullen was mixing him up with other students and other conversations from his decades of teaching.

Cullen shook his head. "It's unlikely you would. Playfair

hasn't visited Edinburgh in several years. He's a minister up near Dundee—though I believe he just resigned the position. Unlike Hutton, he has no head for the countryside. Brilliant mathematician and natural philosopher, needs to feed that bottomless intellect of his. Tutoring students doesn't cut it."

"He's an accomplice of Holm?" George assumed a theological connection existed.

"A little too young for dark chymistry business," Cullen said. "Nor is violence in his nature. But I wouldn't be surprised if he shares some of Holm's theological viewpoints. I suspect Holm intends to use Playfair to discredit Hutton's theories."

"You think it's possible?" From the way Black had spoken, George assumed Hutton's conclusions were air tight.

"If anyone can pick holes in Dr Hutton's theories, it will be Playfair. There are a few other ministers with natural philosophy expertise, but none of them have Playfair's wit or charisma. Holm knows the theological arguments inside out, but Playfair can speak the language of the Royal Society."

George grimaced. If it was enough to worry Cullen, it would worry him too.

"Did you say this Playfair tutors students?"

"Yes, he tutored Simon Argyle as a youth."

George made a series of belated connections.

"Professor, do you mean Simon Argyle is of the Argyle family? The Classics student?" He would be the grandson of the murdered dark chymist.

"The very same."

"Well," George said, taking a long gulp of his ale. "I spy an opportunity to initiate several prongs of enquiry in near-simultaneous fashion..."

An older woman who George suspected was the brothel madam approached the table. If she was surprised her guests seemed uninterested in her girls, there was no sign of it on her face.

"Is everything well here, gentlemen? Can I get the table any more provisions?"

Black politely shook his head. "Thank you madam, but—"

"Actually," George interrupted. "We have a partiality for oysters. So much so in fact that we call ourselves the Oyster Club."

The men at the table looked startled by his forceful outburst, but a more complex set of emotions was flitting across Black's face.

The woman looked confused, but it didn't appear she'd been slighted. "Indeed, sir?"

"Yes, madam." George was angry at Black for dragging him into this charade, and the anger was getting the better of him. "My colleagues came here tonight thinking of oysters, and the larger quantities you can provide, the better."

The woman gave a knowing nod. "I think we might be able to help you."

"Take my good friend, Mr Black, over here. He tells us often how much he enjoys the fragrant juices of local oysters. He insists that freshness is not the quality he values most in oysters. In fact, he says the saltier the oyster's brine, the more he enjoys swallowing them."

The others at the table laughed, but that was more because they were several drinks into the night than because they understood what was going on.

Black held eye contact with George. Then he smirked. He turned to the woman with an expression of utmost sincerity.

"My friend is absolutely correct."

The madam beamed. "Well, I'll tell the girls to come through, then."

He braced himself for what would happen, but the girls who came through a few minutes later were merely carrying brimming plates of oysters, which the men set upon with gusto.

As one of the ladies of the town—a particularly mousey-haired woman with the faintest smudge of freckles under the painted skin—turned to leave, Black's expression changed suddenly. Before George could react, he reached out his hand and caught her elbow.

"I heard from one of my acquaintances you were approached by a man calling himself the Reverend Malcolm Holm a few days ago outside the Theatre Royal." Black spoke so low only George could catch the conversation.

The woman's expression went from confused to guarded.

A flicker of gold in Black's hand caught the candlelight. The woman bit her lip.

"It isn't my intention to accuse you of anything. You've not done anything wrong. But I would like to know more about your conversation."

George could see the calculation on the girl's face. She was assessing the likelihood of re-encountering Holm, of him finding out about this conversation, versus the glow of coin in this other man's palm. A decision was made quickly.

"The gentlemen you speak of affected concern for my welfare, and I assured him my lodgings and landlady were most satisfactory."

"Was Reverend Holm trying to discern anything through his discussion with you?"

"He asked if I'd seen Lord Bennett on the North Bridge. I gather he suspected him of assignations with ladies on the town in this spot—not that I know anything about that. He also wanted to know the current address of Dr John Brown."

"Hmm."

Black extended his hand. The woman took it. When she let go of his hand, the guinea had vanished.

"Thank you, madam. You've been most helpful. I wish you a pleasant evening."

George gave the prostitute space to retreat before turning fully to face his professor.

"Pray tell me, what in the name..."

He didn't have time to make his indignant demand, because at that moment Smith stumbled back into the room, wide-eyed and crimson. The door swung back on its hinges and banged into the wall, causing all conversation to cease.

Smith coughed.

"As I was, um, coming back from the water closet, I couldn't help but notice a bevy of well-dressed young ladies congregating in the adjacent room. They, err, were peculiarly brazen-faced..."

Several of the noblemen coughed and adjusted their collars.

Black remained a picture of innocence. "What are you trying to suggest, Adam?" he asked gently.

"He's saying we're in a brothel!" George burst out, his conscience unable to perpetuate the charade any longer.

There was a hush of conferred whispers.

"What is going on, Joe?" Smith asked, his cheeks red.

"Well..." Black spoke slowly, as if talking through a new chemical theory. "I notice we're in a room that seats fourteen men comfortably, and have spent two and a half hours conversing without once being accosted by drunk singers, impetuous fiddle players or half-witted amateur seditionists. And we're paying three pounds less for the privilege than anywhere else we've gathered this winter."

Every eye in the room was on Smith.

"Oh." Smith plopped down and picked up his drink. "When you put it like that, forget I said anything."

* * *

George and Black walked the last stretch to Nicolson Street in silence.

"Are we quarrelling, Mr Stephens?" Black sauntered beside him with the loose amiability he only acquired after drinking. Once his interrogation of the whore was completed, his restraint dropped several notches.

He would use proculopathy, George thought to himself.

"You always do this! Making fun of me at my expense. You didn't have to drag us all to the brothel just to get those scraps of information from that whore."

"Well, if you had a more meritorious approach you should have shared it with us. I have great respect for your ideas."

"You keep on doing this!" George exclaimed.

"Doing what?" Black remained cheerful.

"This!"

They fell back into silence. At least they'd almost reached Black's house.

Black laid a hand on George's shoulder. Some of his merriment dissipated.

"One of the things I like most about you, George, is that you can handle yourself in any situation, even when you believe you can't. You sped up the process of locating the girl in a way that saved most of the gentleman from embarrassment."

"Ha, most of them."

"The remark about oysters was quite amusing, I admit. Disrespectful and borderline slander, but amusing."

"I'll take my leave of you, Dr Black." George turned to face him. He was still angry, but now his anger was entirely directed at himself for his inability to remain angry at Black.

"Good evening, Mr Stephens. Your company is always a pleasure."

IO

Waking up the next morning in the comfort of his own bed, George wondered if the world had changed. Would Hutton's theories have shaken the city to its foundations? Would people look out of their windows at the new dawn, viewing it in a new light?

Phoebe was sleeping soundly next to him. Four floors down, the street hummed into boisterous life.

Or had George awoken to a world without Hutton in it? Was Black's closest friend already dead?

Safe in the comfort of his own bed, a few errant memories bumped together inside George's head.

He'd wondered why the confrontation on Salisbury Crags stirred a queasy feeling of familiarity, why it felt like he was sleepwalking through events that had already transpired: the whole scene reminded him of Brandywine Creek.

That cursed, damp meadow, with the long grass tickling his calves and heavy morning fog. It created a panorama of misery. The one thing George hated about Pennsylvania and New York: the nights and early mornings were bitterly cold, but either turned to baking heat within hours, or torrential rain.

It was George's first battle. He'd been bored senseless with the marching and hours waiting around while senior officers bellowed about logistics. George hadn't understood why the soldiers needed to stand around in the midday heat or what the hold-up with their supplies was. He was desperate for combat and an opportunity to discharge his rifle.

His uncle had always said he'd make a good solider. "You're brave and principled, lad—any battalion worth its salt would promote you to captain as fast as they could." His father told him similar things—but his father tended to enthuse about everything. Praise from Uncle Roderick actually meant something to George.

His light infantry battalion was tasked with sneaking round the rebels' flanks and concealing themselves in the woods to trap anyone trying to flee or encircle the British.

"Private!" his corporal barked. "Take those men round left to the hillock with the maple tree."

George hesitated. He understood what was being asked of him: the hillock pointed out was one of the most defensible spots in this sparse area. If the rebels came through this way, they'd be funnelled towards it.

"Err...it looks to be marshland behind the hillock though, sir."

"Private Stephens...!"

George rushed to get his words out first. "It will be difficult to fall back from that point, sir!"

The rest of the men cringed. Corporal Laurence's eyes and lips tightened into slits.

"Are you refusing to obey a direct order, private?"

"No...I just..." George scrambled. The fog made it impossible to see more than a hundred metres in any direction. "Wondered if maybe...that clump of elms would be better?"

He was too chastised to even fully raise his arm to point. In any case, Corporal Laurence didn't bother to look in that direction.

"Do you know what would be even better, private? Waking up in a well-furnished brothel with a leisurely breakfast and coffee already brewed. But we don't have that luxury, Private Stephens. Besides..."

"Quiet!" another infantryman hissed. "I heard voices."

Silence dropped in a heartbeat. The thick fog around them lay unperturbed, but a murmur and clicking discernible above the trickling stream was coming from the southwest.

"Get into position! Now!"

It could theoretically have been a squadron of their own men, or farmers coming back from the market. But as he rushed across the boggy ground, George regretted every desire of his to see combat and prove himself a man. He no longer wanted that glory.

His rifle was almost as tall as him and proved cumbersome to balance as they stumbled over marshy ground. The mud pulled him down just as he heard cries breaking through the mists.

They'd been spotted!

"Fire!"

Paradoxically, George thought he should stand up to face the incoming gunfire. It seemed cowardly to recline in the mud, concealed from the rebels' sight.

Then came the first crackle of rifles, followed by grunts and cries. Belatedly, George remembered he could fire back, so he pivoted onto his belly and propped the tip of his rifle on a root.

Ten paces from him, he watched a scruffy lad about his age stab his bayonet right through Corporal Laurence's throat. The blood-slicked blade came out the other side. He was close enough to hear the sickening crunch of flesh and bone spliced, and the guttural pants of a dying man frantically trying to suck air through a mangled windpipe. It was a ridiculous sight: the boy's clothes were barely more than rags. Corporeal Laurence took tremendous pride in shining his boots and buttons. Yet whatever original colour his murderer's uniform was, it was lost to indeterminate shades of brown. Yet his hands didn't even shake.

An eternity later, George was one of four dazed soldiers aimlessly drifting back towards where they thought their army was. With every step, his sodden breeches stuck, then peeled off his thighs.

No one said a word or looked at each other.

I'm to blame for this, George thought to himself, over and over. If we'd got into position a minute earlier, we'd have been ready for the rebels. It's because of my delay that all those men are dead.

II

Black awaited Holm's reaction with jolts of agony in his stomach. He knew a reaction was coming, but he couldn't predict what it would be. Mrs Kitty Holm on his doorstep? Hutton's severed head in a box?

He'd done precisely what the Holms ordered him not to do. At the time his conviction burned with incendiary brightness; in the morning all he was left with was shakiness. At one point he'd believed his friend was too valuable to be killed right away—he tried to bring himself back to that state of conviction.

The act of eating breakfast that morning took double its usual time. Black had to force every piece of buttered roll into his mouth, and chew when he wanted to spit each mouthful out.

He'd managed a few sips of coffee when his manservant came in, brandishing a scrap of paper.

Morris had served Black ever since he moved to Nicholson Street. Black could tell from Morris' expression nobody they knew delivered this message.

This would be it, then.

There was no point asking who delivered it. Holm would cover his tracks.

Where you might expect florid handwriting given the man's egotism, Holm's was sparse and neat. It was ministerial handwriting: you didn't deliver condolences to parishioners in looping calligraphic flourishes.

Ten o'clock this morning. Greyfriars Kirkyard. Lord Argyle
will be the host.

Black didn't suppose Holm would involve the current Lord Argyle in his dealings. He'd have to leave the house now, since he wasn't sure he remembered where the elder Lord Argyle was buried.

By the time Black reached the kirkyard and located the tombstone, it was approximately five minutes to the hour. He retraced his path to the front gate, where Adam Smith was stamping his feet.

"Did you see William?"

"Afraid not, Joe."

It was likely Cullen had already departed his house to call on patients, and Black's hastily scribbled note sat unread in his study. Still, having Smith as protection was better than being here alone.

"I looked around the kirkyard and can't see anyone who resembles Holm. It's probably best you stay here and keep watch, Adam. You have a good view here." Smith would be a hundred paces from Arygle's grave. Not close enough to disturb the conversation—Holm wanted privacy—but hopefully close enough to react if...or when...something went wrong.

Smith nodded.

Back at Argyle's grave, Black studied it for any trace of a message. The urgent rendezvous time might be a misdirection, designed to put Black on the defensive. Holm might not intend to speak with him at all. But there was no half-buried letter.

A gentle breeze blew through the kirkyard. A handful of people, mostly women, were tending graves. No one passed Smith in or out. He craned his neck over the haphazard rows of tombstones, checking no one crouched nearby.

Black flexed his fingers, testing the feel of phlogiston and aether.

Then he saw it. Some of the moss was scraped from Argyle's tombstone near the base. In its place looked at first glance like a smudge of charcoal, about the size of a fist.

Black couldn't help himself: he sprung back. He clenched his hands to his sides and looked around, mindful of everything he'd touched on his way in.

He fumbled for a handkerchief. Touching an unknown dark chymistry sigil was a terrible—potentially fatal—idea, but perhaps if he had a rock or stick...

In the distance, the bells of St Giles tolled. Almost instantly, the sigil glowed orange.

Black took a step back, his hands outstretched. Phlogiston rose inside him. The sigil bulged on the dark stone.

"Ah, Joseph." Holm's voice sounded bright in his ear. "I take it you already spotted my sigil on Argyle's tombstone?"

The kirkyard was deserted.

"Not soon enough to destroy it," Black said with bitterness.

Enemies of the dark chymists tended to end up dead inside locked apartments, with their throats cut. Witnesses swore no one entered or left the murder sites. However, when enquiries were made, it was often revealed a dark chymist or two accessed the rooms in the preceding days under benign circumstances. A discrete charcoal sigil would be inscribed somewhere out of sight, and sometime later a second portal sigil would be drawn, allowing Holm passage from one sigil location to the other.

It made sense Holm retained knowledge of portal sigils.

"We have about four minutes to conduct this conversation before the sigil burns itself out, Joseph." Although clear enough, Holm's voice had a transparent quality to it. Hearing him speak via a sigil wasn't the same as standing in the same room as him. "So let's keep things on track."

Black angled himself so he had a better view of the kirkyard. He could see Smith at the gate, peering in multiple directions.

"Your friend's tenuous grasp of composition is probably what saved his life. Last night you presented a lot of geological history, competing hypotheses and hand-waving statements... but scant proof of your blasphemous claims."

"So what is the harm?" Black asked coldly. "If you think his thesis is so poorly constructed."

His heart hammered. He hoped his voice didn't waver. Hutton was still alive.

"He admitted the second half of the thesis contains the meat of his argument. Alas, he remains very forgetful as to its location."

Holm must be close enough to hear St Giles' Cathedral strike upon the hour.

"You don't need Dr Hutton alive." Every word of Black's was like a cold stone. "All you need are his papers."

"Call it romanticism on my part, Dr Black. My flock loves a good repentance tale almost as much as they love a tale of sin, though they pretend the latter isn't true. But you're right. Dr Hutton doesn't need, say, the use of his legs to repent. He doesn't strictly need the use of his tongue, but most people find verbal penitence more compelling than the written form."

Where moments ago the sigil almost blinded Black, it had faded to a dull ember glow.

"You will return here at noon on Saturday with Hutton's papers. That's a tight deadline, but I prefer not to work on the Sabbath. Besides, knowing you, Joseph—you'll either cooperate quickly or not at all. Non-cooperation at that juncture will lead to irreversible consequences."

Two days.

The sigil momentarily flared, then dissolved. Now it was no more than a smear of dirt on a neglected tombstone.

Back at the entrance, Smith relaxed his vigil when Black reappeared uninjured, but shaken.

"He's still got sigils up his sleeve. Portal ones."

Smith took the news grimly.

"That was always Holm's domain. It's a shame we don't know half of what the dark chymists were capable of. We can only guess at the sigils based on the scant available evidence."

Black filled his friend in on the deadline.

"I'm not being facetious—I don't know where Hutton hid his papers. Given the trouble brewing, I decided it was better not to enquire when he told me he'd store them somewhere safe."

"But he's talked through his arguments with you?"

"We covered the chemical aspects extensively. But Hutton kept his geological arguments to himself. I don't know what rock formations he's discussing in the second half of the paper, for instance."

Hutton preferred to talk that side of his theory out with the late Earl of Hopetoun.

"At least we have some time," Black said. "Let's pray it is enough to figure out what's going on."

He wanted to sag to the ground in relief that Hutton still lived, and there remained hope of recovering his friend. But a deeper unease was setting in. Not a mote of weakness resided in Holm's heart: if he kept Hutton alive, it was because he saw value in doing so. But what value could Holm possibly be exploiting? That his imagination couldn't jump to an obvious answer was troubling indeed. It meant Black was underestimating something.

"You know who I did see on the way over here?" Smith said after a pause. "George Stephens greeted me his on way to the college library."

Black needed to only think for a moment.

"Thank you, Adam," he said. "That's where I'll head next."

<h1 style="text-align:center">12</h1>

Simon and his entourage took up a central table in the Old Library. Ignoring the annoyed looks from the librarian, they continued to laugh and converse as if they were in a tavern.

Even though he was concealed behind a row of shelves, George kept his back to the table as he pretended to thumb through the old dissertations. He wasn't in the medical students' section. But he'd shuffled close enough to hear what they were braying about.

It took a glance for him to recognise the two others with Simon Argyle, for the three were inseparable.

At his left was a young man of extraordinary beauty, with the physique of a weeping willow. This effect was accentuated today by his choice of a three-piece matching suit in soft brown wool. With his long, wavy red hair and near-translucent eyelids, Gregory Bennett was derisively nicknamed 'Ganymede.' George assumed the insinuations were self-explanatory, though it was noteworthy no other men's names were attached to Ganymede.

Simon's other compatriot was a braying dark-haired lump of a man. He towered over the other two, always managing to take up more space than necessary. Jerome Lee was orphaned at a young age, coming into a generous inheritance and a barony somewhere in the Midlands, thanks to his mercer father. His nickname among the students was Diomedes. Although he publicly acknowledged the nickname, Diomedes didn't seem aware it was intended as mockery, skewering his *lack* of wisdom, in comparison to the famous Greek general.

Today, he wore a pea green suit and embroidered silk waistcoat in the French style. This was a bizarre affectation, because even George knew current French fashion was modelled on the leisure garb of English country gentlemen. Why a British gentleman of limitless means would ape the style of a modish Frenchman *as he was aping* the style of a British gentleman was a mystery: perhaps he intended it as irony?

That left the man in the middle. He was a hand shorter than the others, but possessed a steely intensity. Alone, his features were unremarkable and if he was unaccompanied, most people would surely walk by him without noticing. Simon preferred inconspicuous, dark cuts of fabric. Today he wore a navy wool coat with silver buttons. His claim to fashion was forsaking a gentleman's walking cane, instead carrying an oiled silk and whalebone umbrella, even on cloudless days. He must have been one of the first in Edinburgh to venture out in public with such a contraption. No one breathed a word of mockery when he did, though.

Only the deferential glances of his two colleagues indicated Simon was their ringleader. He defied classical nicknames, since no one's derision outstripped their begrudging admiration of the man. How Simon labelled himself was a mystery.

"'Did it please you, great Jove...'" Diomedes boomed, at a tone sacrilegiously loud for a near-empty library. The others tittered appreciatively.

Their voices dropped, but George heard "Virgil" muttered

a few times, leading him to deduce they were discussing a translation of the Aeneid, and Diomedes was performing aloud.

"'The gods in Jupiter's halls lamented the unavailing wrath of them both...'"

"No, stop." That was Simon's voice, a harsh command. "You've translated it wrong."

Even George froze and baulked. He could hear Diomedes nervously clear his throat.

"'Miseror' is closer to compassion than sorrow," Simon continued.

"'Felt sorry for?'" offered Ganymede.

"Pitied," Diomedes added hastily, eager to counteract his blunder.

Simon hummed.

George faced an impossible task. He knew nothing of the Classics beyond cursory outlines. While Cullen spoke lovingly of the ancient texts, he was more likely to wax lyrical on Don Quixote than the Aeneid or the Odyssey. There was nothing George could say of merit on the topic.

"'Unavailing wrath' isn't right either," said Ganymede. "The root is 'inanis', is it not? That's closer in meaning to 'inane.'"

"'Inane wrath' rather lacks the poetic majesty Virgil was celebrated for." George could hear Diomedes' shuffle as he leaned forward, his tone dropping to mock-confidentiality. "Perhaps the word you're looking for, dear boy, is 'ceaseless'?"

Still...

Slipping the book back onto the shelf, George crept closer. He'd forgone binding his injured arm, resolving to keep it as stationary as possible. It stung and throbbed, but the last thing he wanted to do was draw attention to his weakness, or field questions about its provenance.

"But that's not the sentiment Virgil is going for,"

Ganymede insisted, his voice close to a whine. "He's not just saying that war is unending, he's calling it folly."

Thomas' wife Elizabeth had a lot of opinions on the subject of communicating with social superiors. She'd once told George: "if all else fails, resort to confident rudeness, and mirror their accent."

She'd also killed one of the richest men in Britain by kicking him out of a hot air balloon. George hadn't been in Edinburgh at the time, and all Elizabeth would say about the incident was the rich bastard had it coming.

Still focused on the conversation, George's heart rate spiked as the arguing students trailed off. But it wasn't because they'd spied him eavesdropping: instead, Diomedes and Ganymede were waiting for Simon to intercede in their argument.

Yet Simon hesitated, probably unsure of the correct answer himself.

To George's surprise, he was seized by an opinion. It struck him with such force he almost gasped.

Before the strong weight of his conviction could flee, George stepped from behind the shelves and approached the table. "Your carrot-topped friend is correct. Go with 'futile.'"

Simon stared, either too affronted or too stunned to respond. Diomedes whispered in his ear.

Simon turned over the quill in his hand, his eyes not leaving George. "Stephens, is it? The medical student? What do you know of Latin conjugation?"

George moved his facial muscles into a smile. "Nothing. But I know a lot about war."

Another pause. Every eye on the table was on Simon.

After what felt like an eternity, Simon burst out with howls of laughter.

"Quite right you are! Well-played, sir."

George smiled with pleasure, despite himself.

Simon nodded and turned slightly in his chair to better regard this new arrival. Almost imperceptibly, Ganymede and Diomedes adjusted themselves too, flicking their books away.

"Old Monro must be cracking the whip if you're still in the library this close to your dissertation defence."

"Actually, I only came here to see if the treatise I wanted had been returned. Looks like I must wait another week." George affected a loose nonchalance, acting as if he didn't care about the dissertation one way or another. He did a decent job of concealing his nerves, because Simon leaned forward and propped his chin on his fist.

"Lucky for you. We're leaving this stuffy tomb as soon as possible. How about you join us for a drink at the White Horse Inn shortly? I see you around the college all the time, yet feel I don't know the first thing about you."

"Oh, there's not a lot to spoil...but a drink sounds like a pleasant distraction." From what Cullen had imparted, Playfair often socialised at the White Horse too.

"He's a good sight more fun than most of the stuffy medical students," observed Diomedes in *sotto voce*. George smiled obligingly.

Simon's beam widened. He genuinely looked intrigued. "You decided to become a physician while in the military, did you not?"

"I suppose so," George admitted. At some point in his life he went from having no desire to enrol in medical school, to being enrolled in the best medical school in the world, but it wasn't clear when the key decision was made. "My first forays into Mr Pearson's surgeon tent didn't suggest it would be a promising career..."

* * *

To his fellow students, that's all George was: former lobsterback turned man of medicine. From the outside, it sounded like a smooth narrative: the transformation from one lowly state to a higher one. It was a transition all matriculated Edinburgh students accepted when he told them, because it mirrored their own longing to pass through university and become an adult with a degree.

He could smell the surgeon's tent from halfway across the regimental field camp: of blood soaked into churned mud, of lapsed bodily functions, and the stench of slow death hanging like a haze. Like most soldiers, George avoided the surgeon's tent until he had no choice.

"I came to see Lance-Corporeal Biltings," he stuttered, halting a harried-looking surgeon in a blood-stained apron.

"Not a moment too soon, and almost too late," the surgeon muttered, pointing him to a cot.

George didn't know if his dying friend was even aware he'd turned up: aside from feverish mumblings and the occasional twitch, there was no sign that a lucid soul once occupied the now-mangled, charred body. George sat with him all the same, until he realised half an hour had passed since the last twitch.

There wasn't anything he could say or do. So he rose and walked out, nodding to the surgeon as he passed.

"If you're heading that way…" A pile of bloodied, sodden rags was thrust into his hand. "You can take these bedsheets to the washerwomen."

George's tent was on the opposite side of the camp, but he obeyed, grimacing as the blood and effluvia seeped into his uniform sleeves. He supposed the surgeon could have kicked him out at any point during his vigil, because he'd been rushing all over the field hospital and George had to scrunch onto his stool several times to avoid getting knocked onto his dead friend's lap.

With Biltings dead, George found himself back at Pearson's tent within days. He hadn't any other friends in his unit. The surviving members of his squadron had retreated into themselves following the slaughter at Brandywine, as if blame for the ambush would settle onto the largest cluster of men, so better to avoid its gaze.

He'd proven rather useless as the surgical aspects of the role. However, Pearson was always in need of someone to hold down a ruined limb as he took a saw to it, or to evacuate the rags that passed for bedding to the washerwoman, who only succeeded in making the stains set deeper into the fabric. Pearson spent more time snapping at George to rectify this or that mess that George was almost ready to give up on his guilt-motivated assistance.

That was until one quieter night Pearson handed George the dregs of his bottle and motioned for him to finish it. "You have a way with the sick and dying," he said.

"Um, thank you?" George hadn't expected this. In the flickering candlelight, Pearson looked decades older than his thirty years. Old enough to be George's grandfather.

"You soothe the sick and dying. I hear you talk to them. Someone people try to reassure the dying and end up agitating them: they know they're dying, many are tired of fake pretences otherwise. But you manage honesty without upsetting them further."

"I'm awful at surgery, though." Pearson had asked George a few times if he was interested in becoming his apprentice. George didn't know if Pearson was asking to encourage him, or to better talk him out of the idea.

"You'd make a halfway decent physician, I reckon. There's too many puffed-up, rich and indolent bewigged physicians strutting around Britain, if you want my opinion. I think a few more of your humble demeanour might make the country a better place."

George had smiled at this fanciful, yet flattering compliment, and assumed it was the kind of wistful imagining one did in wartime—like fantasising after a plot of farmland and a rosy-cheeked wife who smelled of baked bread, instead of gangrene and stale sweat like he had to breathe in every day. But he couldn't have done a good job of concealing his hesitation, because Pearson became more insistent he consider medical education.

As would reoccur many years later with Cullen and his insistence on writing to Dr Hunter in London, George allowed Pearson to write a letter to his old professor in Edinburgh, reasoning that his inevitable rejection would finally put a stop to the matter.

13

EDINBURGH—OCTOBER 1768

Despite Black's protestations, Hutton insisted on hiring a tavern room for the evening's conviviality.

"Let's get a little bit of space to ourselves—I hate when drunks knock into me."

Black would have been content with a table in the main cellar, but Hutton saw his return to Edinburgh as a special occasion, and he had the coins for it.

Seeing the room in question was Dowie's upstairs room 'The Coffin', Black thought a table in the main room would be better. The Coffin was accessible from the tavern floor via a narrow corridor and stairway. It could fit four men—as the joke went—as long as all four were dead. While quieter than the main area, a few men always loitered in the upstairs corridor to conduct their own private conversations. Black squeezed past a pair of linen-drapers.

Hutton was already beaming.

"Are you back in Edinburgh for good, this time Dr Hutton?" asked the third guest, the Earl of Hopetoun.

Hutton made a spirited denial. "We're readying Sligh-houses for harvest time: I can't let abandon it at this critical juncture of the experiment. Besides, my poor cows would be heartbroken!"

"I hope the new plough prototype is as successful as you predicted." Word had reached the Lothians of Hutton's new lightweight plough—imported from Suffolk—and a lot of Scots farmers and agriculturalists were watching his efforts with interest.

"It seems to be. I can steer the thing myself single-handedly. I think the only hesitation my neighbours have is whether my flimsy-looking steel plough will withstand a full harvest season."

Black doubted there was as much opposition to Hutton's imported plough. He had a way of charming his fellow farmers.

"I'm only in Edinburgh a few weeks," Hutton said, taking a sip of ale. "My sal ammoniac business partner promised to meet with me soon to update our contract."

It was rude of Black to inquire too deeply into another man's financial affairs, but he gathered most of Hutton's newfound wealth came from the chemical works he'd recently constructed in the shadow of Arthur's Seat, as opposed income generated by his farm. As a student, Hutton idly proposed an alternative method of manufacturing sal ammoniac, and the enterprising friend he'd told thought it would be fun to test the idea out. The fact his offhand idea turned out obscenely effective *and* lucrative was symbolic of Hutton's twin talents of wild scientific creativity and accruing heavy doses of luck. It wasn't fair, but he could hardly resent a man as kind-hearted and simply...fun to be around as Hutton.

"Well, we hope the city will provide enough intellectual stimulation to tide you over until you're ready to rejoin us for good," the Earl said. "I don't wish to impinge upon the reputation of Berwick...but its inhabitants can hardly match your curiosity and imagination."

Hutton laughed. This was an argument several years old, well-trodden. Ever since Black befriended Hutton, the geologist had promised to return to Edinburgh, but had never followed through. Could he be imagining Hutton's growing wistfulness when talking about his childhood and student days in Edinburgh? Was it a sign that he might yet act on his promise?

It would be a while before such a thing happened. Right now, Hutton was too preoccupied with his new scientific ideas to dwell on future travel plans. "As a matter of fact, I really started to study the soil around Slighhouses—properly study it—and all sorts of thoughts are churning in my head." Hutton spoke in a slightly breathless way, that indicated he was mustering all self-control to get his exciting thoughts out in a manner comprehensible to his friends. "Urban philosophers like yourself witness little soil erosion in your natural habitats, but it took me aback during my first year at the farm how much erosion took place. It's extraordinary. I'd wake up some mornings shocked I still had fields left! Then I started calculating how much soil was displaced from my farm in a year by rain and such. I can't pretend high fidelity with my numbers...but at the rate the soil was moving, I started wondering why the Borders hadn't vanished into the sea eons ago."

"Soil erosion is truly a blight," the Earl of Hopetoun mused.

"Yes, but you need rocks to be worn down to give us soil in the first place, because you can't plant turnips in granite." Hutton laughed at his own witticism. "And presumably at some point the washed-away soil settles and turns back into rocks."

"Ah, so you see the process as cyclical?"

"I'm specifically wondering how it relates to the Neptunist

arguments about the validity of the Biblical Flood...or rather, does not."

"You refer to the presence of sea-bed fossils on the tops of mountains?" A few Royal Society papers in London had recently mentioned these unusual geological specimens. A lot of philosophers now had strong opinions on a topic they knew nothing about last year. "I thought the sceptics claimed we shouldn't have mountains, since the great flood and erosion should have worn them down to nubs?"

"Well, exactly." Hutton's voice rose. "I was wondering if there was another way to think about the age of the Earth, and if we're being led astray by taking the Biblical chronology too literally."

"I suppose the Reverend Ussher's calculations have been disputed a few times..."

Hutton shook his head, as if trying to dislodge a fly from his ear. "No. Everyone these days is trying to measure, quantify and calculate everything once seen as a wonder of nature. But every hypothesis is set with the Biblical chronology as the largely undisputed starting point. What I'm suggesting is that instead of taking our measurements of the age of the Earth from the Bible, we take them from the Earth..."

A wracking cough interrupted Hutton's thought. In the doorway of The Coffin stood a man dressed in a dark navy waistcoat, clutching an ale. Black thought he was the linen-draper he'd passed in the corridor. Another man stood behind him awkwardly.

They should have closed the door. But Black hated the claustrophobia.

The linen draper spoke to a point a foot above Hutton's balding head, as if he were reciting a memorised speech.

"I overheard parts of your conversation and wanted to remind you of Psalm 119:89. 'Your word, Lord, is eternal...'"

How many men were in the corridor, just out of sight?

The linen-draper stuttered as he spoke, but it was a stutter of a man determined to press on to the end of his point.

"As a student of the Bible, I beseech you…"

Hutton made noises of objection. Black laid a hand on his arm, silently begging him to keep quiet. There wasn't even a window in The Coffin. The only way they could get out was through that door, down that packed corridor.

Hutton didn't have the social dexterity, and a linen draper was too low in the social ladder for the Earl of Hopetoun to adequately communicate with. Black fixed a friendly smile on his face and waited for the draper to finish speaking.

"I apologise, my friend. I see we didn't convey our meaning properly and have offended you." Black spoke slowly, hands raised in supplication. He was seated; the draper and his friends were standing. Such was the cramped nature of the room; he couldn't get to his feet quickly.

Recognising he wasn't posed to deal with this confrontation, the Earl of Hopetoun bit his lip and looked away. Black maintained smiling eye contact with the draper, hoping he wouldn't notice whatever outraged expression was on Hutton's face.

The draper's face reddened, and he grumbled under scrutiny. Black supposed he'd steeled his nerves for a confrontation, and his body now wanted to fight even as his mind had second thoughts.

"God's truth should not be questioned," the man mumbled.

"Of course it shouldn't," Black replied brightly. He stood up slowly, careful not to crush the Earl's knees as he moved his chair. "What is your parish?"

Hutton let out a moan of exasperation, which the Earl did his best to soothe. Now standing, Black could see a half-dozen men in the corridor. Most were simply watching the confrontation from a distance, unaware of what prompted it.

However, they all appeared to be tradesmen. They looked at his black physician garb with suspicion, but none of them could yet see the Earl of Hopetoun in his powdered wig and velvet breeches perched in the room. His presence in an altercation would inflame the situation beyond anything Black could control.

"How about we bring up a jug of ale?" Black asked, keeping the same bright tone. "I saw you as I came in half an hour ago, did I not? How long have you been conserving that glass?"

If the Earl was smart, he'd lead Hutton downstairs while Black sorted out the drinks. Maybe they could continue their conversation, but he suspected the mood was spoiled.

14

The Tolbooth cast a long shadow over the High Street. Black took George by the elbow and steered him to the side of the High Street a few paces from the front entrance.

"I have to warn you, George," he began. "I cannot see how this confrontation won't descend into violence. Even with William staying home."

George, who already spent some time fearing this very admittance, bit his tongue. Having secured an audience with Simon and associates later in the day, he almost collided with Black on the way out the library. The chemistry professor had been waiting for him.

Black kept his eye on the Tolbooth. "The best we can hope is Brown lets slip some useful information, either in an attempt to goad or threaten us. We must keep him talking as long as possible."

George had spent a lot of time remembering his last encounter with Brown. The two had squared off in the Brunonian headquarters. Exhausted by the phlogiston fight that preceding this, Brown resorted to his fists, which proved as dangerous as his phlogiston. Eventually, George had seized

99

an opening and knocked his more powerful opponent unconscious. He'd not set eyes on Brown since.

Nodding at Black's counsel, George's fingers slipped into his pocket and eased into the security of the brass knuckleduster. This was a contraption he'd not relied on since his military days.

He tried to be discrete, but Black's eyes narrowed. The chemistry professor's hand shot out and grabbed George's wrist. George tried to slide the knuckleduster off his hand, but Black pulled his hand out of his pocket before he got the chance.

George sighed.

"George." Black lowered his voice. "You know that metals and phlogiston don't mix. What were you thinking bringing this?"

"We need all the protection we can against that man." George didn't trust himself to speak in a level tone. "He's a brute."

Left unsaid were all his anxieties and fears. That he wouldn't be able to wield phlogiston, despite the presence of Black, and that the only thing he could trust was his martial skills. Except that those were rusty because he'd wasted the past four years training with phlogiston and feeling relief as his soldier days faded into the distance.

"Promise me you'll keep your hands away from these knuckledusters if you even suspect you'll use phlogiston," Black said. When George garbled out an affirmation, his expression eased.

* * *

As a debtor, Brown enjoyed certain privileges not afforded to the condemned criminals. This included certain freedom of movement within the confines of the jail.

Descending into the cellar tavern, Black and George had to step to the walls to let a crowd pass. The young men heading up the stairs, laughing and ribbing each other, put George more to mind of a crowd of theatre-goers than students. Many weren't even carrying quills or paper.

"Looks like we've caught the end of the morning's lecture," Black muttered.

It was quite a small crowd. Maybe that was to be expected, but George assumed the squalid location would be more of a draw than a repellant factor for this calibre of students. At one point, the loyalty of the Brunonians to their figurehead was unshakable.

The students gone, the pair reached the bottom of the stairs and entered the now-empty tavern.

The Tolbooth prison tavern reeked of urine, and from what little George could see in the dim light, every surface was coated with congealed ale, and no table even enough to balance a bottle on.

It wasn't the worst tavern George had visited in Edinburgh.

And there at the front of the room—at a broad table doubling as a lectern—was seated the figure himself.

"Well, here's a sight for sore eyes," Brown chuckled.

Years had passed since they'd squared off in the Brunonian headquarters. Brown looked slightly thinner—but his face seemed more distorted. Puffy and redder. His eyes glinted: his expression one of macabre amusement. Knowing that their last fight ended with George knocking him unconscious, this expression was all the more terrifying.

"You still have unsettled debts, John?" Black asked, inching closer.

"Well, I cannae plead ma belly," Brown laughed, smacking his sizeable stomach. "So one hundred and fifty pounds is what it'll have to be to get me out of here...Joe."

Only the tiniest flicker crossed Black's face.

"I'm surprised your friend, the Reverend Holm, hasn't offered to assist you."

Brown's face darkened to the colour of shadows. "So that's what this visit's about, Joe. Like I'd help ye, even if I had information to share."

"But you know he returned from Paris?"

"Everybody kens," snorted Brown.

"We move in different social circles, it appears."

A steady drip of water onto the cellar floor was the only noise.

"Has he visited you?" Black tried.

"Whit's in this fae me, Joe? Quid pro quo. Dinnae see much point in making yer life easier."

"Well..." Black leaned closer. "Malcolm Holm has a habit of proactively tidying up what he considers...loose ends. Your former patron Elliot Ross was one such loose end."

This didn't have the salutary effect they hoped for. Brown scoffed.

"Yet I'm still livin' an' breathin' while Lord Ross is bedded down in a nice plot a' earth."

Brown was smart enough to recognise Holm could have already killed him, and chose not to.

"He *has* visited you, then?"

George saw the tiniest hesitation in Brown's face before the man's sneer returned.

"The fine folk of Edinburgh were quick to discard Holm when he thought his useful streak over. Ye've got no love fae the man—that's well-established. Unlike some folk we both ken, Holm appreciates loyal friends."

Black ignored the dig at Cullen. "The average citizen need only look at Reverend Holm to know his fanaticism will get innocent people killed."

Brown snorted. "Graham didnae think so."

Who was Graham, George started to ask, only for Black to lay a restraining hand on his shoulder. But Brown had already realised he might have said too much, because he inhaled on his planned tirade and glowered instead.

"All we're asking, John, is for a bit of information about what Holm is planning. I'm sure he was asking you questions, and obtaining as much information as he could. You're smart enough to know that loyalty won't protect you from a man like Holm when—not if—he decides you've outlived your usefulness."

A steady drip from the corner punctuated the long silence.

It was like staring down a wild boar you'd cornered in the forest. In a second, it would either try to flee around you...or charge.

"Ye snobs at the university always doin' this. Pretend ye dinnae need auld Bruno, only tae beg for his help when someone cuts through yer bullshit an' shows how weak ye are. Well, I'll let ye fail. Watch yer weak, flawed doctrines fail ye again and hope mebbe this time, the lesson sticks."

"You say that sir, as if we didn't rout your pathetic followers, destroy your lair and if I didn't manage to render you unconscious while nursing a broken rib." The hot words rushed out of George's mouth before he could stop himself. He'd beaten the puffed-up charlatan fair and scare—what right did he have to prance around claiming he wasn't the loser?

Brown did not immediately yell or curse in response. Instead, his body and gaze momentarily slackened.

That half a second was all the warning George had.

Brown's phlogiston was a more amorphous, messily thrown ball of fire, but he barely seemed to point—it simply erupted from his arm and was hurled straight at Black.

The professor regarded the fireball with cool detachment, but George had already shot forwards, thrusting out his hand.

George was aware of his own phlogiston attack leaving his hand at the same moment he registered searing pain. The two fireballs collided and barrelled into the jail wall. George was stunned for a moment at how bright and swift his reactionary phlogiston was.

As his own left hand curved instinctively around his injured right, the hot metal burned his skin. It took a few swipes to get the knuckleduster off. The skin underneath was already blistering.

He'd been fingering the knuckleduster in his pocket, especially as Brown's temper stoked, but he couldn't recall slipping it on...

For the second time that day, Black's hand caught George's wrist. But this time, his nails pierced George's skin. Before he had time to yelp, Black jerked him towards the door. George's free hand burned and stung in the breeze.

He thought he heard Brown snigger behind them. Without breaking stride, Black clicked his fingers. Cries of alarm rang out through the building as the entire Tolbooth plunged into darkness.

Black deposited George at Cullen's, leaving his colleague to administer a salve on George's burned knuckles. As far as George could tell, Black didn't exchange more than a few words via procolopathy with his friend.

"What happened, lad?" Cullen asked, once satisfied with the poultice.

George explained, trying to construct a narrative that foisted less blame upon himself, though it was clear Cullen saw through his misrepresentation of events.

After all, he'd done the one thing his mentor specifically warned him not to do.

"You're lucky you still have two hands," Cullen noted,

sounding less reproachful than he was entitled to be. "I would have expected brass to not withstand a blast of phlogiston without exploding."

The salve had taken the edge off the pain. "It conducted the phlogiston. It shot across the cellar," George explained. "It must have lost its heat immediately."

"Given the state of your wounds, yes, you were fortunate indeed." Cullen replied. "Reminds me of the Princess and her silver-wired swords."

"Weren't they platina wires?" George asked, relieved the conversation was flowing away from him.

"Quite right lad, yes, they were platina," Cullen agreed. "It looks like your gunshot wound is healing satisfactory. Given you seem intent on not resting, I suppose it's doing better than we could hope for."

"It feels fine," George said. Provided he didn't move his arm much. "I was surprised getting shot garnered me credit with Dr Monro."

Cullen tutted as he dabbed the burns. "It's rare he gets such a clean grapeshot wound to use for teaching purposes, at least on a living patient. I've only seen Sandy Monro that excited twice before. The first was when his favourite actress, Mrs Siddons, greeted him by name at the Lord Provost's dinner party. The second time was when Dr Hamilton found that Cornish weaver with an incredibly rare fungal infection on his genitals."

His fist stung, but George had experienced worse injuries.

"Brown said Holm had been discarded by the dark chymists. Is that true?"

He was sure this was another of Brown's fabrications, but Cullen nodded a confirmation.

"I don't need to bore you with all the details of what happened a long time ago, but Holm was sent to stop Joe one night...and failed. It was the first time any of them encountered phlogiston-wielding, though at the time the dark chymists didn't realise that's what it was. They simply thought Holm had failed through his own weakness. For a long time, that was the last anyone heard of him. He got his revenge in good time, though."

"Is that why there are nobles helping him, Dr Cullen? Because they're afraid of Holm's vengeance?"

"It could be." Cullen wrapped a roll of linen round George's poulticed hand. "Or Malcolm is offering a path for forgiveness. Or there's another factor that's causing everyone involved to pinch their noses and get down to business."

Now Cullen had finished patching him up, he studied George for a moment.

"Do you need to be anywhere now, George?"

"Um, I suppose not." Phoebe wouldn't be happy when she saw his second injury.

"Well, Dr Black briefly summarised your encounter with Bruno, and he suggested I take care of an unresolved question while he investigates another..."

15

EDINBURGH—MAY 1766

Black awoke to the screams of William Cullen.

"Where's Joe? Anna, where's Joe?"

"He's upstairs. He w-w-was sleeping when I last checked on him."

"Get the children. We have to leave. Joe!"

Cullen's voice rose. He was coming up the stairs, Anna's frenetic entreaties following.

"What's going on, William? We can't move him, he's still bleeding..."

"There's no time!" Cullen bellowed. "Grab the purse from under the mattress. We have to get out of Edinburgh this instant. Go!"

The wails of Cullen's youngest three children filled the stairwell. Anna tried to shush them, but her voice trembled. The commotion downstairs increased.

Black had already peeled off the blood-soaked sheet, and was staggering to the bedchamber door. He had his breeches on, but could only grab the topmost blanket to wrap around himself. Even that gesture tugged the stitches in his side open. Getting a coat on was too painful to contemplate. He'd never heard Cullen—his headstrong, fiery, former professor—sound this close to blind panic before.

"Joe?" Black was almost at the door when it flew open. For a moment Cullen stood on the threshold, wide-eyed and pale. When he took in Black stumbling towards him, lips pinched in an effort not to cry out with every step, his features softened into something like relief.

"We're leaving this instant," Cullen said, letting Black collapse against him. "Don't know when we'll be back. There's a carriage in the High Street."

Black felt the thick woollen coat between his fingers, catching Cullen's familiar scent of horsehair and lavender. He hopped down the stairs and out the front door as quickly as he could, focussing on the ground ahead of him.

The sobs of terrified children followed him at a distance.

"Papa's scaring me."

"Hush, Annie..."

"Where are we going?"

"I don't know, sweetie. Hold Mama's hand."

Cullen's eldest were long grown and married. It was the eldest Robert's bedchamber Black had been recuperating in.

Their shambling traverse of South Gray's Close was slow. Black pinned the blanket against his side as best he could and hoped it was dark enough to conceal the bloodstains.

Cullen kept turning his head this way and that as they moved, biting his lip almost hard enough to break the skin.

Black didn't have the strength to walk and ask questions at the same time: movement required too much focus. In a sense he didn't need to know: Cullen feared for his life, and that was enough to keep him moving.

When they reached the promised carriage and Black collapsed against the doorframe, he decided to ask.

"Is it their library?"

"No, that's destroyed beyond trace." Cullen stared at Anna and the children, willing them to move faster.

"Did Holm...?"

"It's not safe in the city, Joe. All of them are dead."

Cullen half-assisted, half-shoved Black into the carriage.

"What?" Inside him, Black's stomach pulverised and collapsed, leaving only a sickening void.

"The dark chymists. We aren't safe in Edinburgh, Joe. Word reached me...all the dark chymists are dead."

16

"The facts were covered up. Merchants left early for the West Indies and died at sea. A Duke retired to his lodge in the Highlands to convalesce but succumbed to palsy. Or stories to that effect. All fabrications.

"On the day Joe and Black destroyed the dark chymists' library, or possibly the morning after, six prominent men were murdered in the city."

The noise of Edinburgh vanished. George stared at his feet.

"It was our fault," Cullen continued. Usually lively, the professor spoke in matter-of-fact tones, as if he were recounting the results of an experiment.

George tried to protest, but Cullen waved him silent.

"Joe fought Holm, and though he defeated him, Holm escaped. By that juncture, we suspect he'd committed some of the murders. Before he fled Edinburgh, he finished off the rest."

Watching Cullen calmly recollect this grisly past, George initially felt anger they'd deceived him about the dark chymist's downfall. But then it occurred to him how little he knew of the events that transpired decades ago. Where was the dark chymists' library of grimoires held? How was it uncovered and destroyed?

Maybe it wasn't deception on the professors' part, so much as a reticence to recall the most horrifying ordeal of their lives.

"How long were you in hiding, professors?" he asked.

Cullen smiled faintly. "We stayed at Slighhouses, Hutton's farm in the Borders, for a few weeks. There were no more killings, and it became apparent the attack was directed solely at the dark chymists, even though Holm was its architect. A little while later, Holm was spotted in Portsmouth. More time passed and reports came he was established in Paris."

"And we still don't know what he's doing now?"

"It's safe to say that when we destroyed the dark chymists' library in 1766, we inadvertently halted Holm's plans, not understanding that at the time. He'd freshly returned to Edinburgh after a period of exile, intent on revenge. It's no clearer now if what we're dealing with today is a continuation of that act, or the writing of a second slate."

Cullen led George back towards the university. The morning's clouds had dissolved into a warm and bright March day.

"Are we looking for another Brunonian?" George asked.

"Not this time." Unlike his colleague, Cullen sounded as cheerful as ever. "I learned Dr James Graham was released from the Tolbooth the other day, and Joe thinks he would have been there when Holm approached Brown. I know the man well enough—he took some classes with me when he was younger—apparently he's in the university Physick Garden at the moment."

So that was the identity of the man Brown mentioned.

"Why was this Graham imprisoned? Are his debts as bad as Brown's?" That seemed to be the usual reason a man of that standing would end up sharing a cell with the disgraced former physician.

It was perhaps surprising that so many Tolbooth inmates could boast of Cullen as their former medical teacher, but George doubted that the point was pertinent to the matter at hand.

"No, it was incendiary pamphlets that did him in," Cullen remarked, speeding up.

George took in Cullen's stony expression, and the tension in his neck muscles. He knew by now Cullen was manifesting reluctance about the upcoming encounter. This was unusual, since Cullen was never intimidated by his social superiors, and possessed a genuine interest in meeting people. This heel dragging actually reminded George of that time when...

"Does this Dr Graham happen to have," George ventured. "A tendency to soliloquise on...carnal matters?"

"It would be bearable if that was all he does," Cullen grumbled. "But any conversation with him turns into an attempt to sell you his latest quack cure for impotency, longevity, and nervous disorders. If he could achieve a tenth of what he claims he can, why, Apollo should hand him his lyre! From what I hear, he was touting the value of procreation in those pamphlets. Perhaps in London he can get away with such brazen statements, but the Scots Kirk aren't known for leniency. Graham currently claims reproduction is the cure for everything."

"He'll have much in common with Dr Duncan then," George said, in an attempt at levity.

Cullen didn't crack a smile. "The two men loathe each other. Andy thinks Jim is a greedy charlatan; Jim thinks Andy is a self-polluting blasphemer."

This is going to be an interesting encounter, rued George.

. . .

The Physick Garden was cordoned from casual wanderers behind a waist-high dry-stone wall. The pair let themselves in through the gate. Students and most of the professors avoided the place, unwilling to enrage the botany professor by trampling his carefully tended flowers.

"Are you sure Dr Graham is in the Physick garden?" George asked, struggling to keep up with Cullen, who was working himself into a fury. "I looked around as we came in, and I'm afraid there's nobody here."

"Ah," said Cullen, not breaking stride. "I suspect I wasn't clear enough. When I said Graham was *in* the Physick Garden, I meant…"

"Hey hey, steady on good sirs!" cried a voice near their feet.

Looking down, George first thought he was regarding a cauliflower, albeit one of a large size and confusing hue. Then he realised the cauliflower was rotating this way and that in the freshly turned earth. Oh, and it was speaking to him.

"Goodness, you two gentlemen walk at quite a pace!" By now, George knew this was in fact a head, but the fact it lay disembodied on the ground conducting a conversation with them was alarming.

"Apologies, Jim," Cullen carefully lowered himself to a crouch, accompanied by groans and creaks. "I should have paid greater attention to where I was going."

Ah, he's buried in the soil, George finally realised. He could now see Graham's clothes folded neatly under the nearby tree, and noticed the soil underfoot was loose and greatly disturbed. He joined Cullen in a crouch.

"Jim, this is my student and friend, Mr George Stephens," Cullen explained. "We had a few matters to discuss with you."

Graham had a cherubic face, with a slightly upturned nose and well-defined features. He possessed a kind of boyish charm, despite appearing to be in his forties. His hair was blond, powdered to bone-white. Notably, his burial in the earth was accomplished without a clot of soil getting onto his head.

"The wonders of earth bathing? Why, I would be delighted. As you no doubt are aware, countless patients of mine can attest to the benefits intimate proximity with our bountiful mother earth bestows. A corpulent fellow in Nottingham earth-bathed six hours every day, and after two months, his dropsy was completely cured! Would you believe it? The marvels of science and nature entwined."

"We understand you spoke with a Reverend Malcolm Holm in the Tolbooth, and we wish to know what you discussed." Cullen spoke loudly and quickly, before Graham could get any more words out. "Holm is up to nefarious business and I fear for anyone associated with him."

"Really?" Graham swivelled. "The Reverend was quite supportive of my predicament—he offered to petition the church elders in the city to withdraw their calls for my prosecution."

"I would expect him to perform the exact opposite service," Cullen noted grimly. "On some religious matters he is fanatically intolerant...but lying is not one of them."

This suggested Holm had extracted something he wanted out of the oblivious doctor in exchange for the pretence of cooperation. George suspected Graham had no reason to believe their warnings over what they'd heard from Brown and Holm themselves. Indeed, he didn't appear daunted by their couched warning.

"In fact, I think Reverend Holm departed our brief conversation a happy convert to earth-bathing. He promised me he'd attend my next public sermon on the topic. It's taking place a week on Tuesday. Admission is two shillings—but who can put a price on good health?"

"I'm sorry Jim, we didn't come here to talk about that."

"Well, then consider my Celestial Bed, which I'm bringing

up to Edinburgh following its resounding success at the Temple of Health at the Adelphi. I know for a young man, fifty pounds may seem a non-trifling sum, but what price can you put on the peace of mind that accompanies guaranteed progeny? You may look disbelieving, but I have studied the electrical experiments of the genius Dr Franklin, and have found the voltage that enables fruitful multiplication when applied to the bed and its inhabitants. One night on the Celestial Bed is all a couple needs. For an additional sum, I can also be at hand to provide proper scientific guidance..."

Cullen's face grew red. "That's not what we're here to discuss either, Jim."

"I attended to every detail of its design, you know," Graham continued, ignoring Cullen's discomfort in favour of completing his advertising pitch. "The mattress is a proprietary blend of stallion hair, wheat, straw and lavender. The sheets are the finest Egyptian silk. After extensive experimentation, I settled on a perfume blend of jessamine, tuberose, rich gums, fragrant balsams; the richest Oriental species to soothe your senses..."

George's nose and arms were itching just thinking about all the plant flotsam he'd have to roll around in.

"...While the sweet notes of organ-pipes, horns, flutes, kettle-drums, clarinets, trumpets, and violins accompany you and your loved one's tender embrace. But I am always seeking to perfect my creation! Just this month I introduced turtle-doves on a bed of roses into the canopy, to accompany the painted fresco of flowers, cherubs and nymphs..."

An embarrassing incident last month when two farriers got into a blazing row one night on the street below his lodging window impressed upon George that a certain amount of noise ruined his concentration. He couldn't imagine trying to block out an entire orchestra. Not to mention the threat of defecating birds from on high.

"With all respect, my good sir," George began. "Please don't force me to start kicking your head."

There was an uncomfortable silence.

After swivelling a few times, perhaps to check the soil hadn't loosened enough to let him spring free, Graham sighed.

"Fine. Yes, Reverend Holm approached me a few days ago, asking to obtain several supplies I would not easily have access to and deliver the goods to my cellar off St Ninian's. I will cancel the orders with utmost haste."

"No, that won't be necessary," Cullen replied thoughtfully. "What supplies did Holm request?"

"I'm not sure precisely. I spoke in general terms about the necessary equipment for my electrical demonstrations, and he got in touch with my supplier directly."

That information wasn't a lot of use, but it was better than nothing.

"When did they estimate the orders will arrive?"

"Tomorrow, as it happens," Graham answered. He craned up at Cullen. "You wish to be informed of the location and time?"

"Correct."

With that information teased out of the recalcitrant doctor of love, the pair took their leave.

"You're sure Mr Graham won't warn Holm we spoke to him?" George asked once they exited the garden.

"It's a low risk," Cullen said. "He wants Holm to pay him for the goods, after all."

* * *

After scraping through his first semester by the skin of his teeth, the next few years of George's medical studies proceeded easily enough. Some of his peers managed to absorb medical knowledge by diffusion: they would hear a lecture once and all the material would be imprinted on their brain. If anything, alcohol seemed to accelerate this process of diffusion. On George, it had the opposite effect.

But the first round of oral examinations—discussing a Hippocratic aphorism in Latin in front of a panel of professors—brought George back to the crisis point he thought he'd got away from.

First came denial: avoidance of study, lacklustre review of notes. Then came the panic, the fear, the catastrophising. Would the Earl of Hopetoun refuse to accept him back for another summer of paid surveying work if he failed this examination? Black and Cullen helped George negotiate reduced fees from several medical professors that year: would they all throw up their hands and ban him from their classrooms?

Calling on William Cullen at midnight on a Saturday wasn't George's finest hour. But George had socialised with the professor as late as this before, and assumed Cullen wouldn't yet have turned in for the night.

"Professor!" George wailed as soon as the door closed behind him. "My oral examination is on Tuesday...and I'm going to fail. I know nothing!"

"What don't you know about?" Cullen asked, closing his book and putting down his glass of wine. In the doorway, Anna watched the proceedings, stifling a yawn.

"About anything!" George hadn't slept in days. He could vaguely hear how hysterical he sounded, but like a disinterested observer, he was unable to stop the words coming out like that.

A lesser man than Cullen would have smirked, rolled his eyes, or given an indulgent chuckle. Even if the hour of his arrival was unusual, Cullen would have dealt with hundreds of unjustly panicking students over his decades as a professor. Instead, Cullen gestured to the chair opposite him in front of the fire.

"Sit down, lad. My love, did you say there was half a bowl of broth left?"

Anna nodded and slipped away. She returned with the warm dregs of her barley and beef broth, then politely excused herself for the evening. Given George wasn't sure when he'd last eaten, he swallowed the soup in a few mouthfuls.

"Right, lad. It's improbable that you in fact 'know nothing about anything' when it concerns medicine, so let's start exploring what you do know…"

George had no idea how long they stayed in front of Cullen's fire. The elderly professor dropped into his gentle tutorial style of asking simple questions, then teasing out better responses through further questions and hints. He never once lost his patience, or showed frustration when George buried his head in his hands and apologised profusely for being such an embarrassment of a student.

"Back to the task in hand…" Cullen would say, clearing his throat.

Eventually, he sighed and stretched his arms. "Well George, I'm not sure there's anything you *don't* know about medical theory and practice. It's all there in your head, and I can't think of anything more to question you about. Your best preparation for Tuesday's gauntlet is to get plenty of sleep and eat a few good meals. You'll be fine."

"Thank you, professor…" George said softly.

"Come on lad, you can call me William. We are friends, are we not?"

"I suppose so…"

Now the panic had been lanced from his system, George felt spent, like a flattened roll of vellum.

"The wife will have my head on a stick for staying up so late. I best get some shut-eye for her sake." Moving stiffly, Cullen guided George to his front door. "Best of luck, George.

I'm very proud of you. Come back afterwards and tell me how you got on."

Needless to say, George was a stammering wreck during Tuesday's examination…but he passed.

"A little less than what I expected from you, Mr Stephens," Monro said gruffly. "But not bad."

On the way home, George fought back tears and sniffles. Partly because he was drained to the point of collapse, and now relief flooded through his broken body, overwhelming it. But there was also a measure of hollowness and shame to his 'achievement'. It was, in fact, several days before he saw Cullen again, and it was at a gathering of the Oyster Club. Apologies seemed laughably insufficient. The worst part was that Cullen didn't seem upset George hadn't stopped by to tell him the good news personally: he repeated his claim he was proud of him.

In the following weeks, every time someone congratulated George on passing his oral examination, he wanted to shrink into himself and pretend the words weren't meant for him. If they knew how close he'd come to failing, that it was only Cullen's undeserving patience and encouragement that he scraped through, they wouldn't sound so pleased for him.

17

In need of a distraction as much as his fulfilling his sense of urgency, Black took off briskly back up the High Street. His next avenue of inquiry was such low-hanging fruit he wondered if it was a waste of precious time to even chase it.

He drew his coat tighter around his frame, touching his hat to familiar passersby.

Goodness knows what had got into George these past few weeks. Paralysis when faced with armed opponents Black could understand—even sympathise with—but swinging from that to burning himself over John Brown of all people was beyond his comprehension. He'd told George he had nothing to worry about with his final examinations, but the more Black and Cullen tried to counsel the boy, the more agitated he appeared.

Black made his way past the old Society buildings to Brown Square, and a shabby yet genteel lodgings house perched on the precipitous slope down to the Cowgate.

The lodgings owner let him in with barely a murmur—a screaming baby in the back room suggested she had enough to worry about already—and Black made his way to the first floor.

Over the past ten years he'd made social calls to most of the lodgings-houses in Edinburgh, though they tended to blur together. The Brown's Square lodging looked vaguely familiar, but couldn't remember the name of the students he called upon here. It might come back to him in a minute if he didn't concentrate too hard on it...

The parlour door was ajar, so Black eased his way in.

He found the door blocked by a body.

Squeezing into the room, Black first thought he was viewing a murder scene. As his eyes moved around the room, they kept sweeping over bodies, tossed around like discarded clothes. Some on the floor, others slumped against the wall, several half-fallen out of sofas. It was only when he registered a bespectacled student placidly sitting in the corner with a mangy copy of *The Life and Strange Surprising Adventures of Robinson Crusoe* propped on his knee that Black decided the situation was more complicated than mass slaughter.

"Oh...good afternoon, Professor Black." The student blinked in confusion. "What are you doing here?"

"Good afternoon Charles," Black echoed, no less confused. "What on earth is going on?"

Charles' blinking continued. "Nothing much. This is just the tail-end of Samuel's opium experimentation."

Now that Black was adjusting to the bizarre tableau, he could take in more details. Namely, that the five students— and they were all medical students—were alive. A few appeared in deep slumber, but Phil from Leicester in the corner had his eyes open and was transfixed by the ceiling.

"Samuel Hyde?" Black wasn't sure this was the most fruitful line of questioning, but even a morsel of knowledge would hopefully start to resolve this mystifying eyesore.

Charles nodded, beaming.

Maybe this line of questioning wasn't leading to clarity, because Black now identified Samuel Hyde as the body upside-down on the settee, his cheek scraping the rug, and legs flung into the air.

"Yes, he's writing his thesis on the effect of opium on body temperature. I'm recording their temperatures every hour."

Black felt he had an unwelcome handle on the situation now.

"Ah, but why is Samuel himself receiving the opium?"

Charles looked anxious, as was the tendency of students when asked to defend their colleague's barely understood research program. "For completeness, Professor Black. He already tested me at a quarter grain."

Black looked again around the room.

"But why dose five of you at once? Surely that's a challenge to measure all your temperatures accurately upon the hour."

Charles pushed his spectacles up his nose. "Um, well, Professor Monro said he needs Samuel's dissertation draft tomorrow, professor. He's already given Samuel two extensions and said he refuses to give him more or he'll miss graduation."

Black took a long inhalation through his nose, letting the air sink to the bottom of his lungs before trickling it out through his mouth. "I see."

Charles fingered his book.

"Opium is a powerful drug, Charles. It can be dangerous if not dosed correctly. You and your friends are putting yourself at no small degree of risk."

"Oh yes, we know all about that." Charles nodded his head vigorously. "Samuel promised us a round of ale at the Mermaid Tavern for helping him."

Another long inhalation. "Well, if the moral calculus works for you all, who am I to judge?"

"Professor Monro gave him the opium," Charles added, eager to avoid an interrogation he was unprepared for. "Said that he could use some of his supply from the Infirmary provided Samuel help him with patient calls next week."

"A perfectly fair arrangement. It's quite right of Dr Monro to have stipulations when he dispenses large quantities of narcotics to his students."

Black had now identified all the unconscious students.

"I actually wished to speak with Michael Grangemore. Is he in?"

"Um, I think he's in Midwifery right now, Professor Black."

Black had been counting on this. But before he had time to say more, Charles interrupted, perhaps sensing the interrogation was over.

"I hope you don't mind me asking, Professor Black...but would you be willing to look over our experimental notes? Professor Monro was giving Samuel such a hard time with his earlier drafts and if he was awake now I'm sure he'd tell you same as I...err, I know you're not our dissertation supervisor, and we're not supposed to ask other professors for help writing our dissertations...but perhaps...?"

Black paused. "I'm afraid I consider that unethical, from a medical and academic standpoint," he said sternly.

"Oh." Charles hung his head.

"That said..." Black took a last look at the scene, deciding it made as much sense as it ever would. "I don't wish to trouble the young laird Grangemore while he's so studiously occupied, so I might just take a look in his lodgings room and see if I can find the answer to my trivial question myself. Then perhaps...I can come back downstairs and review Samuel's notes?"

Charles' expression brightened. "You would? That's so kind Professor Black. Samuel will be incredibly grateful once he regains consciousness. He's barely slept a wink this past week, what with all the stress."

Michael's room—which he shared with Charles—was more orderly than Black expected, with fewer possessions. From the scraps he'd overheard of Michael's comings and goings, he might still lodge with his family most of the time. The Grangemore estate was only half a day's ride away from Edinburgh, and the family probably rented an apartment in Edinburgh too.

With Charles back downstairs in anticipation of his next temperature reading, Black took a cursory rifle through Michael's possessions.

His reverie was disturbed by a heavy thump from downstairs, which was probably Samuel falling off the settee. Before coming upstairs, Black had insisted on checking the pulses of the students and found them within acceptable ranges. If Charles had dosed them accurately, it would be an hour or more before they came to.

There wasn't anything remarkable. A few bound lecture notes. Cream silk stockings tossed carelessly on the bed. A miniature portrait of a young woman who might be his amour, or perhaps a beloved sister. An enamel snuff box.

What letters Black found weren't of particular interest— the usual youthful bragging about the beauty of Edinburgh's women and complaints about boring lectures. Several of James Graham's obnoxious pamphlets had found their way into Grangemore junior's possession. Black flicked through them with a sigh, since he supposed many scholars would be titillated by Graham's rants on earth-bathing, procreation and the curative powers of electricity.

Black didn't want to be caught reading those, because he understood Graham included borderline slanderous depictions of the medical faculty when touting the restorative powers of the earth.

"It was too much to suppose there'd be a note, 'This is where we're hiding Dr Hutton'..." Black muttered. It didn't rule out the culpability of the Grangemores, but either their son didn't know what was going on, or he knew better than to commit anything incriminating to paper. That he was out of the building at lectures while his friends lay drugged in his parlour suggested the latter was a reasonable likelihood.

Back downstairs, Charles had helpfully laid out his friend's dissertation draft on the table for Black to examine. He'd even refilled the inkwell. Charles' expression was one of guileless hope: perhaps it didn't occur to him that Black shouldn't be rifling through a student's personal possessions. He kept his expression neutral, since his investigation of Grangemore junior was far from complete.

Black pushed his own reading spectacles onto his nose and stared at the frenzied scrawling.

"I'm having a little difficulty following this, Charles. Where are the baseline temperatures?"

Charles looked puzzled. "We took the first temperature reading five minutes after dosing, then at the half hour, then once every hour..."

"Yes, yes—I am, however, asking about the temperature readings you took before dosing the opium?"

Charles' puzzlement deepened. "Um, I don't think we took those readings. Were they important?"

"Well, you can't make a conclusive statement about the effect of opium on body temperature if you don't know what temperatures you started from." Sighing, Black pocketed his glasses and re-buttoned his coat as he headed for the door. Behind him, Charles unleashed a howl of frustration. "I'm afraid today's experimental results are useless."

<h1 style="text-align:center">18</h1>

George had never visited the upstairs floor of the White Horse Inn. He was ushered into an airy room overlooking the close, decorated with hunting tapestries and gleaming silver candlesticks. A faint aroma of yeasty alcohol floated up from the tavern below, but the room itself smelled of fresh rushes and beeswax.

There were at least ten men already there, most sat around a large circular table. As he approached, George heard the click of dice.

"You'll rub the numbers off if you caress those dice any longer, Ben."

"Hauld yer wheest."

Though the players had been in their places for a while, it was a more subdued poker game than George was familiar with. Moving closer and taking in the seated men, he realised who controlled the table.

Playfair was a moderately attractive man in his late thirties, with a long nose and a shock of dark brown hair, artfully modelled to appear carelessly tousled. He was a big-framed man, slowly losing the leanness of youth. From the way he held himself, Playfair knew he was the smartest man in the room, and intended to enjoy it.

At the man's feet lay a mottled grey and brown hound. Upon seeing George it roused and let out a warning growl. Without looking up from his cards, Playfair issued a warning hum and shushing motion with his hand. The hound resettled with a whine of complaint, eyeing George with what looked like resentment. Taking a breath, George stepped forward.

The murmurs of conversation trailed off as Playfair's eyes swept over George. A faint sneer passed over his lips, and the conversations picked up again.

He doesn't think I'm even worth a public put-down, George thought.

Unfortunately for Playfair, George had a formative experience being humiliated by Brown and his stooges in a public house during his first semester. Stung in the aftermath, he'd made a point of hardening himself to prevent a repeat of the encounter.

"I wished to introduce myself to you, Dr John Playfair," George said loudly as possible. "Though I wager you already know who I am."

The tiniest gap between Playfair's lips sealed shut. He regarded George with an irritated air.

"I confess your actual name has slipped my mind." His voice had the nasal twinge of educated Scots men who'd been tutored out of their coarse native accent. "I merely identify you as Cullen's farmer-boy fart-catcher."

This had enough air of a performative insult for George to shrug it off.

"It does one good to keep both feet on the ground and engage with nature. To better anticipate seismic geological shifts."

Playfair sighed and tossed down his playing cards.

"I wish Hutton's friends would stop enabling his fanciful

ideas. I have to put my penning of several mathematical papers on hold to read and respond to his atheistic drivel. Not that his ideas occupy the bulk of my concentration: whoever pretended to teach that man grammar should be lynched, in my opinion."

George hadn't wanted to admit he found some of the paper Black read to be tricky to follow. Hearing this insult from Playfair implied the fault didn't entirely lie with him.

Still, he didn't respond. It wasn't as if Playfair wanted to hear his opinions here. The gathering around the table uttered an appreciative titter.

"Hutton has left the learned men of Edinburgh scratching their heads over the place of caloric heat in rock formation. It appears he changed the definition of 'heat' to better suit his arguments, to the point where the definition has lost its meaning. Of course you can claim 'heat' explains those rock formations when you twist its definition like that."

The only mercy here was Playfair didn't expect George to respond, because he deemed him too stupid to understand the chemical complexities. It rankled George, precisely because his understanding lacked.

"It will take an hour at most before a space in our game becomes available," Playfair said, shifting most of his attention back to the cards. "Besides, you don't look rich or smart enough to make the gambles interesting."

"How unfortunate. If the gentlemen don't object, I will take my leave. I have business later today that I cannot be late to."

Simon, Ganymede, and Diomedes were laughing in the corner. They'd not once glanced at him.

"I once saw Alex Inglis passed out drunk in a field near Colinton, snoring loud enough to be heard over the church bells. I must have kicked him five times before he roused. How can he claim his father's ceiling renovations are keeping him awake?"

"What were *you* doing in a Colinton field with Inglis, of all people?"

"Goodness knows. Worst night of my life. Swore I'd never drink gin again..."

George thought Alexander Inglis was ten years older than Simon, if he was referring to the family who owned a mansion called Redhall in a nearby village. Surely Inglis—currently a colonel in the 23rd Highland regiment—had better things to do than socialise with this lot?

"Perhaps you can rejoin us later this evening," Simon said, when George approached. "The old man takes his time with cards, but the real merriment begins later."

"Well, if you aren't going anywhere..."

It wasn't like the three had clinical rounds or a physician to shadow. Lectures were concluded, and the bare minimum of studying had been accomplished for the day.

George was halfway back across the room when Playfair coughed. Surprised, George looked up. He was beckoned closer.

"Don't presume your intimacy with young Simon affords you anything," Playfair said, his voice slightly lower than before. "He and his chums like to tether along useful idiots for amusement, discarding them when their novelty wears off. While I tried to counsel moderation to him as a child, I suspect your longevity is measured in weeks, perhaps less. A swift tossing aside is the kindest outcome you can hope for."

19

EDINBURGH—AUGUST 1773

The two men stood at the foot of the cliff, studying the cracked pillars. Hutton enjoyed coming to this section of Salisbury Crags, where the parabola of the Crags sank into the earth, giving way to the precipitous rise of Arthur's Seat. This little cove shut out most of the distant sounds of Edinburgh. The cliffs with their honeycomb rock formation leant back in a state of relaxation close to 45 degrees. On a warm autumn day like this, hours chipping at the rock face passed in pleasant seclusion.

Hutton fiddled with the brim of his tricorne hat.

"I've struggled to find a convincing explanation for mineralisation, and without it, I have no theoretical legs to stand on. How are rocks formed? Well, they can't all be precipitated from the world's oceans. If they were once solutes floating around in the sea that turned into solids once the water dried up, we should be able to dissolve all rocks if we leave them in water long enough."

"We *can* dissolve some rocks with enough water and time," Black reminded him. "Albeit over a period of thousands of years."

"Yes, but not *all* rocks and sediments are eroded by water," Hutton pointed out. "Even on a thousand-year timescale. So maybe some of them came from the ocean...but not all of them did."

Black wiped the grime off his pickaxe handle and studied the face before him.

"Take Salisbury Crags, for instance." Hutton gestured with his pickaxe towards the cliff face. "The rocks here are considerably younger than the surrounding strata. And they're coming out of the earth practically perpendicular. Tell me, Joseph—how could a receding, gradually evaporating universal ocean account for such an uneven distribution of rocks with new below old, and none of them at the same angle to each other?"

"The Neptunists would say their universal ocean was rather choppy," Black replied with a sly smile. "That storms and disturbances accounted for the uneven deposit of layers." Hutton barked a laugh of objection. "They'd also say you were mistaken about the darker rocks being older than the sandstone."

"So how else can we form rocks? Everyone who's heard my ramblings about soil erosion—or who takes the Neptunists' fancies to their logical conclusion—want to know why we don't live on a flat plate of a world. Otherwise, the balance of soil erosion and rock creation doesn't add up."

"Did you come up with any better ideas, Joseph?"

Pausing with his small pickaxe, Black regarded his friend. He'd debated whether launching into his hypothesis right away, or waiting to see what kind of mood Hutton was in. Was his friend too excited and irritable to reason through new ideas? However, since Hutton asked, he wasn't going to change the subject. Black wanted to share his idea.

"As a matter of fact, I may have..."

Hutton beamed.

Black picked up a handful of soil. As his friend watched, Black squeezed the loamy earth in his palm. With comprehension slowly washing over Hutton's face, Black theatrically opened his hand to show off the now-compact ball of soil.

"Now you just need to bake it, and pliable dough turns into hard crust."

"Latent heat and pressure!" Hutton exclaimed, his jubilation echoing off the Crags. "Sediments must be pressurised and heated under ground, forming them into rocks. You're right, Joseph—that explains geological motions beautifully."

20

"You see that, friends? Stephens is back!"

"Well met," said George, slipping across the close to join them.

It was approaching midnight when he returned to the White Horse Inn, and George was sure the trio and Playfair would have long departed. Instead, he found Simon, Ganymede and Diomedes loitering outside the Inn.

His wife hadn't wanted him to do this.

"How many hours will they have been drinking?" she'd asked, her lip curled. "I hope they've drunk themselves unconscious, because if they're still awake...it's bad news, dear."

"I need to find out what they know," George insisted, taking her hand. "I promise you I'll slip away if there's a serious threat."

He knew he wouldn't to win over Phoebe this time, but she allowed him to depart without obvious sulking.

Diomedes clapped an arm over his shoulder. "Good ol' George," he said jovially.

The young men were obviously drunk; it was a level of

drunkenness that conferred looseness of their limbs, but not a staggering gait.

"Were you waiting for me? Has the gathering finished?" There were still lit candles in the private room, but most of the noise and merriment now came from the main tavern room. He peered through the window, but George didn't immediately spot any other card players.

"It was getting tiresome. Let's head off." Simon turned, and the others fell in behind him.

George tried to act as jovial as the rest, but he felt a tug of unease. His plan was to interrogate them over a shared bottle. He hadn't expected them to leave.

"Where are we heading?" he asked.

"Somewhere fun," Diomedes replied with a smirk.

"Is St Cecilia's Hall your idea of fun?" George asked, staring at the building they skirted towards. He didn't think Simon and chums had the sophistication to appreciate music recitals.

Ganymede chuckled, taking no apparent offence to George's remark. "It's what inside that's fun."

Come to think of it, wasn't St Cecilia's closed this month? There were no lights in the building, nor were there the chattering crowds George would expect when a show was on. But getting closer, someone emerged from the shadows of the doorway and nodded them inside.

They followed a loose crowd into the elliptical concert hall. Only half the lamps and candles were lit, casting the auditorium into thick amber shadows. Chairs were pushed haphazardly to the sides, and a pack of rough-hewn men formed a circle in the centre of the polished wooden floor, right under the cupola.

Simon and his cadres appeared to be the most affluent individuals in the hall. Far from being a genteel gathering, their appearance and coarse accents put George more to mind of a dingy tavern than concert hall.

Then he heard a rooster crow.

Ah.

"Ganymede—go see if Todd has some bottles." Simon pointed towards a bedraggled man in the corner wearing a suspiciously long greatcoat. He looked around. "We might need to stand on some chairs."

It seemed pointless asking if the hall proprietors knew cockfighting was taking place here tonight. They almost certainly didn't.

George had neither the money nor discernment to gamble on cockfights, and he didn't know enough about the state of the sport in Edinburgh to tell if the names of the roosters or owners bandied about meant anything.

Simon found suitable chairs and reclined—sticking the muddy heels of his shoes onto the back of the second. He barely glanced at the two combatants strutting into the makeshift ring—a jewel-red claret and a hefty Old English game, whose blond neck feathers were already tinged pink from an earlier bout. It was as if being in the presence of violence was sufficiently entertaining for Simon.

Ganymede returned, passing green bottles to Diomedes and Simon. He didn't offer one to George.

"Have you heard of a Reverend Malcolm Holm?" George asked, raising his voice loud enough for the others to hear, while trying to avoid everyone overhearing. "He just moved back to Edinburgh?"

Diomedes and Ganymede looked at Simon. After a moment's thought, the ringleader broke into a grin.

"No, we're all Catholics."

That was certainly more sarcasm than truth.

"He was a man who made a lot of enemies among rich

families like yourselves," George tried again. "I thought he might have been mentioned."

If the three were deceiving him, their performance was more convincing than most of the shows he'd seen in this hall. Simon shook his head.

"He might be more of a friend of mine than an enemy, in that respect." A bellow and responding cheer from the ring signalled the end of the bout.

"Got coins weighing you down, Stephens?" Diomedes asked, nudging George before he had a chance to ask what Simon meant by that. "Want to add a bit more gentlemanly sport to the proceedings?"

George knew nothing of cockfighting, and the next pair of fighters were flapping and writhing so hard he couldn't discern who had the upper hand. He shook his head.

"Once the cocks are finished, there might be a bareknuckle round or two, depending on how the crowd is feeling," Ganymede added, sensing his reluctance. "Want to try your luck, Stephens?"

"Most certainly not," George replied, with enough confidence the others shrugged and looked away.

At the other side of the room, someone tossed the limp remains of the Old English game onto an intricately painted harpsichord, lined up besides its fellow losers. A solitary blond feather fluttered to the floor, kicked away by scruffy boots a heartbeat later.

"I believe John Playfair met with Reverend Holm recently." George tried to press the matter, watching Simon closely. "Which was a surprising turn of events."

"If this Holm thinks he can outsmart Playfair, he's got another thing coming," Simon said, looking more bored with the conversation than anything else. "Come on, we can get a better view round the other side of that corpulent loafer."

This wasn't proving very informative. It could be—like

he'd discussed with Cullen—that Holm was coercing his former handlers and they were keeping their involvement with him secret. Or the three families genuinely had no involvement in Holm's scheme.

Still, they were tolerating George and his questions right now. He may as well keep pushing. A rooster flapped free of its handler and pelted towards another bird, squawking. The crowd laughed at its pluck.

"What do you think of Dr James Hutton and his geological paper?"

This got more of a reaction.

"Dr Black's peculiar friend?" Diomedes scoffed. "The pair of them are a thorn in the side of Edinburgh families. The whole Oyster Club can in fact go to hell."

"Really?" Quite a lot of rich patrons attended Black and Smith's convivial gatherings, with all-apparent enthusiasm.

"There's money and there is *money*, Stephens," Diomedes retorted, recognising George's confusion. "A world apart: mix-ups between the two made lead to misunderstanding, misery and death. You need to understand these blindingly obvious nuances if you want to be as wealthy as us."

An entire night in their company was proving tiresome.

"Dr Black set Dr Hutton up to promulgate that blasphemous nonsense he calls 'geology.'" Ganymede added, less as an informative aside to George, and more as a way to air his own grievances. "The man himself was too scared to read his own paper! Dr Black engineered it as an attack on the leading families of Scotland."

George had expected fanciful ramblings from Ganymede, but behind him Simon was nodding in thoughtful agreement.

"I don't understand how that can be..."

"He's trying to convince the world that God's natural order does not exist. That man is not lord of his domain. That one-legged beggars are equal to lords. Or maybe we should put beggars and rocks above kings in Hutton's new order?" Ganymede huffed. "Ludicrous."

George wanted to ask more, but he was seized with the sudden fear that further questioning on the topic would expose the fact Hutton had been kidnapped. As far as anyone in Edinburgh knew, Hutton was still recuperating from illness at home.

"I don't feel bad about all the families Hutty is disparaging," Simon mused, tracing his thumb round the rim of his gin. "Some of them deserve what's coming to 'em."

Ganymede cleared his throat and took a swallow of gin. Simon's comments seemed to disturb him; even Diomedes looked awkward for a moment, before his excrement-licking grin resurfaced.

In any case, another round of cheering went up, followed by a rooster's shriek, indicating the next bout was underway. The others craned forward to watch.

A quartet of ruffians jostled a step too close to the seated Simon, who cleared his throat and glared. George expected the four burly interlopers to sneer at the slight, poised figure lounged like an invalid across two chairs. Instead, they mumbled and shuffled aside.

For a moment George blinked at this perplexing interaction, until it occurred to him the four men smelled wrong. They were dressed like tradesmen, but there was no patina of stale sweat under the frayed waistcoats. Their breath reeked of gin, but was there a hint of cedar and nutmeg perfume in there too?

He scanned the room with dawning suspicion. How many nobles were here in similar coarse masquerade?

"This is wearisome," Simon said, stifling a mock yawn. "Let's go have some *proper* sport."

21

They made a slow procession up the High Street, since Diomedes and then Ganymede stopped to empty their bladders against convenient doorways, laughing as passersby wrinkled their noses.

Simon guided them past St Giles and the Tolbooth, up into the Lawnmarket. George thought the three stayed in the Potter Row area, and tried to decide if he was mistaken.

"Where are we going?" he asked, eventually admitting ignorance.

Ganymede and Diomedes laughed, but Simon tugged his coat sleeve. "Come on, I'll explain. Let's move out of the street first."

By now, George's senses were on high alert. The close they wandered into appeared deserted, but it was one of the more spidery Lawnmarket closes, with plenty of shadowy corners and nooks.

"I thought you resided on Bristo Street, Simon?" George said.

"No, where did you hear that?"

George fell silent as the others laughed. He hoped to draw

out some information about Simon's address, but it seemed the trio wasn't going to share.

Simon clapped a hand over George's shoulder and steered him closer to the wall. George gritted his teeth as his shoulder burned under the pressure. He wanted to swipe Simon's hand away, but didn't want to reveal he was nursing an injury. While even a lanky man like himself was physically stronger than Simon, George remained acutely aware there were three of them...to one of him.

Simon's teeth glinted in the grubby traces of a distant oil lamp. The trio drew closer. "You know, I grew up loving the hunt. Foxes, deer, pheasants—I enjoyed nothing more than a long day in the forest tracking them all. But we are men of the city these days. I can go months without stepping on grass. So it occurred to me, why not bring the hunt to the city?"

Simon pulled out a brace of flintlocks from his coat pocket.

"It's not good for a man, slipping into idleness. The thrill of the chase and its stimulation of the blood is what keeps us healthy."

A few paces away, Diomedes and Ganymede tugged cloths from their pockets and wrapped them around their faces.

George wished spoiled aristocrats had the capacity to surprise him with their inventive cruelty. "Why are you sharing this with me? I see no foxes."

"Oh, there are more interesting things than foxes to hunt within the city walls of Edinburgh."

All eyes were on him.

"Am I the target?"

Diomedes chuckled. "Do you want to be? We had in mind more entertaining prey than you, Stephens. Let's see how much of a warrior you are."

"And what if I don't wish to play your reckless games?"

"Well," said Ganymede, eyes narrowed. "You better hope you can run fast."

Simon unhitched the safety mechanism on his pistol. For all his youthful bravado, he held it steadily. This wasn't the type of man to bluff with an unloaded flintlock. It was pointed at George's head.

George paused. Eventually, he'd have to run, but he knew before the masks came out that a confrontation of some sort would happen. The time for conversation was over.

He ducked under Simon's arm and delivered an elbow to his stomach. At the same time, his right leg lashed out and caught Ganymede in the inner thigh. This only caused the man to stumble, but in that second, George grabbed Simon's elbow and delivered a second kick to Ganymede's stomach.

He wrenched the flintlock from Simon's hand, discharged it, then tossed the smoking metal into the close.

Simon swung his fist, but George anticipated it fast enough to sway back so it only grazed his chin.

Before he had time to right himself, the hefty bulk of Diomedes sent him crashing into the close wall. George landed, winded. His shoulder exploded in pain, momentarily paralysing him.

The last thing he wanted to do was be on the ground, but he couldn't jam out his arm to prevent himself from sliding down. Diomedes pulled back only far enough to prevent his own head colliding with the stone, then swung back his leg for a kick.

Twisting, George hooked his left foot behind Diomedes' other ankle, stamping his right heel into the boy's knee as hard as he could.

"Fuck!" Diomedes tumbled, momentarily sending Simon and Ganymede back two steps to avoid him.

The uneven stones dug into his neck and skull as George

kicked himself upright. He was halfway righted, but still against the wall, when Ganymede rushed in.

Whatever rumours about his effeminacy bubbled around the college, Ganymede delivered a competent downward hook to George's face, sending him down and sideways again.

For a moment George's legs were moving of their own accord: he had no control over how they stumbled further right. If it wasn't for a brick protrusion by his hip, he'd have toppled over.

Ganymede caught George's collar, but this time George twisted himself in and upwards, sending an elbow to Ganymede's chin. Ganymede dropped—instantaneously out cold—and George used his momentum to dive over the dropping body and roll past Simon.

He was almost too slow—Simon moved towards him as he rose, and there was a deafening crack of a pistol discharge.

Rising into a cloud of gunpowder smoke, George spun and struck out where he thought his attacker was. Simon had in fact stepped aside, and dizziness from the roll almost blinded him.

Simon smashed his pistol down towards George's shoulder. It appeared as a sudden blur in the smoke cloud, and George had no choice but to drop to the ground to avoid it. His knees screamed as he slammed back onto the cobbles, but the pistol butt barely grazed his injured shoulder. The fight would be over if any of them landed a blow on that side.

Keeping his feet underfoot, George shot himself up and sideways, catching Simon around the waist and driving him to the ground. He thought he heard the spent flintlock clatter onto the ground. Diomedes was now the only one armed, and George hadn't the time to locate him.

Ganymede was stumbling to his feet, and Diomedes was hobbling back towards the wrestling pair to land another blow on him.

The fight was getting nastier. George looked down at the rabidly struggling Simon, wondering if he'd be able to end this fight without inflicting injuries the brats could never recover from...

"Halt, you rogues!"

Emerging from a turnpike brandishing a pistol was a sweaty Town Guard captain.

Quarrel forgotten, the young men scattered around George into the High Street and down the slope towards the Nor Loch basin.

This was the hour that the Town Guard night watch ended. Simon had chosen a position in the shadows that concealed them from anyone entering the close.

Scaling the lumpy wall and dropping into the adjoining close, George mused that what he'd assumed was to be a random attack on passersby might not be so random after all.

<h1 style="text-align:center">22</h1>

Smith looked up from his correspondence.

"That's an impressive bruise," he said, studying George.

George wasn't in the mood for sympathy. "Which one?"

Black was watching him expectantly.

"The Argyles aren't sheltering Hutton. The antics of their scion have isolated them from the other dark chymist families."

Smith looked to Black. After studying his student for a moment, Black nodded.

"Well..." Smith pulled out a list. "That narrows our search down by...one location. What proof do you have the Argyles have lost influence?"

"The aforementioned scion is occupying his time with mugging them. He has quite a lot of repressed petulance concerning their treatment of him."

George explained what had transpired in the close last night.

"They fled as soon as Captain MacBride of the Town Guard appeared, alerted by our scuffle. I wager they were hoping they'd have the advantage of surprise upon him, not the other way round."

The bruise was only one of the reminders of the fight. His shoulder was aching, and George supposed his entire gait was lopsided to compensate for the pain on that side of his body. His back was scraped raw from where he'd slid along the rough-hewn wall, as were his palms.

Still, it could be worse.

"At one point in this city's history, Argyle would yell 'jump' and the Inglises, Bennetts, Grangemores, MacBrides and Rosses would upend tables in compliance. How the mighty have fallen." Smith did not look particularly sad.

"Does this rearrangement of the board change your predictions?" Black asked, studying the unrolled map of Edinburgh on the table.. "It looks like Hutton must be held at either Calder Hall, Grangemore Estate, or Redhall." His fingernail tapped three locations.

"I refuse to believe the MacBrides know nothing about the kidnapping. Mrs Holm may affect ignorance—or perhaps genuinely requested information be withheld from her—but her brothers and surviving male relatives will have negotiated with Holm. If they're not holding our friend, I refuse to believe they're unaware of who is." Smith craned over his vellum.

"There are no MacBride students," Black said, anticipating George's next question. "The youngest family members are studying in Oxford."

It was disappointing, but George doubted he could pull off the same trick twice. Besides, Kitty and her brother-in-law would be on the alert for this kind of interference.

"However, we can move onto the next likely family on the list, and maybe clarity will assert itself. We need to think of some questions you can pose to Gregory 'Ganymede' Bennett."

"It's a little too late for that," George said, wondering if it wasn't clear where his black eye came from.

"Nonsense," said Smith, impatience rising off him like steam. "He's the oldest son of the Bennetts. The family moved to the west coast of Scotland thirty years ago to escape the dark chymistry business, but his parents recently started renting an apartment on the High Street again. Ostensibly to visit their son, but it could herald a tentative resumption of Edinburgh politics."

"I got into a fight with Ganymede and Diomedes last night," George said haltingly, worried he would come out of this exchange looking like an idiot. "Ganymede pulled a flint-lock on me."

"Really?" asked Smith.

"Yes, a 50-bore pocket pistol. Probably a Griffin & Tow model—it was too dark to see clearly."

"No matter." Smith waved his hand. "The situation is urgent and we have a scant twenty-four hours to recover Dr Hutton."

"Yet if he's going along with the mugging of Captain MacBride, surely that's proof his family isn't supporting Holm?"

"Are you certain that Ganymede Bennett knew what Simon was doing last night?"

"I assume he doesn't carry a flintlock and mask out of habit."

"No." Black rubbed his eyes. "I meant, was he aware who Simon Argyle had selected as a victim that night?"

"Well, I'd assume..."

"A man's life is at stake, George," Black said, snapping slightly. "You need to stand on firmer footing than 'assuming' and 'surely.'"

That was a little rich, given George was privy to an argument where Cullen accused Black of precisely that same care-lessness, but he wasn't in the mood to poke that leopard.

"No, professor," George said with only a hint of a theatrical sigh. "I cannot say with certainty that Ganymede knew Captain MacBride was Simon's intended target."

As much as he hated to concede an argument two seconds after making it, it wouldn't surprise George if Simon's friends went along with his nasty schemes without questioning all the particulars. They'd orchestrated similar attacks before, that was obvious, but that didn't mean Simon was telling them his full plan.

"Good," Smith said. "I better not detain you any longer."

George turned to Black, mouth agape.

His former professor was frowning, arms folded and hand on chin. But it was the frown of contemplation, rather than annoyance.

"Professor," George beseeched. "In what world can I stroll back to the men who, last night, tried to murder me, and jovially put questions to him as if nothing were amiss?"

Black sighed. "In what world, you ask? The answer: in academia."

George emerged from Black's house into a pleasantly overcast morning. It was the kind of grey weather that didn't threaten rain, with a fresh breeze cleaning away some of the rotten meat and vegetable smell of Nicolson Street.

His injured arm continued to pulse, and he was constantly fighting the urge to poke his puffy eye, but he'd got enough sleep last night to feel alert.

Stretching his arms, George made his way back to the College.

The hunt was on.

• • •

George cut through the smaller Quadrangle, around the new Anatomy theatre and came in to the library building through the back way.

It was ten minutes past the hour, and the college had already settled into its first class of the day. A few straggling students rushed past with their heads down, paying no attention to him. Classroom doors were eased shut, and the murmuring of a dozen lectures filled the corridors.

He didn't expect Simon and company to be on college grounds after the beating they received last night. Not that they rose at this hour in normal circumstances, either. But plenty of their hangers-on were the kind of anxious boys desperate to please somebody—it didn't matter whether that was their professors or overbearing fellow students. They would be somewhere in the college building, no doubt awaiting orders and cramming in more study before their final examinations.

Keeping his head down, to avoid drawing attention to his bruised face, George headed into the Old Library wing and ascended to the first floor.

At the end of the corridor sat an empty classroom, used for materia medica lessons in the winter months. Since it was particularly small and leaky—its ill-fitting windows brought nature into the classroom in all seasons—other professors avoided using it unless all other rooms were occupied.

Inside, a student was splayed on a desk in the corner, snoring fitfully. Had he been here all night? It seemed preposterous that he would saunter to college before nine o'clock, then collapse into such a deep sleep.

George tried clearing his throat. No response. The snoring didn't even sputter.

He shook the student's shoulder.

"Wahhh?"

"Wake up." George shook the shoulder faster when it

looked like the student was dipping back into slumber. "Please."

Not raising his head from the desk, the boy regarded George with bleary confusion, no doubt more concerned with what the time was than what George might want with him.

"I'm looking for Ganymede Bennett." George said. "What is he doing today?"

"Ddddnnnn..." the student mumbled out a disavowal and tried to rearrange his head on his cloak.

"You're his friend, are you not?" George persisted, tugging the student's shoulder to prevent him from drooping. "Simon, Ganymede and Diomedes come in here to smoke tobacco when the weather is bad, do they not?"

The student was slowly realising George's intentions towards the trio might not be wholly friendly, and thus, it was a mistake trying to go back to sleep and ignore him. Unfortunately, he was still too dazed to school his reactions.

"I only wish to speak to them," George said, doing his best to conceal his rising temper. "But their location eludes me."

"Did something happen to your eye?" the student asked, squinting up at his tormentor.

"I don't know. Which eye are you talking about?"

"The bruised one?"

"Unconnected to the situation at hand, I promise you. I'll let you get back to sleep if you can tell me where I'd find them."

His one advantage in this interrogation was that he didn't look like a bruiser, nor like he owed them money. Satisfied George didn't pose a threat to his friends on either of those counts, the student nodded.

"Ganymede has a clinical lecture in the Infirmary at 1 o'clock. I believe he'll head to the White Horse tavern for dinner afterwards."

George released the student. This time he didn't slump back to the desk, but glanced around with a guilty expression.

"Where will they be before then?" He'd have quite a few hours to kill, and didn't feel comfortable leaving them unaccounted for that long. If they had any sense, they'd avoid the tavern where they met George last night and were known as regulars.

The student shrugged, a genuine lack of knowledge. "They'll be doing as they wish. Most people don't know what they're up to half the time. I think Ganymede is meeting with Professor Grenville before his class, though."

"The natural history professor?" As George said this, he realised it wasn't that bizarre a proposition. He'd seen the three students walking across the Yards with Grenville before, hadn't he? The oddest collection of students seemed drawn to that professor and gushed about him in rhapsodic terms; George couldn't see the allure himself. Given the trio took classics, there was no reason for them to be friendly with a professor of natural history, but he supposed there might be a family connection, or a one of them had a relationship to Grenville outside the academic setting.

No doubt sensing his surprise, the boy nodded. "The three of them just like talking to old Grenville. Simon reckons he's the smartest man in the university."

Now *that* couldn't possibly be true. But George stood up and sighed.

"Well, thank you for your assistance. I'll take my leave." George headed back to the door. He didn't want to cause alarm among the student body by being too aggressive in his questioning. The clinical lectures it would have to be, unless George could catch his quarry with Professor Grenville, wherever his classroom was.

23

EDINBURGH—FEBRUARY 1778

Old Professor Grenville set the publication of Hutton's theory back by about five years.

He'd been a semi-regular at Black and Smith's Poker Club that winter: attendance obviously wasn't a top priority for him, but he came by often enough to be greeted by name, and greet the regulars with cordial familiarity.

As Black recalled, he'd either not been in attendance when Hutton was speaking about his geological theory, or he'd been in the room but not felt the need to engage. However, this particular evening Black, Smith and Hutton had been so engrossed at the table they hadn't noticed Grenville scrape his chair over.

"Has a new volume of Gulliver's Travels been released?" Grenville asked. "I don't think I've heard of this adventure before."

"No, this discussion sounds fantastical," said Smith. "But I can assure you, it's soundly rooted in fact." He jabbed a knuckle in the Hutton's direction.

"Mountains rising from the ocean and then falling into wheat fields? It certainly sounds fantastical." An expression that might be mistaken for mirth played across Grenville's face, but Black could recognise an undercurrent of cruelty in the fixture of his smile. "Well, it certainly sounds like an entertaining tale, and maybe I didn't catch enough of the beginning of it? Perhaps Dr Hutton can start from the beginning?"

Hutton blinked. "Um, I'd be...honoured?"

Then he looked around and realised at the same time Black did, that the rest of the gathering had fallen silent and was watching him. While Hutton had spoken about his theories during Poker Club meetings, it was usually as part of a private conversation between Black and his closest friends. There were about twenty men crowded into the side room of this tavern, the small space turning them into a sea of onlookers.

"We might be better arranging a formal reading at a later date..." Black began hastily, seeing Hutton's eyes widen.

"No, no, Joseph." Hutton held up a hand. "It's alright. Are you all listening to us? Oh, right. Well..."

He rose.

A number of chairs and stools scraped in unison as the Poker Club attendees swivelled to get a better view of this impromptu lecture.

Grenville's eyes crinkled into his face, and his smile steadily exposed more teeth.

"Um, alright." Hutton seemed transfixed by all the eyes suddenly on him. Sweat beaded his brow. "When you consider the...no, sorry..." With that, he turned and vomited onto the floor.

It gave Black only a meagre sliver of satisfaction to know some of Hutton's oysters and roast chicken hit Grenville's shoes, because the entire gathering immediately dissolved into laughter.

It's surprise, not malice, Black consoled himself as he helped a pale and swaying Hutton from the room, hoping fresh air would be all he needed. They didn't mean to laugh at him.

Still, though Hutton would laugh off the incident and claim there were no hard feelings, it was several months before he dared speak about his geological theories again, even in the privacy of his own home.

24

A long time passed between George knocking on the natural history classroom door and its occupant answering. After a period of silence almost convincing him the room stood empty, George heard the slow, deliberate shuffle of someone reluctantly crossing the floor. When the door creaked open, he hoped his impatience wasn't showing.

The professor he sought was a stooped, frail creature in a heavy orange dressing coat thirty years out of fashion. He blinked at George, as if he too had been disturbed from a slumber.

"Professor Grenville?" George asked. "I was told Ganymede was coming to speak to you this morning."

"I'm sorry," he said in a mild voice. "I'm quite busy this morning and I'm afraid I don't understand what you want. Did we arrange to speak?"

He barely looked strong enough to close his classroom door shut in George's face, let alone slam it.

"Apologies." George tried again. "My name is George Stephens. I was looking for Gregory Bennett and thought he was meeting with you right now. Perhaps he arranged to meet with you later?"

He thought perhaps his force of personality would get Grenville to help him, but the natural history professor countered with the same mildness as his first reply.

"I don't wish to disappoint you greatly, but Mr Bennett is not with me at this present moment." He sealed his mouth shut, stopping George from attempting to ask—again—when Gregory might show. While now obvious signs of impatience showed—tapping of feet or sighs—George received the clear picture that Grenville wanted him gone and had no interest in entertaining him.

Well, if conventional diplomatic enquiries didn't work...

"I apologise for intruding upon your time," George said. "It's just that Mr Bennett and I got into a disagreement last night, and I'm rather afraid I hurt him."

Grenville glanced shrewdly at George, no doubt assessing his swollen right eye in this new context.

"Hmmm, you better come in." He opened the door.

Grenville had a personal desk in the classroom's corner, which he directed George towards. The room was filled with taxidermied animals, giving the impression one had stepped inside a zoo or museum of antiquaries. An eagle in mid-flight was suspended above Grenville's desk, appearing to glare at the rows of seating where students would usually sit.

"I've seen you in the company of Dr Black and Dr Cullen, have I not?"

He beckoned George into the room and bade him sit by his front desk.

"Yes, sir. I'm a medical student."

"Indeed. I remember you now. Mr Stephens, you called yourself?"

"Yes, sir."

Grenville eased his stiff bones into a frayed leather seat, stretching as if he had all the time in the world.

"What was the nature of your disagreement with Mr Bennett last night, if I may enquire?"

"Oh, it seems foolish to recount now. Since you are close with him, it might be fairer to hear the tale from his mouth when he arrives."

"We have a bit of a wait until then," Grenville said with a twinkle in his eyes. "He intended to see me right before his clinical lecture began."

Ganymede might not show for another hour, in that case. If he was intending to show at all. But Grenville clasped his hands on his sternum and regarded George with the full weight of his attention.

"You young scholars get into quite the scrapes. To an old fusty gentleman like myself, it's hard to see what the hot tempers are about."

"You were young once though, sir?" George had a sense polite and diffident behaviour wouldn't grant him much headway with Grenville.

The professor chuckled. "Quite right, Mr Stephens. Quite right indeed."

"I understand you don't teach Mr Bennett?"

"Never taught him natural history, and I doubt I ever will. Not that I hold it against him. I used to be fond of Greek and Latin in my youth, too." Grenville sighed. "They're good boys; indulging an old man with their company like they do. I enjoy hearing of their high-spirited antics."

George suspected a connection between Playfair and Grenville was hidden in here, as well. Playfair the mathematician was a more natural acquaintance of a natural history professor than obnoxious classic students.

It was as if Grenville had never tried to dissuade him from entering. The professor regarded him keenly.

"And what of yourself, Mr Stephens? I don't think I've seen you outside the context of the medical school."

It wasn't like George could afford to pay for tuition in courses unrelated to his degree. He shrugged and gave a half-smile instead. "It seems medicine has taken up most of my time."

"That's the nature of physicians; always thinking themselves more important, just because their knowledge is *applied*. All learning is important, I say, even learning for the sake of it. It's important to expand your mind, is it not?"

Grenville's old woollen coat was dirty at the cuffs: he'd probably owned his shirt and waistcoat for the better part of two decades.

If Grenville knew George associated with Cullen and Black, he probably also knew that George's financial circumstances weren't great, and that the late Earl of Hopetoun's patronage had kept him afloat for most of his studies. Perhaps Grenville was deliberately trying to make him feel inferior, because taking university courses merely for curiosity's sake was never something he could indulge in.

"It's generous of you to support such discussions," George said, thinking of Ganymede and his chums sitting where he was now. "I'm sure Gregory enjoys spending time with you."

"And you clearly enjoying spending time with Dr Black," Grenville laughed. "I can hear his voice in your words."

That was probably not a compliment, though George knew to pretend it was. He wondered how long he was supposed to sit here tolerating Grenville. What if Ganymede heard him at the door and snuck away before he noticed?

"I may have my disagreements with his companion Dr Hutton, but I can't fault him for trying to make geology a respectable course of study. When I was a lad, if any professor discussed geology, it was an after-thought in their natural history lecture. Until I began lecturing on the subject, no one thought geology could form a course in its own right. Look at us now." Grenville chuckled, motioning to the empty, dusty classroom.

"However, Dr Hutton is a little...eccentric in his viewpoint that the Biblical truth can be tossed aside. You'll see among respected geological circles that the biblical age of the Earth is accepted without controversy, and that calculations of the Earth's age and formation by serious philosophers support the Biblical timeframe. You'll know that a philosopher no less renowned than Sir Isaac Newton made his own supporting calculations of the Earth's exact age."

Hutton had made a spurious remark on this topic that 'to a hammer, everything is a nail', which George took to mean no other geologists dared to think outside the 6,000 year paradigm, and thus their arguments would always wind back to supporting it.

Grenville continued. "Certainly, I teach the stated biblical doctrine in my geology and natural history lecture courses. Man is created in God's image, and he holds dominion over land and the creatures that share his world."

That would explain some of his opposition to Hutton: this amateur geologist was contradicting everything Grenville taught.

"I met Sir Isaac Newton as a boy, did you know?" Grenville paused, though this wasn't something George could have possibly known. "I was born in Southampton, and my father took me to see the great philosopher at his country residence nearby. My recollections of the day are vague: he's nothing more than a shadowy figure earth my mind's eye." Grenville chuckled to himself and the folly of infancy for not remembering such a momentous occasion.

"Was your father interested in natural philosophy?" George asked awkwardly. Grenville was expecting him to say something in response, and he had no idea what.

Grenville ignored the question and resumed his soft chuckles. "Sir Isaac and the Honourable Robert Boyle built the bedrock of modern science that men like Drs Black and Cullen stand on today. You'll still see their little scribbles in use as chemical notation. It always surprises me how much intelligent men like Dr Cullen seem to disavow that older generation, not acknowledging how much they owe to them."

A queasy tingle rose from the base of George's spine. The words might have sounded harmless were it not for a peculiar glint in the old professor's eye, similar to when he was studying George's bruised visage.

"I...understand some of Newton's theories tended towards the...mystical..." George ventured, unsure how much he should admit. He wasn't equipped to handle a conversation like this. Black would know how to respond.

Grenville's lip quirked in response to George's flailing attempts at subtlety. Then abruptly it vanished.

"I know you are expecting Mr Bennett here, but duty calls me away from the classroom this morning. I'm afraid we must cut this conversation short."

George lowered his gaze so as not to let his frustration show. Smugness radiated off Grenville's wiry frame. He'd known from the moment George arrived Ganymede wouldn't show in his classroom today. Here was a man who enjoyed sowing confusion, and revelling in the sense of control he gained from doing so.

Well, his games worked. George rose and inclined his head. Grenville made a show of tidying his desk and donning his hat.

"I wish you a pleasant day, Mr Stephens, and hope you and Mr Bennett can resolve your difficulties without my intercession."

. . .

From a vantage point on the other side of the Yards, George watched the professor amble down Jossie Steps, fiddling with his coat buttons, until he disappeared from view.

Then he leant against the wall and rubbed the parts of his temples that weren't swollen and tender.

Could there be any chance he'd misunderstood that exchange? The undercurrent was frightful, but he was running on negligible sleep, with a mounting toll of injuries.

The sight of Cullen generated an audible cry of relief. The professor stopped to talk with a bunch of faculty members, then four paces later he waylaid several students, pressing them gently about something, hand on each elbow in turn.

By the time he'd concluded that series of conversations, George's mind was made up, and he jogged over.

"Good morning, George." Cullen did a barely perceptible double-take at George's bruised eye, then decided to leave it unacknowledged. "What's on your mind?"

"Are you busy right now, Dr Cullen?" George asked, looking around.

"Hmm, nothing urgent." Cullen folded his papers. "I had a couple of boys to chase down regarding their submitted dissertations, but that can wait until after the clinical rounds." He eyed George, his head cocked in a question.

"It's just that Professor Grenville said a few things to me that made me wonder if...oh, maybe I'm wasting your time... alright, fine...if maybe he's got a hidden link to the dark chymists and Reverend Holm."

25

The pair found Grenville's classroom unlocked. Once inside—satisfied no one saw them enter—Cullen gestured to a heavy table.

It took George an embarrassingly long time to get the table barred against the door: he couldn't pull with his injured arm, so he had to bump it with his hip across the uneven flagstones, almighty shrieks of wood against stone ruining their attempt at discretion.

Far from laughing or dismissing George's rambling concerns, Cullen had grown deathly serious.

"Grenville came to Edinburgh from Cambridge a while back. He missed most of the dark chymistry squabbles, so Joe and I never saw him as much of a threat. Not that we liked the man," Cullen added, surveying Grenville's immaculate desk. "His doting mother must have told him he was cleverer than everyone else at too delicate an age. Don't spoil your future children too early, George. It breeds insufferable men."

Setting aside that concern for thirty years hence, George joined Cullen in surveying the classroom. Grenville kept the place sparse. There was little of his own correspondence or personal effects in this dusty museum.

"Maybe I overreacted or misunderstood..."

"Don't question yourself, George. All the learned men in Edinburgh know enough about the dark chymists and their sigils to know it's *not* a thing to joke about."

"But supposing Grenville wanted to give the impression of being affiliated..."

"Then he's dangerous for a whole host of other reasons. Like how a burning cart sent down a hill towards livestock is dangerous. He's made no secret of his hostility to Dr Hutton's theories, which puts him as a potential Holm sympathiser."

So even if Grenville wasn't in active collaboration with Holm, he was an obvious target for the reverend's manipulations. That made George feel slightly better.

"This is Grenville's temple; he spends more time in here than at home, as far as I'm aware." Cullen prodded the skirting boards with his cane. "He doesn't like other faculty coming in, either. Which makes me suspect if he's hiding anything, this is where it'll be."

"He was giving funny looks at the eagle," George noted, pointing to the creature suspended in the centre of the classroom. "Though I'm not sure why he'd try to make his secret so obvious."

Cullen didn't share George's skepticism. "Oh, I'm sure he thought he was being subtle, and it tickled him mightily knowing you'd never guess the truth."

They circled the eagle from below, looking for clues.

"Should we cut the strings?" George asked, looking around for any sharp objects.

"I doubt he's concealed anything in the eagle, lad," Cullen said breezily. "It's not trivial to access."

George supposed not. He'd need a ladder to reach the ceiling; standing on a desk or chair wouldn't be enough. A doddery man Cullen's age wouldn't reach it unassisted.

He spent all of ten minutes in the professor's company. Had that given him any insight into how the man thought? Stuffing valuables into his prized taxidermy didn't seem in-keeping with him, it would be more subtle...

"Hmmm...Dr Cullen, does the eagle strike you as looking at that wolf?"

Cullen burst out laughing. "Oh, a trail of clues around the room? Following the eyes? Grenville must have kept himself awake, sniggering at his cleverness. There's what, thirty taxidermied animals in here? And they're all looking at each other?"

"Well, the wolf is either looking at that dusty jaguar, or preening at itself in the mirror."

Cullen froze.

"Professor?"

He was watching the blood drain from Cullen's face, and he could hear the professor's breathing turn shallow and quick. Cullen stared at the mirror, as if he'd seen a ghost.

"Oh no, not this again," Cullen moaned, almost to himself.

George had half a mind to bolt from the room crying for help. He'd seen Cullen in a variety of strong emotive states—angry, elated, morose—but he'd never seen the old professor *scared*.

But then Cullen regained control of himself. He swallowed once and lurched forward towards the wolf.

"Providence help me. I hoped Joe and myself would never have to deal with one of these again. Careful, lad—don't touch it." George had taken a step towards the mirror.

"Sorry." It looked like an ordinary mirror, with nothing to George's mind differentiating it from any other, fixed to the wall with a much-tarnished, unadorned brass frame. It was a little unusual to have such a large mirror on college grounds, but to George, the whole natural history classroom was a monument to Grenville's eccentricity, so in that respect, it wasn't out of place.

"Thought so…" A small rattle came from Cullen's side of the room. The professor adjusted the collar round the wolf's neck—a jocular accessory, George had assumed—to reveal a silver tag no larger than a pound coin. "You can come over, but be careful, George."

Cullen held the tag with the aid of a handkerchief, presumably to avoid it coming into contact with his skin. On one side was an intricate carving of overlapping circles, lines, and triangles.

"It's a dark chymistry sigil?" George whispered.

Cullen nodded. "One class of sigil is only activated if you draw its components in the correct order. That's the class they most often used. But there's a second class of sigils drawn inverted. They're inactive until…" Cullen turned and nodded towards the mirror.

"They're reflected?"

"Yes. We have to be careful, because I'm not entirely sure what will happen…" Cullen shooed George several steps away.

"Dr Cullen, are you s—?"

George didn't have time to fully question the wisdom of his plan, because Cullen turned and twisted the tag to expose the sigil to the mirror. At once there was a flash of light, like the sun reflecting on metal. George couldn't say whether it leapt from the sigil to the mirror, or the other way round, but a second later, the surface of Grenville's mirror flickered and darkened.

George's eyes took a moment to make sense of this transformation, before realising the mirror no longer reflected the classroom. Instead, it portrayed a spiral staircase.

"Mmmm…" Cullen let the tag drop and approached the

mirror. As George moved closer, the mirror did more than show an image. There was genuinely a stairwell behind where nothing had been before.

"Is it real?" This side of Grenville's classroom was the outer wall of the Old Library. In fact, there were windows on either side of the mirror. If George was to look out, he'd seen an uninterrupted wall a couple bricks' thick.

"As real as these things can be. The conniving bastard. He's hidden this for decades..."

Given Cullen's behaviour so far, it shouldn't surprise George that he also intended to plunge through the magical mirror portal down a stairwell that may or may not exist. "It is possible this stairwell exists in an entirely different location, and the mirror connects to this classroom."

"So the stairwell might be on the other side of the college grounds?"

"Or in Coventry," Cullen said. "Doesn't matter." He jabbed into the frame with his physician cane. It plunged in and out of the stairwell space without a flicker of resistance.

George drew close enough to smell the earthy mustiness of the old stairwell. Its stones were brown-sugar granite, worn with grooves.

Cullen held out a hand. A small ball of light appeared in his palm.

"Well, let's get this investigated before Grenville sneaks back. Now let your heart be strong!" He paused to take in George's disbelieving, wide-eyed expression. "It's alright, lad. I doubt Rev Holm is at the bottom right now."

It proved the lack of cosmic justice George thought, as he stepped over the brass frame into the mostly real stairwell, that a man as reckless and impulsive as Dr William Cullen could survive almost to his eightieth year with facilities intact, and a cautious person such as himself now had a ruined shoulder and wrecked limbs. Cullen hadn't even suffered a broken nose in his eighty-odd years.

It took them a while to creep down the stairs, since Cullen found it difficult to navigate the steep steps with his cane in one hand and aetherial light in the other.

Fortunately, it took only a few turns of the staircase before they stepped out into a low cellar space. The ball of light in Cullen's hand expanded.

"Goodness gracious…"

It looked like every other neglected storage cellar on university grounds. Broken furniture was crammed into the back of a space maybe ten metres wide.

In one corner was a bundle of blankets.

"Someone's been staying here." George took in a clutch of candle stubs, bottles, and cutlery on one table nearest the blankets. He picked up a bottle and tilted it.

Liquid sloshed inside.

"Holm, no doubt."

"That means he's been coming and going from the college?"

"Maybe. Maybe not. It's possible there's more than one entrance to this cellar."

"Oh, so a second mirror connected somewhere else?"

Cullen nodded.

George hoped they'd be able to walk out of this strange place. He craned his senses. No noise reached them down here. The cellar smelled only of cobwebs and mustiness— there were no clues to help him deduce their true location.

"We'll deal with Professor Grenville later. It might be best he doesn't know we've discovered his secret yet. Besides, I want to hear what Joe and Adam make of all this."

George was glad Cullen didn't intend to spend more time down here than necessary. He took another look at the seem- ingly abandoned objects in Holm's den.

There was very little dust on them.

In fact, on one of the surfaces a set of polished carpentry tools was neatly arranged.

Perhaps this was less an abandoned cellar, and more a workshop?

"Is Holm practicing sewing?" George asked, gesturing at a dismembered spindle wheel. It had clearly been disassembled down here, because the constituent parts were set neatly beside it.

Cullen frowned. "Goodness knows what he's doing. I can't make head nor tail of this."

Aside from some small tins of wax polish and oil, they couldn't see any chemicals stored down here. The experimentation seemed purely mechanical.

"Perhaps Mrs Holm is involved in this also?" Not that Kitty Holm seemed the type for large sewing projects, from what he'd made of her.

"I wish we could bring Joe down here and see what he thinks of it. Whatever Holm is planning, it doesn't look dark chymistry is the only weapon at his disposal."

26

After George departed Panmure House the two conferred, but Smith was adamant their list remained unchanged.

"Calder Hall, Grangemore Estate, or Redhall are still the most likely options. I visited a number of properties in Edinburgh and Costorphine yesterday, just to confirm my reasoning. I told the servants the commissioners received word their master was storing boxes of undeclared imports on site, and was obligated to investigate such rumours."

"And you were let in without question?"

"Yes." Rummaging in his coat pocket, Smith pulled out a palm-sized ledger, bound in black leather. "I've found the majority of Edinburgh citizens are more terrified of a solitary tax commissioner carrying a very small notebook than one with an armful of ledgers."

There *was* something intimidating about hatchet-faced Smith furiously scribbling minuscule handwriting into that tiny notebook—Black had seen it for himself. But he hadn't realised his friend used that perception to his advantage.

"Did you find anything of interest, Adam? Anything at all?"

"I'm afraid not, Joe. Those weren't properties belonging to the main dark chymistry families, and there was no scent of Holm or James. Nor of anything else being concealed from me."

Few things escaped Smith's notice, so Black had to trust his assessment. It was good that only a handful of locations remained under consideration, but they were all larger estates miles outside Edinburgh.

Having bid Smith adieu, Black donned his thickest wool coat and headed out in the brisk morning.

The Grangemore boy hadn't proven particularly useful, but Black admitted information on Hutton's location wasn't going to fall into their lap. It was possible Holm had bypassed the noble dark chemist families entirely, and his friend lay trussed up in a Gorgie inn cellar.

He wished either Princess Dashkova or the Earl of Hopetoun were around to help—they had ways of cracking open the aristocracy he did not. Sadly, he didn't have much in the way of patrons right now.

Taking the familiar route across a blustery North Bridge into the New Town, Black kept his head down, hoping to avoid the need to greet anyone.

He never understood how Holm managed to worm his way into the dark chymist circles in the first place. The story was that Holm came to Edinburgh as a theology student of modest means: son of a village schoolmaster or something like that. Cullen's pet theory had Malcolm the bastard son of a dark chymistry Lord, his unsavoury origins disguised. Black put little stock in that: Holm had always demonstrated an aptitude for killing, gleaming off him like a dark light. That kind of talent would have been seized upon and cherished, no matter the boy's origin.

At one time, it felt like the less he knew about Holm the better. Now Black was staring at a solitary loose thread, using it to try to re-construct the garment it came from. What did Holm want?

Instead of having a useful and informed aristocratic patron to rely on, Black would need to ask...

"Ah, Louis—you're looking well."

His former chemistry student turned man of leisure, Louis Grey was the kind of affable New Town gentleman of whom little was expected, beyond tasteful extravagance. He managed some safe portion of his father's estates and threw much-lauded dinner parties during the Season.

These parties took place in the neoclassical splendour of his new accommodation on St George's Square. Louis had lately succumbed to Greek antiquities: Black had to weave around several statues abandoned in the entrance hallway. Crates of vases partially blocked the stairwell. He wasn't sure where his former student would house all these antiques. But since it wasn't his money being frittered, Black decided against voicing his opinions on the extravagance.

Once he'd squeezed into the drawing room, Louis bade him sit. "You can manage a pot of tea, Dr Black?"

"I would be much obliged, thank you."

The younger Grey belonged to a dark chymist family, but to imagine this scion getting involved in the deceitful dealings of the dark chymists was like imagining a retriever committing arson. Louis was too amiable to lust after power.

Unfortunately, this made him an outcast among the suspects Black was now pursuing, because Louis could only be expected to tell him things he'd sworn to keep secret.

"Did I see your father and Lord Argyle together the other day?" Black started blithely.

Louis frowned. "It's unlikely, Dr Black. My father said the Argyles extended overtures for a bit—dinner invitations, what have you—but Pa says he's too old for all their nonsense."

Black had seen no such thing, but he'd hope to bait some

insight from his oblivious friend. Deceiving Louis was like pretending to throw a stick to a dog: very easy to repeat, but it made Black feel increasingly guilty to the point it caused physical discomfort. So he changed tack, giving away as much information as was safe to do so.

"I got the impression some of the older Edinburgh families were becoming a bit shiftless. I wasn't sure if there'd been a quarrel or something similar."

"Not that I'm aware of." Louis shrugged. "But you know how I am." It was true he tended to associate with merchants and new money: to the traditional Scots families such behaviour was gauche, but Black supposed that was where all the money and influence were these days.

"You're too modest, sir. I've never seen you on unfriendly terms with anyone."

Louis took a sip of tea to conceal his smile.

"If you want gossip, Dr Black, I hear the Argyle boy took a beating the other night. He was set upon by muggers...apparently."

This was sadly the one bit of gossip Black already knew about. "You doubt the veracity of his story?"

"That Simon Argyle was coming home from church and violently robbed of his cherished family bible? No, the boy attracts wildness, and that wildness came close enough to bite."

That was a surprisingly perceptive observation from the usually blithe Louis. Black was momentarily taken aback.

"In other developments," Louis said, leaning forward on one elbow. "I hear the eminent Dr Black is being canvassed for opinions on Town Council nominees."

"That's unfortunately a less interesting development," Black mused. The change of subject wasn't a welcome one. "I demurred on the subject."

"Yes, and I hear the Lord Provost was disappointed, and

intends to ask you again. You are quite close to the young Earl of Hopetoun. Did you not teach him?"

"I did." Black took a sip of tea. "Young John is a good man, very thoughtful and enterprising, much like his departed father. I'm sure he'll do well in any elected position...but I don't think my opinion is worth as much as the tattlers would have you believe."

Louis laughed and slapped the table, as if Black had uttered a great witticism. "You are far too modest, Dr Black. Of course your candidate endorsement will count for something—that's why they asked you."

"What I mean is, the Earl is likely to secure a seat on the Town Council through his own merit without input from me."

A frown passed across Louis' face, which was an unusual sight. "But Dr Black, even I know his rival is not fit for the position. He's another English lord stuck in the old-fashioned way of doing things, who's made no secret of his intention to meddle in the running of the university. When I last heard, he seemed to brag about how little he knew of academic matters."

To Black, that seemed all the more reason to assume the election would fall in Hopetoun's favour, but he didn't want to agitate Louis further. "Well, if the Lord Provost approaches me a second time, I will be sure to state my positive sentiments towards the Earl."

* * *

Two weeks after moving to Edinburgh in 1752 to complete his medical degree, Black first heard the voice.

He was still fumbling his way around the college. On that day he was trying to find his dissertation supervisor Prof Alston: he'd been told by a fellow student Alston was in the

New Library wing—of course that meant nothing to him because both library wings appeared ancient—so he was creeping down an empty second-floor corridor at three o'clock on a Thursday, sure to be embarrassed when somebody pointed out how far from the New Library wing and Alston he actually was.

"Good afternoon, Joseph."

Black turned slowly to find the source of the voice. He couldn't immediately put a name to the voice, but part of him recognised its owner and warned him of danger. Heart slamming in his chest, Black turned and found Holm standing by the stairwell.

Black was barely through his twenties; a gawky young man almost alone in a bustling, hectic city, struggling to adjust to the rigours of Edinburgh medical school after a leisurely course of study in Glasgow. There were only whispers of what Holm—then a theology student—did in the small hours of the morning at the behest of his handlers.

More to the point, Black and Cullen had barely come into their power as phlogiston-wielders. No one knew Cullen had developed such a system or shared it with his student Black. To brag about such powers was to challenge the dark chymists and their sigil-based hegemony over Scotland. Standing in that silent corridor in 1752, Black had no idea of the power he was to come into, and that Cullen and he could topple the dark chymists.

Instead, Black reached out to steady his hand against the nearest doorframe. His palm was already slick with sweat.

Cullen had carved out a reputation on the West Coast as an outspoken chemistry professor with eccentric pedagogical techniques and a blazing anti-authoritarian streak, and Black's arrival in Edinburgh had been greeted with much gossip and speculation among the medical school. But it startled him to realise Malcolm Holm knew his name.

Even worse, Holm had recognised him from behind, from the other end of a long corridor. Had Holm followed him here?

For a moment, the two stood silently regarding each other. Then Holm smiled, raised a hand in farewell and vanished down the stairs. Black clung onto the doorframe for several minutes after, not trusting himself to walk without collapsing.

He emerged from the building an eternity later, expecting to find Holm waiting for him, arms folded, in the Yards. Yet of his tormentor, there was no sign.

A few days later, a deacon's newborn son vanished from his Lawnmarket tenement, while his mother dozed a few feet away. The baby was returned a week later; placed back in its cradle one evening as if nothing were amiss. The child seemed healthy, and not a cut or blemish was found upon it, but the deacon resigned from the role the next day. No one knew why he was targeted by the dark chymists—apart from the deacon, presumably—and everyone whispered speculation about the business lines he had crossed, or the nobles he had slighted, to warrant such a warning.

That Holm played a part in the brazen abduction was obvious. Black found himself wondering if Holm also assumed care for the infant over that week. One detractor of the deacon's family acidly noted that the babe came back in better health than it was taken. It didn't seem like a paradox to Black: Holm had no quavers in his moral conviction, and would see keeping a stolen infant healthy as important a duty as stealing it in the first place.

* * *

The only other exchange between them came a few months later. Again, Black departed the Royal Infirmary and found Holm standing by the front gate, possibly waiting for him.

181

It was too late for him to retreat into the building, but there was no way to leave without passing Holm. So Black squared his shoulders and tried to look confident.

"There is a natural order to things, Joseph," Holm began, as conversationally as if they were old friends meeting in the tavern. "God has placed Man at the top of nature's order. So within mankind exists a natural order: kings rule over beggars, not the other way round. Your former teacher has cultivated a foolish disrespect for these natural orders. I would encourage you to pray and reflect upon such follies before they become dangers." This little speech concluded, he nodded, smiled, and departed. Black stood there for a minute, straining to think of a reply. But of course Holm had not expected a reply, nor did he desire one.

The warning seemed to coincide with an influx of Cullen's charity students back in Glasgow, and their entry into professions hitherto reserved for a wealthier class of men.

At the time, Black was probably counted among their number: a foreign-born middle child of Scots-Irish wine merchants in Bordeaux, halfway through his medical doctorate. Not impoverished, but a noticeable social rung below most of his peers. Thirty years later and medical students of Black's modest background were as common as fruit flies. You could almost forget it hadn't always been so.

Until you caught the look of disgust in Holm's eye.

27

If the students in the corridor were surprised to see Prof William Cullen and a random medical student emerge from Prof Grenville's classroom, accompanied by scraping of heavy furniture and the distinct absence of the professor whose room it belonged to, they were too polite to say.

Cullen nodded to a few of them and exchanged jovial remarks, as if nothing was amiss. George could only stare at his feet and hope he didn't look ill.

Once they were back in the Yards, Cullen decided what his course of action would be.

"I'll go and find Joe right away, and see if he had any inkling of this." Cullen tutted at the audacity of his natural history colleague. "It's a veritable hornet's nest we've uncovered, but I worry it doesn't get us any closer to finding poor James."

"I suppose it could mean Professor Grenville knows where Hutton is being held, if he's working closely with Holm."

"Why did you say you were speaking to Professor Grenville in the first place?" Cullen asked.

George wasn't sure he had. "I heard Gregory Bennett was

going to speak with him this morning. Um...how long were we in the room, Dr Cullen?"

"It couldn't have been longer than five minutes, could it?"

"I suppose not." He heard no one knock or try to open the door. "Doctor, where does Professor Grenville live?"

"I think he has an apartment in Carrubber's Close," Cullen remarked. "Or at least that's where he lived a few years ago."

It was easily within walking distance, and Grenville didn't move fast.

"Maybe I'll try to catch up with Prof Grenville."

"Good thinking, lad."

Sprinting, George cut through College Wynd into the Cowgate. He wasn't even out of breath before he caught sight of Grenville, making his careful way down the Cowgate.

But instead of continuing to St Cecilia's and turning up Niddry's Street, which would bring him onto Carrubber's Close, Grenville turned left onto Stevenlaw's Close.

What if Grenville lied about going home? Perhaps he was going to find Ganymede or Holm and warn them? Slowing into a brisk walk, George followed.

The natural history professor sauntered as if he hadn't a care in the world, turning right onto the High Street and heading downhill. But again, he didn't turn left again onto Carrubber's Close, instead passing the close where he lived and continuing onwards.

As George got a little closer, he saw something white flutter from Grenville's pocket and land next to a doorstep. The professor didn't react and kept walking, but a clump of journeyman carpenters leaning against the windowsill chatting spotted it. One reached out and picked up the object—George was close enough to see it was a scrap of paper—flick it over with a shrug, then return to his lively conversation.

The scrap of paper vanished from sight—either discarded

underfoot or shoved into a pocket. George had to step a few paces to the side to avoid walking suspiciously close to the men.

But now his attention was caught, he saw a second scrap of paper flutter from Grenville's coat near the cobbler's. Again, it seemed aimed towards the doorstep. This time there wasn't an obvious target close by, so George scooted forward and caught the scrap before it could blow away.

The paper was barely the size of a shilling, with the '9 DSA' written in minute crabby handwriting.

That was worse than useless. Could it be a scrap of a longer message? Was Grenville dropping the same combination of letters and numbers on every doorstep? George dropped the paper into his coat pocket and hurried on, hoping his interception wasn't noticed.

Reaching the next corner, as Grenville turned off the High Street into St Mary's Wynd, the gap between them widened. George had to weave around sedan chairs and mounted guardsmen. St Mary's Wynd would take him back onto the Cowgate, so what was the point of going around via the High Street?

This seemed like an evasive manoeuvre to shake off pursuers, unless Grenville had spoken or indicated to someone and George had missed it? While it was unlikely Grenville had spotted George in pursuit, he was passing into quieter wynds and lanes, and no doubt worried about his increased visibility.

Indeed, St Mary's Wynd was almost deserted when George jogged down it. He hadn't figured out where Grenville was headed. Perhaps a roundabout route to the Royal Infirmary? Or was he intending to sneak back up towards the Grassmarket? Or maybe this sudden spurt was a sign he'd almost reached his destination?

"Hold on a minute, friend," croaked a voice to his left. "Can you tell us what time it is?"

Two figures emerged from the doorways. Both moved slowly to block his way. The one who'd spoke had already unsheathed his pistol.

For a moment, George fought to control his annoyance as the object of his pursuit strolled away into the distance. Then he paused to remind himself there were more pressing issues at stake. He'd been so caught up he'd not noticed those two thieves laying in wait, and he'd rushed straight into their trap.

He craned over his shoulder. There didn't appear to be anyone sneaking up on him from behind. Yet. He'd need to act before a third or fourth man got into position.

"Right you are, gentlemen..." George kept his left arm outstretched to show he wasn't holding a weapon, and reached into his coat pocket, wincing as his injured right hand rubbed against the woollen fabric. "I don't want no trouble."

He only had two items on his person: his purse and his decoy purse. It was the latter he gingerly extracted, keeping his eyes on the thieves in the hope they wouldn't look too closely.

The thief in front of him nodded slightly and took a shuffle forward with hand outstretched. The other hand still pointed a pistol at him. He may well decide to shoot George anyway—there was no benefit in letting a victim get away and identify him later. But for now there was the polite pretence they'd let their cull live.

George's ruined knuckles wailed, and it took everything to stop himself from flinching with the pain. But his left arm wasn't as good as throwing.

He leaned forward as if to toss the purse, then threw it sideways at full force. It caught the second thief on the shoulder, and he pitched to the side with a howl. Before he had to time to realise a purse of coins shouldn't cause that much acute pain on impact, George had skipped to the side and delivered him a kick to the head. The thief dropped, his scream cutting off mid-fall.

George heard the crack of the pistol, but the first thief had only reacted to the sudden motion, not tracking him properly, so the shot went wide.

George let momentum carry him away from the first assailant and out of the gunpowder smoke cloud, kicking away the purse loaded with a sharp-edged rock. He steadied himself as his assailant took a cautious step forward. He didn't bother trying to reload his pistol, but it could still cause George a lot of pain if it struck him.

They started a wary circling of each other. Any other week than this, George wouldn't have worried about his chances against a man like this. The thief was wiry as a leather strap, but his face was lined, and his age showed in his slow reflexes. But today, George's right arm was useless. A strike to his injured shoulder would send him falling to the ground screaming. It was already a shrill cry of pain in his mind. If the old thief had any savvy, he'd no doubt see George favouring his right as soon as he attacked, and capitalise on that weakness as quick as possible.

Looking at his opponent as he took another step around, George supposed he'd have to...

"Rrrrr-aAAAHHH!"

Glancing over George's shoulder, his assailant froze mid-step. Eyes wide, he hesitated for just a second before backing into a run, almost tripping over a front step in his hurry to get away.

"Rrrr-AHH! Rrrr-AHH!"

A grey and brown hound pelted down the close after its quarry, the sharp edge to its bark and glint of teeth warning them he wasn't playing.

Striding up the close, his coat whipping around him, Playfair whistled sharply. Without hesitation, the hound whirled around and rushed back to his master's side, circling Playfair's legs and looking up at his face with beatific anticipation.

"Heel, Vulcan."

Playfair slowed his stride. George wasn't immediately sure if he was slowing to converse with George or to step around the unconscious thief. He glanced the direction his attacker had fled. There was no trace of him now.

"Good afternoon, Dr Playfair." George wondered about making a smart remark, but he couldn't think of one. His right arm was throbbing, and he'd strained his hamstring with that kick. "Your dog is well-trained."

"Naturally." Playfair spoke as if only fools would raise a dog to a lesser standard than his. "I would have said you were lucky to get away from Simon and his chums with only a scratch last night, but now I see you have a little more than luck at your disposal."

"It's been a long time since I donned a red coat," George replied. The thief on the ground groaned, but didn't stir. "Do you happen to know where Ganymede Bennett is?" Goodness knows what Grenville was playing at: George doubted Playfair would be much help with whatever was going on there.

Playfair laughed, perhaps despite himself. "That would be a Cullenite display of nerve if you seriously wish to seek him out. But no, fortunately for both of you, I don't."

There wasn't much point in arguing. George didn't fancy his chances against Vulcan, who kept glancing at his master, probably hoping to be allowed to go sniff the unconscious thief.

"Well, I'll let you go about your business, Dr Playfair. I imagine you concluded drafting your rebuttal of Dr Hutton."

Playfair chuckled, as if admiring George for his lack of subtlety.

"I don't intend to let Dr Hutton ruin my day. His laughable arguments don't require that much of my attention."

It was another put-down, but George detected a note of falseness in Playfair's sneering tone. Maybe he was imaging it

—he'd only met the man once before—but this insult wasn't as fluent as his other ones.

"Perhaps there's a chance you don't appreciate the full sophistication of Dr Hutton's arguments," George said as politely as he could. "There is a nuance in his definition of heat that deserves careful scrutiny."

"Nuance, good Lord!" Playfair laughed as if George had delivered a witty jest. "I suppose 'nuance' and 'convoluted mess' might produce the same head-scratching dismay in the reader. Dr Hutton is quite a phenomenon: I don't know how he can claim an eternal Earth with a straight face. It's either a joke—not funny at all—or whole-hearted blasphemy. His argument about heat causing mineralisation outside the ocean make little sense when you think about the calculations for over five seconds. Which he apparently hasn't. You don't need to be a mathematician to see that." Playfair chortled at his remark, then turned his attention back to George. He tapped his walking cane once on the ground. Vulcan's ears perked. "Good day to you, sir."

George watched him until he'd passed through the close. The thief he'd knocked out was making more noise and movement, so with a sigh he returned the way he'd came. He'd have to catch his quarry's trail elsewhere.

But he felt a cautious stirring of something akin to hope. Playfair tried to downplay Hutton's theories, mocking them as easily rebuttable. Yet it sounded as if Hutton's Theory of Earth was putting up more of a fight than Playfair expected.

28

The wait by St Ninian's proved tedious. Having crawled under an abandoned horsecart—at least he hoped it wasn't in regular use—George was stuck until Holm appeared later that day. They had only Graham's vague recollections to go on about what time Holm intended to visit the Marlin's Wynd cellar, and goodness knows whether that lined up with their quarry's real intentions.

A light drizzle was now settling in. A few specks of rain were making it onto George—the damp dirt under him would be oozing mud before long. He didn't know how long passed, and he didn't want to start counting the minutes.

At least the threat of rain thinned the crowds. Finally, several hours after he'd told Graham he would arrive, a man in a dark cloak sauntered up the street.

From Black's description, George identified Holm without a problem, even in the dimming light. He was a broad-chested man with a strong face and confident stride. Black claimed they were of a similar age, but Holm looked closer to forty than fifty. He unlocked the cellar door and slipped inside him without a backward glance.

No one had entered or left the cellars that afternoon.

About ten minutes later, as the drizzle morphed into rain, Holm emerged, slinging a bundle across his shoulder.

From his place of concealment, George watched Holm button up his coat and head down the slope into the Cowgate.

The door to the cellar remained unlocked.

Cullen had advised him to follow Holm—if safe to pursue —or get him and Black if it wasn't. The wynd and Cowgate were annoyingly empty, which made George reluctant to pursue. Today wasn't a market day in the Grassmarket.

But it seemed silly to leave and get Cullen just to investigate the cellar. George had seen Holm arrive and speak to a few tradesmen in the street, and a few more exit the cellars while Holm was inside. If anybody was still working in there, he could come up with an excuse for his presence. They didn't know how long Holm would keep his supplies here.

Holm would be adept at evading pursuers: it was likely any attempt to follow him would end up a waste of time. Or worse—with George being spotted. It made more sense to take a look in the cellar and see if any clues about Holm's plans could be pieced together.

George crossed the street and slipped through the cellar door. It immediately dropped out to a ladder, which brought him several metres underground into the Edinburgh hillside.

The street noises faded to muffled vagueness. Fortunately, there were lit candles and oil lamps on the wall to guide him through a tunnel. It was only as wide and tall as George, and probably led to a couple of small several cellars.

This kind of underground vault warren wasn't unusual in a city this crowded: every morsel of space was at a premium, and there was so much uneven ground it seemed a shame not to dig holes in it.

He moved as swiftly and soundlessly as he could, hugging the tunnel walls. Which was why, when something collided with the back of his head, George's first thought was a brick from the ceiling fell on him. Then a second blow landed before he had time to reach up for his head, and he did no more thinking for a while.

Coming to, George was relieved to discover himself uninjured —excluding the pulsating head blow—and tied to a chair, hands behind his back. A rawness in his back suggested he'd been dragged a short distance out of the tunnel into a cellar.

A few candles were lit in alcoves. It looked like a storage space, though puddles covered the floor, making George suspect rising dampness caused its abandonment. Beside a few sacks and pieces of dusty furniture, the space was almost empty.

Dripping water caught on the edge of his hearing. But there were no hushed voices or footfalls.

Yet.

This had the disturbing feel of a planned interrogation. Deep under Edinburgh, screams would go unheard. Holm might not even have been the one who knocked him out, but his attacker certainly was on his way to fetch him.

George tried to move his hands. He couldn't even wiggle his fingers because his hands were bound so tightly. More struggling got him nowhere, apart from twisting pains in his ligaments.

Curse Holm. He understood enough of how phlogiston worked to prevent George from accessing his power.

But George could feel an object in his pocket, swinging as he thrashed helplessly in his chair. Whoever bound George hadn't retrieved the brass knuckles from his pocket.

Not that its presence did him much good. How was he supposed to get it out with his hands and feet immobilised? George looked around the empty cellar for good measure, but it was as empty as it had been a few second ago. He was stranded in the middle of the room, but the chair didn't appear to be lashed to the ground.

He'd have more freedom of movement if he were on the ground. Easy enough to knock himself over, but his body parts were certain to hit the ground and get crushed under his weight.

Was it worth shattering his wrist over? On an intellectual level, he knew Holm would do worse than break his wrist once he arrived, but George still hesitated to inflict injury on himself.

Instead, he angled the chair until he was facing the wall, rolled onto the toes of his feet and worked his way to kneeling on the floor, using his shoulder and forehead to slow his descent.

Once on the floor, George contorted himself half upside down until the brass knuckles dropped from his pocket. More crawling until one hand closed around the warm metal.

He thought the brass knuckle was in contact with his bindings, but the muscles in his side were aching from his contortion.

This time, the phlogiston bubbled from his fingers and palm, and he felt the brass heat. George twisted his whole body to get more of the binding into contact with the metal.

There was pain, but he felt his hand free.

George reached down to his feet and tugged at those bindings. Two feet loose.

Then saw George saw the torch near the door flicker. As if the air in the corridor was disrupted.

He scrambled to his feet, chair still dragging behind him, and flung himself against the door a second before he heard the lock click.

"Is that Mr Stephens?" a baritone Scots voice called out. "Delighted to make your acquaintance at last."

George fought to reassert his balance. Another shove of the door knocked him away, and he struggled to get his feet back underneath him. The door was now a few inches open.

"There's actually a few things I wished to speak with you about concerning your friends," the voice continued, unhurried. "I hope you can calm down enough for that to happen."

George wrenched his tied hand back and forth. His other hand was pushing against the door to keep Holm from entering. Shifting his weight to his shoulder, George reached behind his back and grabbed the cloth bindings. He didn't even consider the possibility of scorching his hands again.

As if sensing his concentration faltering, Holm shoved against the door again. This time George had managed to ignite the cloth restraints which smouldered. He jerked his hand back and forth while his feet slipped on the wet floor.

He regained his balance and paused against the door, finally kicking the chair to one side. In a second, Holm would smell the smoke and know he'd broken free.

George redoubled his pressure against the door, then let it falter for a second. Then he dived to the side.

Holm crashed through the door, expecting resistance and finding none.

George used the moment Holm was off-balanced to push past him into the gap between Holm and the open door. He felt Holm twisted around after him, but momentum already carried George into the corridor and ducking around the corner.

He could hear Holm's laughter echoing behind him. "Well played, George! I'll see you soon."

29

Black always felt secure in the darkness. Tonight it fitted around him like a blanket, securing him from sight and earshot of anyone who happened to be on college grounds after sunset.

Grenville's classroom made him uneasy. There were so many glinting *things* poised around the room; contortions of the darkness, frozen in motion with open mouths.

Instead of using aether to illuminate his way, Black waited for several minutes until his eyes became accustomed to the shades of blackness, and started to deliver a spectrum of greys and dark browns.

He stood in front of Grenville's mirror with only a slight frown.

A single stroke of the pen or hand, Holm had said. It was hard to believe when he taunted Black in Greyfriars kirkyard that he knew his lair would be uncovered...but ever since Cullen described what he'd found with George, Black felt the pull of the room.

The dark chymists loved their mirrors. He'd encountered in his youth a few that served as portals, and those like

Grenville's which relied on mirroring to activate their sigils. Grenville's mirror connected his classroom to a cellar...

...But maybe that wasn't all it did.

Black eased a folded handkerchief from his pocket and carefully unparceled it. A pinch of powdered charcoal was secured inside, and he smudged it onto his forefinger. With his other hand, Black held up a single finger, which glowed white.

It didn't take him long to spot a daubing of charcoal on the side of the mirror at shoulder height. To the casual observer, it would look more like patina than a deliberate marking. But having seen one close-up recently, Black knew what to look for.

This could go terribly wrong. The dark chymistry sigils depended on a precise order of strokes to work—a different order of strokes could change the sigils' purpose.

Still, he could see a downward dash on the mass of circles, loops and triangles that looked a little more substantive than the others. Black traced it.

Then he stepped back.

The sigil began to glow.

It was quiet enough in the room that he could hear the sigil hum: a faint ringing like a glass harmonica, a note that neither faded nor wavered. The surface of the mirror began to ripple and glow, as if stars were trapped inside it.

"I know you're there," Black said levelly.

"This is rather late for you, Dr Black?" A fully dressed Kitty Holm stepped into view where Black's reflection in the mirror had been once before. A white linen cap and shawl indicated she was at home for the evening. Behind her, the swirling firmament concealed any trace of the room she was standing in.

"It was your husband I had a particular interest in speaking to. He never had trouble staying up late."

It had been too much to hope, that he could reach Holm

this way. But his wife wasn't a fool; she certainly knew more about her husband's activities than she pretended.

"My husband never liked staying up into the wee hours, Dr Black. The dark chymists summoned him with the click of a finger, like he was their hound. What choice did he have?"

"So why is he working with them to hide Dr Hutton?"

Kitty drew the shawl tighter across her shoulders. "Again, another supposition. Several suppositions, in fact. Unless you have the gentlemen's scientific papers, Dr Black, I don't see this conversation proceeding further."

"I don't. And you didn't require them until noon on Saturday—a day and a half from now. I hope you don't find the extended stay with your sister tedious."

"To tell you the truth, we left Paris not a moment too soon." Kitty glanced over Black's shoulder for a moment, and he wondered if there was someone else in her room. "The French have been sliding towards collective, national atheism for decades. Their Second Estate is bloated and corrupt, and it's a rite of passage of their philosophers to decry Christianity. But I admit we tolerated Paris as long as we did because...well, I've never expected much from the French. Arguably, my husband could also do good there, because we never had a shortage of like-minded friends in need of spiritual replen-ishment."

The sigil was beginning to lose its lustre, and the mirror its glow. Black reached out a palm and let a small quantity of phlogiston flow towards the sigil. The glow expanded again.

If Kitty Holm noticed Black leak more power into the portal, she did not react. She continued speaking.

"I expected better from the British, however. I heard plenty of mutterings from English visitors to Paris, but while their reports concerned me, I suppose I swept some of my alarm under the rug, reasoning they were exaggerating the state of our native country. Now that I'm back in Scotland, I can see—if anything—the situation is worse than was stated. Perhaps because those who dwell here don't notice the rising rot." She sounded like her husband—Black wondered how much of what she said was an echo of his sentiments, or if they predated her marriage.

"Just fifteen years ago, not a soul would dare be caught outside church on the Sabbath. On my first St Giles visit I could barely hear the minister because of the cacophony on the street: grocers hawking wares, young women giggling over dresses, drunkards arguing, and harlots soliciting trade! Shame has quite deserted Edinburgh's parishioners. I asked the minister if such collective disrespect didn't trouble him, and he all but shrugged. No one in the Kirk is listened to any more, they have been taught to feel powerless and expect scraps.

"It's not all Dr Hutton's fault. He's merely a symptom: the swelling over a deep abscess of atheism and moral corruption. But the while we do not blame the abscess for existing, we still have to drain it."

"How many innocent lives do you intend to cut short in pursuit of this noble goal?"

"As many as necessary! Of course it won't be pretty. My husband is lancing an abscess, is he not? I guarantee blood will be mixed in with the pus...but the patient will thank him later."

To Black, change was inevitable. As soil would be washed into the sea and one day become a mountain once more, so science would elevate Man's understanding of his place in the world. Stemming the tide of progress was as futile as scooping handfuls of sentiment back into the cornfields. Next time it rained, they'd run right back into the river.

He bowed.

"In that case, I bid you good evening, Mrs Holm. No doubt our paths will cross soon."

Kitty inclined her head with the barest required courtesy.

"Good evening, Dr Black. I have a number more pornographic tracts from the circulating library to burn." A worn copy of *The Fortunes and Misfortunes of the Famous Moll Flanders* appeared in her hand.

"I thought the author was providing a condemnation of the narrator's ungodly, sinful lifestyle."

"Only a man would think that." Kitty snorted. "I guarantee the writer had one hand down his breeches the whole time he was writing it. Why else would he expend so much ink chronicling her sexual depravities?"

He'd ignored the sigil for a minute too long, and it faded rapidly. With a flicker, Kitty Holm vanished, leaving Black to stare at his reflection and a silent mausoleum of beasts.

The deep silence was broken by the shattering of glass.

30

How could everything fall to pieces so quickly? George cursed himself with every footfall as he sprinted down the Cowgate in the vague direction of safety. Black said he'd reconvene with Cullen and Smith at Panmure House, and George hoped that's where he'd find them.

He dared not glance behind him to see if he was being followed. Holm seemed content to let him go...this time. He felt a tug of conscience telling him to warn Phoebe, but a colder, more rational part of his brain told him to avoid leading any pursuer straight back to his living quarters.

George kept jogging along the Cowgate past The Pleasance and St John's Hill, planning to cut through the Canongate wynds to Smith's house. There was less foot traffic down here, but it was also a less predictable route for him to take.

It was only after he passed the road to St John's Hill that he realised his planned route would take him right past Hutton's sal ammoniac works.

As George turned into the lane, part of him hoped he'd stumble across the man himself, sleeves rolled up, talking to one of his workers or business associates. It was a wild fancy, but George's tired brain wanted to believe the professors were all operating for a misunderstanding and Hutton was safe, cheerfully going about his Edinburgh business with no inkling of anything amiss.

At first he thought he was imaging the pervasive smell of smoke. Then he wondered if a tenant was burning rubbish in the next close. Vaguely, George registered the din of alarm and men rushing past him.

But it wasn't until he jogged in the direction of the loudest cries and saw the building he'd glanced at scant minutes ago consumed in flames, that the magnitude of the upheaval struck him.

"Water! Water!"

"Is anyone trapped inside?" George asked, grabbing the coat sleeves of a dirt-streaked man in an apron.

"Doubt it." The man swatted George away. He was just another nuisance getting in the way of damage control. If George wasn't rushing into Hutton's burning factory to look for trapped workers, he wasn't any use to him.

Stung by the rebuke, George staggered away from the heat, which was now an uncomfortable rawness on his face.

A few buildings down, a washerwoman stood leaning against a barrel, watching the blaze with folded arms. There was an expression on her face that suggested a grim lack of surprise at the unfolding events.

George cautiously approached.

"Good-wife, do you know what caused the fire?"

"Elliot Sanders and the boys is what started it," she said, scowling at the ground.

The name didn't mean anything to George.

"Did you see them just now?"

"Aye." The woman heaved herself upright, still watching the men congregating outside the works and yelling at each other. "Marched down 'ere bold as Colonel Brass, so they did.

The workers who saw them coming in had the good sense to walk out before the first torch was dropped."

"How many?"

"Elliot brought ten of his boys, so it appeared."

The shouting was still going on, but no one appeared in a rush to tackle the blaze. Since Hutton's chemical works was its own building, there seemed little risk of the fire spreading to the adjoining breweries. Presumably the onlookers had decided to conserve their effort for preventing the spread of the fire, rather than trying to put it out. Seeing the flames licking out of top and bottom storey windows, George recognised there wasn't much point.

"Elliot was tellin' everyone in the Mermaid tavern 'bout Hutton's blasphemy," the washerwoman continued, a glint in her eyes indicating she considered George a safe outlet for gossip. "Or so I heard. Such shocking things." She shook her head and tutted.

George had been convinced Holm engineered this destruction of Hutton's property, but he belatedly supposed the minister might not need to.

From the washerwoman's reaction, she considered arson a proportional response to whatever she thought Hutton was claiming.

"George?"

Black stood in the middle of the lane, clutching his physician cane and staring at the unfolding scene.

"Professor?" As he turned away from the fire, Black's face was bathed in glowing orange then pale white.

"Do you know if anyone is injured?" Black asked.

"Not that I'm aware of...I suspect not."

Black nodded grimly, taking in the loitering workmen and drawing the same conclusions George did.

George fingered the scrap of paper in his pocket.

"Errr...Prof Grenville was walking down the High Street earlier today, dropping these into the street."

His professor frowned as he studied the scrap.

"It's just gone nine o'clock, hasn't it?"

"D-S-A: Davie's Sal Ammoniac," Black murmured. "Not quite as spontaneous a riot as one might assume. We may as well depart. I arranged to meet William at Adam's."

Black led him back onto the Cowgate and further down the street, before turning left in Bakehouse Close and cutting onto the Canongate near Panmure House. It felt like the smoke was following them.

"I didn't have any luck today, professor. I'm sorry." George filled Black in on his thwarted pursuits as swiftly as possible. Black merely nodded and kept hurrying off, as if he hadn't expected good news.

"How are your injuries?" Black asked as they approached Smith's front door.

George shrugged his good shoulder. "I've handled worse, professor."

"Poor James," said Cullen, shaking his head at the news.

"It could be a year before his building is rebuilt," Black said. "I doubt anything is salvageable."

It should have occurred to George before that moment, watching a fire burn out of control and seeing everyone decide to let it raze the building. But the sinking sensation only just struck him with an icy wave of despair.

There would be no sac ammonia works for him to get a job at.

Sure, maybe Hutton and his partner could rent another warehouse, or the damage wasn't as total as it appeared now. But if today's events were a reflection of the city's sentiments towards Hutton...he'd find it difficult to rebuild in Edinburgh.

George sank into the chair next to Cullen. The old professor didn't notice his rising despair, or sense of hopeless. Why would he? The other men had enough problems of their own.

"I...I think I should return to Mrs Stephens," George said, rising. "She'll be anxious, no doubt."

He was tired, hungry, aching. He reeked of smoke. When had he last eaten? Goodness knows.

"Quite right, lad," said Cullen, stretching his legs. "Happy wife, happy life...or something like that. Pass on our regards."

"I'm sorry I couldn't be of more help today."

"Well, if anything occurs to you," Black said, slowly unbuttoning his coat. "I doubt we're going anywhere this evening. Thank you for trying. We'll figure something out."

The trudge home from Panmure House took double its usual time tonight. Smoke from Hutton's sal ammoniac works now permeated the city: a lingering acridity on the air.

George didn't want to look at the ruined shell of the chemical works, so cut onto Cowgate from Niddrie Wynd. He kept one eye on his surroundings in case he was being followed or watched, but couldn't rouse himself to fear. If Holm spotted his hunched, tired form, he'd not consider George worth the sport to kill.

A good chunk of Edinburgh had headed inside, barring their leaky doors and window frames against the smoke as best they could. It gave him an uninterrupted walk through the dank recess of the Cowgate.

Despite the late hour, a solitary cart loaded with timber was making its way down the Cowgate towards the city walls. George supposed it was meant for one of the myriad construction sites around the city. It felt like every noble family was redoing their interiors this spring, didn't it?

He crossed his threshold five minutes later with a mixture of relief and guilt: relief that he was no longer on the hook for Dr Hutton's recovery, guilt that he hadn't been up to the task of recovering him. He'd spent the last few days running around Edinburgh like crazy, barely stopping to breathe...and what had he got to show for it?

Phoebe greeted his arrival with a frown. She'd mostly forgiven him for burning his hand.

"They're still looking for Dr Hutton. Haven't found him. There wasn't anything I could do." George sank into a chair, then rose and dragged it closer to the fire.

"That's terrible." Phoebe's breath caught. She'd only met Hutton once or twice, but he had a way of charming people with his strange yet heartfelt mannerisms. "Poor Dr Hutton. His friends must be worried sick."

George had tried not to think how Hutton's absence would affect Black, a man he'd long ago decided was too strong for emotions. "I'm sure something will come up. There are only a few locations around Edinburgh where he could be: they've narrowed the list down at least."

Phoebe opened her mouth, but George cut her off, suspecting the question she'd be about to ask. "They're spread out on opposite sides of Edinburgh, all a few miles out of town and owned by different families. The professors can't just drop by and listen for screams."

"Don't feel bad, sweetheart," Phoebe said, putting a pot of stew onto the stove. "I know the professors are grateful for what you did."

George shrugged. He let his wife bustle through supper preparations, stretching his legs and angling his chair to get more heat onto his aching limbs.

After a while, Phoebe said something.

"Pardon, love?" George brought himself back to the contents of the room as swiftly as he could.

"I always know when you're working through something you don't understand," Phoebe said with a wry smile. "Because you start muttering under your breath and counting on your fingers."

"Really?" George had caught himself doing that once or twice, but never struck him as a habit. He had been thinking about those three estates, turning over their names and pertinent facts in his mind, but his thoughts just tumbled over each other.

"Ever since I met you." Phoebe looked more amused at her husband's fluster. "I hear you asking yourself a thousand questions until you calm down."

A memory surfaced. Cullen sitting in front of the slowly receding hearth, fingers outstretched. "Right George, you remember the three principles of medical dogma? Let's go through them...Now, when might you apply those principles? Which leads us on to..."

"I think it's an affectation I caught from Dr Cullen," George said.

"Well, if habits are infectious, that was a good one to catch."

Phoebe spoke lightly, spooning stew into two bowls. Then she looked properly at her husband and froze.

"George? What's wrong?"

"What? Nothing." George smiled weakly. He tried to brush off her concern and reach for the stew, but his wife raised the bowls out of reach.

"That wasn't 'nothing' on your face, and you know it."

It looked like food was dependent on his confession. George sighed.

"I've never considered myself good enough...but at the same time, I've never *allowed* myself to succeed. I thought the mess I made of my oral examinations was proof I was stupid and would struggle to be a doctor without constant hand-holding from Dr Cullen...but it turns out I absorbed what he taught me and I was applying it this whole time without noticing to get through difficulties."

How could he be so utterly lacking in self-awareness?

"I remember shortly after marrying I saw you converse with the late Earl of Hopetoun in Mackie's Oyster Cellar." Phoebe smiled wistfully. "I couldn't believe how confident you were, talking with one of the richest men in Scotland. It was...impressive."

She'd been surprisingly amorous later that evening, George reflected. He hadn't understood why at the time.

"I'd known the Earl for years by that point. He'd just... stopped being intimidating."

"But still...don't you see, sweetheart? That's how confident and self-assured you *can* be when you're not second-guessing everything. The Edinburgh physicians all respect you —I'm sure they see you as an equal. Why would you worry about failing at Hunter's London school? You haven't let yourself to fail at anything since you arrived in Edinburgh."

Would smacking himself on the forehead repeatedly help him feel better about his stupidity? He'd talked himself down from even trying at a physician career, like how he berated himself in the aftermath of the Brandywine ambush. His corporal had been the one making poor decisions and delaying his men getting in to a safe position: when George stood up and tried to suggest moving to a more defensible position, he was ignored. The ensuing bloodbath hadn't been his fault at all, but he'd allowed guilt at the delay he thought he'd caused to consume him, and taken it as a sign he wasn't suited for military leadership. No wonder he was passed over for promotion: he didn't even believe in himself.

Well, there was still time to recover from this mess.

"So, what should be done?"

"Can you deduce where Dr Hutton is being held?"

"Probably not..." Phoebe glared at him. "But I think I've figured out something the learned gentlemen have not, because they weren't there when I saw the clue."

A memory from his passage up the Cowgate ten minutes ago had bumped into another memory, lodged slightly further in the past.

"Well then," Phoebe snapped. "Go back to those erstwhile gentlemen and tell them that."

George was momentarily too stunned to reply.

"Sweetheart, if you don't go back and try to save Dr Hutton's life it'll eat you up, until there's no trace of the man I married."

"If it's alright with you..."

"Just leave. Don't come back until Dr Hutton is rescued. I'm acting for the benefit of my sanity as much as its yours; not out of the kindness of my heart."

As Cullen always said, George mused as he re-buttoned his coat: happy wife, happy life.

31

"Redhall is in the midst of major construction works," George explained. "I overheard Simon and Diomedes laughing about how disruptive Alex Inglis the younger was finding it. They're tearing down interior walls and installing new ceilings." He'd got his breath back now, after sprinting across town and pounding at the door of Panmure House until Black let him in, unmistakably wary about who would seek them out at this hour. He'd garbled out his deduction before Cullen coaxed him into a chair.

"When did you hear them discuss this? I didn't know any construction was going on there." Smith looked pained at this admittance.

"They were talking about it in the White Horse where I met Dr Playfair. At the time, I forgot they were talking about it, but I was reminded about it on my way home."

Smith tapped the nib of his quill against his bottom lip. "That kind of renovation work would disrupt the entire household and mean a lot of tradesmen were coming and going. You couldn't hide a valuable hostage under conditions like that."

With bated breath, George watched Smith strike a line through 'Inglis—Redhall' on all his papers. He'd done it.

"Where does that leave us?"

Smith cleared his throat until the others had pulled back far enough from the table for him to set a map down.

"Since Redhall is discounted—we are left with the properties of Grangemore and Calder House." He prodded the map twice.

"Those are on opposite sides of the city," George whispered.

"Almost forty miles apart," Smith concurred.

Cullen tapped his cane on the floor. No one looked at each other.

"If we split up..." George began, knowing he wouldn't reach the end of his sentence.

"Too dangerous," Black shot back. "It's you and me, George."

That was true. Given the short work Holm made of him, George didn't want to confront the dark chymists alone. Right now, he would happily collapse on the floor and drop into a fitful doze. The past few days had taken a heavy toll on his strength, and Black probably doubted he could hold his own against any more attackers.

"You're sure about those two estates, Adam?" Cullen asked, rapping his knuckles on the parchment. "You think there's an equal probability Dr Hutton is kept at either location?"

"I don't think," Smith replied. "I know."

"A completely balanced, toss-a-coin, equal probability?" Cullen persisted. Smith frowned.

"That's impossible, William. What I'm saying is that based on the dearth of evidence available, I can't narrow down the likelihood to a position where I can comfortably state one option over the other."

The way Smith glared at Cullen, and the nervous energy in Cullen's hands, meant an argument would certainly erupt within minutes.

"If we leave now," George said quickly. "We can reach the first estate sometime in the night, and if we're wrong, we can change our horses back in Edinburgh before..."

"That's perilous," Black said, his voice hardening. "If we're wrong and caught, the dark chymists will get a message to the true location faster than us." He didn't have to add that this spelled death for Hutton.

"How much evidence are you missing?" Cullen pressed Smith again. "Adam, tell us what information you need that will allow you to say with any measure of confidence—any whatsoever—that you think Dr Hutton is being held at one estate over the other."

"This isn't a patient case history," Smith snapped, his self-control finally lost. "How am I supposed to tease out economic motivations from the meagre sketch of each man's business dealings and personal ties I have at hand? There are untold variables to consider and rank. Maybe some inclination would present itself, but I'd be working all night, and I don't have the energy to spend the next eight hours scribbling notes."

"With two minds, the process would be a lot quicker," Black said carefully. George observed his former teacher. The harsh tone from a few minutes ago was replaced with something much steadier. The lines on Black's face smoothened to nothing. "We've done similar exercises for the Scottish Industries Board a dozen times together, Adam."

"That's true," Smith admitted, tugging the map back to him.

Cullen nodded with approval, as if he'd personally suggested this plan of action.

George stood awkwardly at the table, wondering if he

should say something or offer to help. Meanwhile, Smith marched to the door of his study and gave a few irritated coughs for emphasis. Black stayed seating. After a moment's hesitation, Cullen and George rose and walked out.

"Give us a bit of time, George," Black said. "Adam and I are going to figure this out." With that, Smith closed the study door behind him.

There wasn't much George could do beside trudge down-stairs and slump into a dining room chair beside Cullen, who now appeared as relaxed as if Hutton had already been recov-ered. Smith's ageing mother came by shortly to offer them drinks. Cullen accepted a glass of wine and cradled it as a man who sensed he'd be enjoying it over the course of a long night.

George wasn't in the mood to talk, and Cullen seemed content to sip his wine and leaf through the books Smith left with them.

In the study above their heads, voices rose.

"...But if you get out of Edinburgh and listen to what the common people think about the issue..."

"Adam, I say this with the deepest affection: no one cares what they think in Kirkcaldy."

George didn't understand half of what was necessary, other than it wasn't obvious which local family held Hutton and where he was kept and the two men needed to think more broadly about their situations. Nor was the two philosophers' path of reasoning clear.

"Doctor," George whispered, tugging at his sleeve. Cullen's chin bobbed to his chest and then snapped up. "Doctor Cullen, they're arguing about the effect of Pitt the Younger's hat tax on silver imports from Holland!"

Cullen placed his empty glass on the table, rubbed his eyes, and stared at George. "And?"

"And...shouldn't we remind them to keep their discussion on the matter at hand?"

Cullen rubbed his eyes again. "They're on track, lad. Undoubtably. Adam and Joe can sustain this sort of complex discussion all night without losing focus. I don't know how Honest Billy's taxation policy influences their deductions, but I have faith it does."

Cullen was down to the last drops of wine, which he seemed intent on holding on to. George regretted declining Mrs Smith's hospitality and hoped she would return, but Panmure House fell into silence, the old lady retired for the night. He headed to the stairwell to focus on the continuing argument upstairs.

"But that's a complete contradiction of your own treatise!"

"Joe, I wrote the treatise—I think I know what I said about domestic imports."

"No, look here. Book four, part two, middle of the page."

"Hmm…Well, I guess I've changed my mind."

"There's a build-up of phlogiston in there," George insisted, trying to keep his voice from wavering.

Cullen rearranged his legs. "That sometimes happens when Adam gets too excited. You might want to try getting some sleep, George. They'll be at this a while longer." He looked at George's worried face. "Under no circumstances am I stepping foot in that room."

Aware that if he stayed still slumber would claim him, George crept up the stairs to get a better view.

Peering into the study without pushing the door more than an inch ajar, George saw a frustrated Black scrunch up the paper he was writing on and toss it towards the hearth. From the opposite end of the table, Smith flicked his hand. His miniature fireball caught the paper in midair, incinerating it before it hit the carpet. From the faint aroma of smoke drifting into the corridor, George assumed this wasn't the first time Smith amused himself with such petty trickery.

Afraid of getting caught snooping, he settled back into the dining room and tried to doze off, but George was never adept at sleeping in chairs, and the voices in the study blurred in and out of hearing.

Unsure how long he'd been trying to sleep—Cullen was dozing fitfully—George gave up and returned to the study door, feeling like a child sneaking out of its nursery after bedtime. The tableau in front of the fire appeared unchanged.

"...But that's another fanciful idea..." Black muttered and crushed another sheet of paper in his fist.

This time, Smith leapt out of his chair. He caught Black's wrist and shook his head. There was a glint in Smith's eyes as he eased Black's hand back to the table and smoothed out the scrap of paper.

"You think...?" Black asked warily.

"Yes, yes...if you just..." Leaning over Black's shoulder, Smith continued to mutter and point. A few seconds later, Black pushed out of his chair and rushed to the bookshelf.

George slunk back into his chair. Cullen raised his eyebrows.

"It looks like they've had a breakthrough."

Shortly after he said that Smith departed the study with a flutter of his coat.

"Good work everyone. Now if you'll excuse me sirs, I'm off to bed. Make use of my guest bedchamber and pull-down pallet if you wish, or go home. I don't care. Just keep your voices down."

"Goodnight, Adam," Cullen responded to the departing figure with cheer, unfazed by what passed for hospitality in the Smith household.

A minute later came the sound of a closing door upstairs, and Black stepped into the room.

"Hutton's being held at the Grangemore Estate outside Haddington," he explained. "Adam realised Liam Grangemore's fortunes are more volatile than we first assumed: his in-laws' mercantile business is being hit hard by the latest round of import taxes. He stands to gain the most from the return of the dark chymists, and projecting strength in front of them."

Cullen yawned. "Good deduction, you two." He looked at George. "Have you visited Haddington before, George?"

George knew the village was a few hours east of Edinburgh.

"It's best we stay here tonight," Black told him. "We need to depart before sunrise."

32

Spring sunlight added colour to the endless East Lothian countryside. To the left, farmland sloped imperceptibly towards the silver Firth of Forth; to the right, the fields rolled up into gentle hills. George had never ventured this far east of Edinburgh—if Black had any uncertainty about their route, he gave no sign.

Black rode easily, in perfect concert with his horse.

"I trust your injuries are healing well?" Black asked once the sun had risen enough to provide the warmth conducive to conversation.

"Yes, sir. Professor Cullen dressed the wounds before I departed." George was able to move his arm, and the sting of the burn was no longer distracting, provided he didn't re-break the skin. Black murmured in acknowledgement and fell silent.

The roads were well-trodden and wide enough for the three horses to fit abreast. They took it in turns holding the line to the third saddled horse, a chestnut palfrey of Hutton's. When the pair headed out from Smith's house at four o'clock in the morning, it took some time to encourage the horse to follow its friends, and George suggested they borrow a more compliant animal.

"We can't," Black said. "Dr Hutton refuses to ride any other horse than this one."

"Even if he...?"

"Yes," Black repeated. "I'm serious about this, George."

After a while they settled into a rhythm of changing the horses they rode at intervals, and the Lothian countryside flattened and broadened. Few people were on the roads this early, and it felt like they had the whole of the Lothians to themselves.

"Does it not worry you what will happen when Dr Hutton's theories are out in the world?" George asked. "A lot of people seem shocked and dismayed by their implications."

He thought of Grenville's malicious sabotage, and the mocking reaction of Simon and chums. Not to mention the homicidal fury Hutton's geological theories drove Holm and Playfair to.

Black shook his head. "That's a natural reaction to such a revelation, but it's exhibited by the vocal minority. If you give the general populace time, they will adjust."

"Is the Reverend Holm overreacting?" George didn't think he was. "He seems to think Hutton's theory of earth will cause great disruption to the social order."

He didn't need to look at Black to hear a smile creep onto the professor's face.

"James Hutton will upend nothing that doesn't deserve to be upended."

George couldn't think of a pithy response to that.

By the time they crossed the rounded bridge over the River Tyne, it was shaping into a promising morning. George's fingers had not only recovered full sensation, but he was warm.

"It's less than a mile from the village," Black said, nodding to a village washerwoman.

Now they'd passed through Haddington, George felt his stomach quiver. He had no idea what they'd find, and whether rescuing Hutton was a foolish endeavour. For all they knew, Hutton was already dead.

The Earl of Grangemore's country seat was located on a ridge overlooking the Tyne river, looming into view as the pair got closer. Casting around, George noted they'd have to ride past the house and turn right to reach the main entrance of the estate.

"You're sure about this, Doctor?" George asked, realising he was lowering his voice as he glanced at the mansion. He couldn't see anyone on the grounds, but his eyesight wasn't great at this distance.

"I suspect we arouse less suspicion on the main road than if we're caught sneaking on dirt tracks round the back," Black mused. "Plenty of travellers use this road to reach Dunbar."

The men slowed their horses to a leisurely pace, which gave George enough time to study the mansion and its grounds. Most were minimally cultivated. The entranceway was concealed by a clump of woodland.

"How are we supposed to get into the house without detection?" George whispered. He should have asked Black about this earlier, but he assumed the course of action would appear more obvious than it currently did.

"Actually, I think we may be able to avoid a direct attack," Black said with a smile. "If my sense of time is correct, Hutton takes his late morning stroll around now."

"The walled garden, then?" George asked. They'd probably have spotted Hutton if he was wandering the lawns.

Black led the horses off the road and into the woodland a

few metres before the entrance gateway, tying them to trees deep in the thicket. The horses grunted.

Less than a hundred metres away rose a thick wall, soaring above the trees. Creeping closer, it looked to George like they stretched a considerable distance. The corners of the walled garden were capped with circular citadels, more militaristic than classical in their design. There was no way a man could scale them.

"The Earl of Grangemore boasts this is the largest walled garden in Britain," Black whispered beside him.

After careful snapping of undergrowth, George was in a position where he could hug a beech tree and peer round to spy on the garden entrance.

At a small iron gate just past a citadel, several men hovered about, dressed in mismatched, dirty clothes. George spied at least one sword.

"They look like hired guardsmen," George whispered. The men were out of earshot and seemed more concerned about blocking the doorway than looking out for intruders.

"Four of them?" Black asked. He slid his spectacles up his nose. In a few years George would need to swallow his vanity and purchase eye glasses of his own. He wasn't looking forward to it.

"I think so."

"Well, we may as well wait. I doubt they're in any rush to get James back to the house."

George nodded.

He wasn't sure how long Black and he stood watching, but his legs were cramping by the time one man peeled away from the group and strolled in their direction.

George tensed, but the fact the man was fiddling with his breeches buttons suggested his approach was motivated more by the call of nature than investigating suspicious movement.

"I think this is when we act," Black told him. "I'll make the first move."

Whistling to himself, the guardsman selected a tree to the left of where George was concealed to perform his business. The heavy scent of pine soon reached his nostrils.

Black was already emerging on the opposite side of the guardsman, curving behind the guardsman while staying out of line of sight of the gate. The stream of urine began to abate.

Then Black pounced, noiseless in the damp undergrowth. The guardsman didn't have time to react before Black pressed two fingers into his neck. There was a tiny flash of pale light and the guardsman crumpled. Black partially caught him and redirected his fall between two trees.

George glanced over to the remaining guards, but they remained engrossed in their conversation, and now their colleague was stowed out of sight.

"Let's move through the trees and come out over there." Black pointed to a spot nearer the men. He was already moving before George could react.

Now two of the men were looking in the direction where their colleague went. They called out a name. One of them rested his hand on his sword.

"Ready?"

"Yes."

Black strode out from behind the tree, his arms raised. Two flashes of light shot out from his fingers as the guardsman noticed him. A pair of distracted guardsmen dropped soundlessly, but the third let out a yell. There was a glint of silver at his torso.

"Look out!" Black and the guardsman simultaneously ducked and fired at each other. The bullet struck somewhere in the forest; Black's phlogiston blast exploded against the stone wall.

George hurtled through the cloud of gun smoke and

tackled the guardsman. A headbutt was enough to loosen his grip on the pistol. Now holding the barrel, George struck the guardsman across the face before he had time to recover. The men stumbled, raising his hands defensively.

Another blast of phlogiston from his Black put the guardsman out of his misery.

"At least we know we have ten minutes until they all come to," Black remarked. George fumbled under the guardsmen's coats, tossing two pistols into the undergrowth and keeping one for himself. "We'll probably have to separate."

Inside, the walled garden spread out for what looked like miles. George jogged off in an anti-clockwise direction, alert for other threats. He wondered if it was safe calling for Hutton, or whether Black wanted him to remain silent. Much of the central grounds were unkempt or incomplete, with ankle-height hedgerows and seedlings jammed in the fresh soil. Banks of pink and purple flowers fluttered against the walls, with apple trees lining the pathways into the centre.

"James!" Twenty metres away, Black was hauling the confused figure of Hutton to his feet, where he'd been kneeling in front of a rose bush. "Drop the cuttings, we're getting out of here."

"Joseph?" Hutton blinked in surprise. "George!" he exclaimed when he saw who else was with Black. "What a surprise to see you both."

"We've come to get you out of here," Black said in firm tones, anticipating what sorted of conversation he'd need to have with his friend. "We brought your horse and are taking you back to Edinburgh."

"Today?"

"Right this minute. I'm afraid we had to knock out your gaolers, who'll be waking any minute."

Black steered Hutton towards the entrance they came

through without breaking stride, but was looking Hutton up and down as they moved, checking for injury.

"If you're sure," Hutton said slowly.

"Yes! Come on."

The guards were lying where they'd left them, to George's relief. Hutton followed them through the woodland to the horses.

"Ah, you brought Emmanuel," said Hutton, patting his palfrey. "How nice to see you too, old friend."

George untethered the horses' bridles. The road they came on was empty, and he couldn't see any carriages approaching from either direction. They'd have to gallop past the estate, and there was a risk that riders would rush to intercept them, but once they got a few miles away from Haddington, they could slip onto a less direct road. They could cover miles of ground before the guardsmen woke up and realised their prisoner had escaped.

Hutton was half in the saddle when he froze.

"The fossils, Joseph..."

Black pretended he hadn't heard. Agitation spread across Hutton's face.

"Joseph, I left the rocks in my bedchamber."

Realising the problem wouldn't go away if he ignored it, Black turned to face Hutton.

"What are you talking about, James? We must leave this instant."

"No, I found these fascinating geological specimens in the garden and set them aside in my room for my collection." Hutton still had only one foot in the stirrup, anguish creasing his features.

Black rarely appeared angry, but George the limits of his patience rapidly overrun. A single sharp rebuke from him would probably be enough to force Hutton to spur his horse into motion.

Instead, Black lowered his gaze and hissed.

"Fine, James. I'll go to the mansion and get them. Promise you'll keep riding until you reach Smith's house. Do not stop...for any reason."

Hutton finally remembered to swing his leg over the saddle. He sagged with relief. "Yes, Joseph, of course...thank you...I will."

"I better come with you, professor," George said, easing his horse in a circle. "I think you'll need my help more than Dr Hutton."

Right now he had no idea how many men were in the mansion, and the sentries in the garden would regain conscious within minutes.

Black curtly nodded, then spurred his horse. He didn't look at Hutton.

He took off along the driveway at a gallop, leaving George struggling to keep up. The Grangemore mansion loomed behind the hedgerows in all its Rococo glory, a picture of creamy stateliness in a sea of manicured greenery.

As George's mount reached the front door, Black had already dismounted and was smoothing his hair. While not deserted, the house seemed quiet: there were no carriages in front of the house, and they'd passed few servants on the grounds.

They wouldn't have long before the guards came to. Then, they'd either come back here to raise the alarm, or because they'd track Black and him this way.

He didn't have time to raise the myriad bad scenarios with his companion, because two valets were hurrying down the steps towards the pair. Time for action. George leaped from his horse and landed in front of the first, pistol jamming into his stomach.

"Making any kind of noise will end painfully for you," he

snarled. The servant, a white-haired, stooped gentleman, cowered and raised his hands.

"Where are Dr Hutton's chambers?" Black asked. He avoided mentioning they'd already liberated the gentlemen.

No doubt aware he was sending the assailants on a false pursuit into the house, the valet raised a shaking finger towards a window in the corner of the second floor.

"Stay here with the horses, George. Don't let these servants leave."

"Are you sure...?" George asked. Hutton told them there were at least ten hired guards who worked in shifts, as well as a lean complement of servant staff.

"The worse outcome is we lose our horses." Adjusting his hat, Black headed inside.

George flicked his pistol at the two men. He led them and the horses to the corner of the building, away from the ground floor bay windows.

An awkward silence settled over the three.

"It's shaping into a nice day," George commented brittlely.

Any further social niceties were swept out of mind by the sound of musket fire.

33

Black was relieved to enter a silent lobby, the marble colonnade above him cool.

There were a few servants milling around, but Black swept up the staircase without acknowledging them, affecting the haughty indifference of an aristocrat. With any luck, he would move with enough purpose that the servants would assume he was meant to be there. They were unlikely to recognise who he was.

At the end of the second-floor corridor, Black found an unlocked door leading to a bedchamber possessing a state of mild disorganisation that suggested its occupant had been Hutton. His captivity hadn't been a cruel one, since he had stacks of books on the desk, bed, and sofa. Three fossils were on the bedside cabinet, and Black slid them into his pocket without a hesitation. The house felt empty, but the thick carpets could muffle a lot of noise.

He almost reached the grand staircase when voices from around the corner pulled him up short. They were getting louder, and the tone was more aristocratic than servile. Fortunately, the door next to Black yielded to his touch, and he slipped into an airy dining room.

Black hated not having a plan.

He had only a moment to inhale with relief before spotting a second doorway on the far side of the dining room, leading to an antechamber. The dining table in front of him glittered with silver and crystal decanters filled with blood-red claret. Though the room was empty—at present—Black suspected it wouldn't stay that way for long.

Sure enough, the voices rose, flowing into the antechamber. Genial laughter, the rustling of coats and thump of boots. Some of the booming voices were on the edge of Black's recognition, even if he couldn't put names to them just yet. He froze with one hand on the corridor door, then gritted his teeth.

The first waves of nobles spilled into the dining room. They laughed amongst themselves, joyous and in excellent humour. Many of them had hunting rifles still clacking against their shoulders.

All these men knew Grangemore was holding Hutton a few rooms down the hall. How could they not?

One man exclaimed, and the entering party stuttered to a halt. They'd spotted Black, a statue blocking the door, the weight of the nobles' complicity sinking in. His face betrayed the hurt and anger he felt.

For a few moments, there was confusion, with no one knowing what to say.

There was no point fabricating a story. Everyone knew the professor of chemistry had broken to in Grangemore Estate in search of his friend James Hutton.

He'd been expecting dismay once they uncovered him, but Black noted their dominant reaction was closer to derision.

Black's hand was on the doorknob. He could pull the door open then make a run for it. He'd have enough time to get halfway down the stairs before the confused pile of men could quit the adjoining room in pursuit.

But that wasn't what he wanted to do. He recognised these men: he'd taught chemistry to their sons, he'd conversed with them at evening clubs and dinner parties. He expected more than Grangemore to be swayed by Holm into carrying out this scheme...but to see this many men?

Most of them were men his own age, and a couple of their offspring. There were at least ten of them.

He'd puzzled what could induce the richest men of Edinburgh to re-enter Holm's malevolent orbit, despite their vicious history. What could prompt them to go along with the kidnapping of Hutton?

Black could see the smear of his reflection in the empty silver platters and candlesticks.

He'd laughingly dismissed the Lord Provost's solicitation, even as Louis Grey warned him not to underestimate his influence in the upcoming Town Council elections. To Black is was all posturing, but the nobles in front of him didn't see it that way. They saw Dr Joseph Black as a threat, wielding enough influence in Edinburgh and abroad to unseat one of their own from the Council.

How could they hurt Black? Through his friends, of course. The elections had clean slipped from Black's mind these past few days, hadn't they?

One of the younger men's expression had shifted from perplexity to rage. He was reaching for his shoulder strap, swinging his rifle to bear.

The key was still in the door.

Black pushed the door shut and twisted the key in the lock.

He grabbed the display cabinet to his left with both hands and tugged it as the first rifle shot burst into the air.

The dining room exploded into chaos with the crash of porcelain and a rifle shot taking up all the air.

This jolted the nobles into action and they surged forward, some with their rifles still clanging against their back.

Black couldn't win this fight without phlogiston. The closest two men were struck with an immobilising blast, causing the others to stumble. Pushing up from one knee, he was shoved into the dining table by someone he'd not seen flanking him.

His hands closed around something cool and solid on the table, which moved as he pulled it towards him. The noble pulling back his fist was surprised to be struck in the face with a silver platter. Black's second strike to the side of the knee sent him falling.

Another gunshot sent shards of glass billowing up from the table. Black tried to regain his focus: where was everybody in the room? He needed to move away from the table.

Fortunately, the nobles were trying to surround him, and most therefore were on the opposite side of the table.

Seeing a man in the corner aim his rifle, Black thrust his palm forward in a scooping motion. The force made a cherry wood chair fly into the man's face, who ducked with a squawk.

Black had to decide how serious he was about teaching these arrogant pricks a lesson. If that was his intention, he'd have to get more violent. Knocking them out with phlogiston would end the fracas quickly, but that could hardly be considered a salient lesson.

Black blocked another swing with the silver platter. It buckled under the impact. That man was further inconvenienced by a kick to the shins.

Someone grabbed his neck and yanked. Black twisted to the side, suspecting a dagger was in his opponent's other hand. In fact, his comrade held a drawn sword.

There was more clattering as someone vaulted onto the table and tried to rush him.

Black sent a low wave of fire across the table's polished surface. The man awkwardly threw himself to the side, sending a blaze of dollies onto the floor. The room was already filled with gunpowder smoke, and Black suspected once the carpet caught fire he'd need to escape as fast as possible. Fortunately, the flames were contained on the table linens for now, and someone was trying to smother them out.

A blow of the face disrupted his entire sense of self, but the man made the mistake of grabbing his collar to inflict a second blow. A quick white flash laid his attacker out.

The handful of men still standing must have realised the danger lay in getting close to Black, so they'd fanned out around the room and drawn their swords and pistols.

Black dropped under the table. He was aware of pain and twinging in his extremities, and it felt like his body was ringing with the aftershocks of the blows. His power wouldn't last much longer.

A sweep of his hand sent a blast of force rippling out, pushing the men into the walls, and sending chairs after them.

Seeing a clear run to the door on the other side of the room, Black took off. Once of his knees screamed, causing him to hop. No one had struck that knee: he must have dislodged the tendon when he knelt on the ground.

Several servants were huddled in the adjourning room, unsure how to intervene. Black being unarmed confused them, which gave him time to get to the door leading to the hallway. Would he have to run back towards the dining room door to get to the staircase?

Instead, Black vaulted the railing and leapt into the marble atrium. Pushing his hands towards the rapidly approaching ground. The quick succession of phlogiston blasts almost spun him in the air, but he was buffeted against gravity just enough that he sprawled onto the ground at an almost gentle speed.

Getting his legs under him, Black scrambled on the smooth marble floor—still in a half-crouch when he burst through the front door.

He found George standing almost on the threshold, looking pained. He'd not wanted to leave the horses alone, but must have heard the disturbance and wanted to intervene.

"Avoid the windows!" Black managed, grabbing his horse's bridle and trying to slow down enough to mount. He hoped George would already understand this from hearing the rifle shots.

Dropping low against his horse's neck, Black spurred him into a gallop. They'd have to cut across the manor gardens, a feat he hoped would be as straightforward as it looked from the road.

With the ringing fading below his frantic heartbeat and gasped breaths, and ears straining for shouts or gunshots, he didn't bother to glance to see if George was following until they'd cleared the brook at the edge of the property.

34

By the time George stumbled into Smith's study, Hutton was already reclining with his shoes on the table, engrossed in a book. He didn't immediately look up when George entered.

A few steps behind came Black. His left eye socket was the colour and lustre of a plum, and the braids of his queue were working loose. Sensing Black in the room, Hutton disengaged from his reading material with a beam.

Black dropped the rocks into Hutton's lap, from what George considered a greater height than necessary.

"Ow! Careful, Joseph!" Hutton yelped, scrambling to stop the rocks from falling onto the floor.

Black spun on his heels and was almost out the door when Hutton reached out and caught his arm.

"No, Joseph—these fossils are for you." He pressed the rocks into Black's open, unresisting palm.

Black's expression was a composition of blankness. "I beg your pardon?"

"The Isla Rose," exclaimed Hutton, returning his feet to the floor. "We both agreed the Isla Rose in your cabinet was rather small and lacking in hue, remember? Even after your garnet broke in two as I transported it back from the Outer Hebrides and you insisted on taking it? Well, when I saw these fine specimens in Lord Grangemore's garden, I knew it could be years before either of us stumbled upon better replacements..."

George decided he didn't want to look at Black's face anymore.

"You raised this fuss about three rocks...none of which you actually wanted?" Black uttered every word with the tightest self-control.

"Well," Hutton said, bouncing his leg up and down, "I lied when I said they were for my collection, because I knew you're too modest about your own fossil cabinet, and retain sub-standard specimens without complaint. You deserve fossils as good as mine, Joseph. Did you look at the Lewisian gneiss on your way here? Isn't she a beauty?"

Black dropped the rocks back into his coat pocket. Wordlessly he left the room, leaving George and Hutton with the crackling fire.

"I don't know how a man of such genius can act like such a simpleton," came Black's proculopathic voice from the next room. *"I have half a mind to bash his brains out with those damn fossils. Come on George, he'll be safe with Adam."* As George rose, Hutton shot him a meek look.

"I don't know if I would have survived the encounter on Salisbury Crags without your quick thinking Dr Hutton," George told him. He took a steadying breath. "I intended to protect you with phlogiston, and my courage deserted me."

Hutton waved a hand. "You're a brave lad, George, but you wouldn't have survived a fight with six men. So it's probably best you avoided pointless heroics." He twisted into what looked like the least comfortable position for reading and picked up his book again. "Lovely seeing you, George."

· · ·

Groaning, George ambled back up the High Street and headed for home. He could smell musty sweat pooling under his clothes, and was desperate to drag a washcloth across him before he fermented.

He'd been surprised to hear how many accomplices Holm acquired—Black had filled the ride back to Edinburgh with his fuming.

"I don't understand why they'd *all* get involved," he kept repeating. "There's something else at play that we're missing."

George couldn't help him there, but promised he'd be of assistance if Black needed him. Not today, though.

Late afternoon was stretching into early evening, with the sunlight taking on a golden tint and the shadows in doorways and under awnings lengthening.

Smith wouldn't have minded if he fell asleep on the settee in Panmure House—and George was sorely tempted—but he wanted to see Phoebe, and hated to think of her getting more agitated while waiting on him.

A few years ago he would've been surprised at how much joy welled up on during into his close and heading towards the familiar turnpike entrance. Just one more doorway...

The shadows leapt to consume him, but George's fist was already hurtling through the air, connecting with Diomedes' sternum before he had to time step out of the doorway. His other elbow was driving sideways into Simon's stomach.

For a second he was disorientated, but then Ganymede made the mistake of cocking his flintlock a pace behind his friend. George kneed Diomedes and pushed past him, grabbing Ganymede's raised arm.

He was just a second too late, because Simon had regrouped and was coming towards him with a hand reaching into his waistband, as Ganymede stepped back. Which meant...

George allowed himself to fall backwards, rolling to avoid the wall. Seeing him fall, the others pressed together...

"Argh!" There was a collective scream as the boiling contents of a kettle poured from the first-floor window and drizzled across them. They were screaming more from shock than pain, but the hesitation gave George enough time to get onto his feet and land a couple more blows and a kick.

"What is the pleasure in knowing what's going to happen...when and by who?" George vented, picking up Ganymede's flintlock before his grasping fingers caught it. "It's all pre-determined. There is no narrative tension, just a dull, relentless predictability to the unfolding tragic events."

"Damn you Stephens," groaned Simon, covering his face. "Why do you have to be so *difficult*?"

"Consider it my blithe longing for the picaresque at all cost," George muttered, steadying himself against the wall and aiming the pistol. "None of us are perfect."

He wouldn't allow himself the distraction of looking up, but he imagined he'd see Phoebe leaning on the windowsill, probably biting her lip while trying to look threatening.

Most of the questions he intended to pose to Ganymede had been answered today, which made this moment rather anticlimactic. Still, there were some outstanding data points.

"Does your family rent an apartment on the High Street, Ganymede?"

"Yes, in Carrubber's Close," Ganymede said sullenly. He was probably annoyed he'd spent a day waiting for George and the extraction of revenge, only to get beaten within seconds.

"Good. I'll let you be on your way." George holstered the pistols and smiled brightly. "I'd advise you against hunts within this city walls in the future."

. . .

"I thought you'd be gone longer," Phoebe commented, reaching to take his hat.

George took in the comforting smell of drying linen, and a meat stew bubbling over the hearth. It was soothing: he felt like he'd been gone for weeks, rather than a day.

"They were muttering loud enough outside to raise me from slumber," Phoebe commented, grimacing at the dishevelled state of her husband. "I'm not sure why they thought discretion wasn't necessary. I know you said the chamberpot would be a better weapon, but honestly I've been worried sick about you all morning and had no time..."

"You did well, love." George smiled and tried to look comforting. "I'm alright. No serious injuries; I'm just dog-tired."

* * *

George told himself he'd sleep. Even though he knew it was unlikely, he hoped by keeping his eyes closed he could admonish himself into a necessary rest. Instead, he grew irate at every minuscule disturbance—creaking floorboards, laughing drunks on the street corner, two cats screaming—until he was even more alert than he'd been before retiring for the night.

Taking care not to rouse Phoebe, George slipped to his desk by the window. A crack of grey moonlight came through the shutters, alighting on the piles of letters. George took the smallest candle stub and tapped it with his index finger. A small crimson flame grew and settled into yellow.

His letter to Dr Hunter was folded on top of the pile; addressed, but not yet sealed. His eyes ached, but George squinted through the words he'd left to dry earlier that day.

He was certain. It was for the best.

So why was he still awake and fretful?

He'd chosen the route with less risk, with the greatest familiarity. Or so he'd thought.

Black and Cullen were getting old. Here was Hutton proposing that everything man knew about Earth and the universe was wrong by a factor beyond comprehension. The very ground below them was upended. There was no path without risk, disruption, and change at the end. Change was the only constant. Why did he waste so much energy on trying to avoid it, instead of doing his best to adapt to it?

George scrunched the letter into a tight ball between his palms. He felt the paper catch light, let it drop to the stone floor at his feet.

He felt Phoebe's hand on his shoulder. A single squeeze.

"I'm not sending this," George said. "The one I wrote. I'll write a new one."

He didn't want to elaborate; he didn't want her to crow or ask questions. Talking would take too much effort, too much time.

Phoebe set her larger candle on the desk next to George's stub and lit it. Then she stood back, but didn't return to bed.

He loved her. He really did.

George picked up his quill.

35

If Black and Cullen argued about the second Royal Society reading, they did it out of sight of George, who elected to sleep off his injuries at home.

It was with considerable trepidation he returned to Smith's house, unsure what state he'd find the others in, and how far back they'd set his tentative recovery.

Alarmingly, the first sight that greeted him was a twitchy Hutton, rearranging his legs in front of the fireplace as if he was worried they'd catch alight. Black and Cullen were regarding each other darkly over tea. Every clink of their saucers set Hutton's legs off.

Smith, meanwhile, spoke a lot without saying much. And no one was listening to him anyway. George slotted himself onto the sofa and picked up his own protective cup and saucer.

"...We'll need Mr Stephens' help regardless..." Smith continued, effortlessly switching from discussing George behind his back to discussing him to his face. "I don't trust any of the attendees."

George doubted his injured arm would ever be back to

243

what he considered 'normal.' It ached when he moved it too quickly, and there were certain movements he caught himself avoiding. But he supposed the aches and twitches were becoming more bearable.

"It's just that I'm unsure what good James reading the second half of his paper will accomplish," Cullen said, clearly restating a point he'd already made ad nauseam.

"It sets out the bulk of his geological argument," Black replied, annoyance at having to repeat himself creeping in. "Without those arguments, his geological theory is just another set of assertions."

"But Playfair and the others don't care about the validity of his arguments, do they? They just want to discredit and humiliate James."

"Which is why we need to get our side of the story out there!"

George wondered if it would be impolite to leave and come back in a couple of hours, in the hope this argument would have resolved itself. While this wasn't as bitter as their initial argument, a childish part of him was terrified of being subjected to another painful Black and Cullen fight.

"But today? Joe, I've been on tenterhooks waiting for the other shoe to drop with Holm. He's out there in Edinburgh somewhere—I can feel it. If he doesn't attempt to murder Dr Hutton while he sleeps, it means he's planning something with the Royal Society. It's a trap, is what I'm telling you."

"Well, what are the alternatives? If we wait until next month, or do what you're suggesting and wait for the printers to distribute his theory, I guarantee Playfair will get his rebuttal out before us. Can you not see how damaging that would be? In the court of popular opinion, Holm would win."

Most men wouldn't care about the intricacies of Hutton's theory. Nor would they understand it. But they would remember who made the most bombastic, spirited presentation, and who appeared confident enough to strike first.

"Well, we can leave George here to guard Dr Hutton while Joe reads the..."

"Incorrect." Hutton sprung to his feet with such vehemence he almost fell over the coffee table. "I'm reading the second paper, Joseph."

Cullen started to protest, but Black silenced him with a glance.

"Don't argue with me, William. It's my damn theory."

"Playfair will have had time to prepare his objections," Black noted, keeping his voice neutral. "I imagine he will try to discredit you." Left unsaid appeared to be Hutton's tendency to take criticism badly and his lacklustre oration.

"Let him!" exclaimed Hutton. "We know what he's going to argue. Don't tell me you didn't hear his snide comments. Besides, Joseph is better keeping an eye on the proceedings than trying to complete a reading."

"I'm not going to argue with you," Black said, retaining the same careful tone.

* * *

The library was packed by the time George pushed his way inside. He passed countless men conversing on the spiral staircase: some engaged in idle business chatter they'd not found the time to complete before the afternoon, but others were clearly gossiping about the upcoming speech at what was likely to happen. There was no sign of Playfair, but his presence was felt by every man on the College grounds.

Hutton sat at the central table next to Black and Smith, staring into the middle distance. He brandished his papers in front of him: by the looks of their rumpled, greasy condition, he'd fiddled with them endlessly.

"Where is he?" George asked.

Black moved his chin to the right. Sure enough, Playfair was sitting near the front, surrounded by smug men. That was a little oasis of silence in the chattering noise, but George could see how much tension emanated from a single man.

"Don't say anything—I want to avoid stressing Dr Hutton out."

"He's more stressed than I've seen him before." This included the time George watched Hutton being kidnapped at gunpoint.

"It's been thirty minutes since he last threw up. I think he's stabilising."

"I'll get behind Playfair, keeping him in my sight." The Royal Society secretary peered around the room, and George suspected that meant they were minutes away from calling the meeting to order.

"Keep your eyes peeled, George. Holm might have more sympathisers in the room." Black took a step away from Hutton, who licked his lips like an agitated cat.

Just looking at the state of Hutton was enough to drive George into anxiety, so he had to look away. Would Hutton faint? Piss his breeches? Clam up completely? All humiliating options seemed plausible.

"I ask you to find your seats, Gentlemen..."

George pushed towards the edge of the library, leaning against the wall. He had a line of sight to Playfair—who seemed to be showing off the lack of notes on his person—but could see most of the audience too.

He also kept his eye out for the diminutive, hunched frame of Grenville, but saw nothing. Would the natural history professor really miss an opportunity to gloat over his opponent? He'd wracked his brains and couldn't recall if Grenville showed at the March Royal Society meeting or not.

Holm was a cipher. Black and Cullen spoke knowledgeably about him, but they couldn't claim to know the man. The way Cullen spoke, he'd not had more than one or two encounters with him, what, twenty years ago? They treated him like an unchangeable evil, and George had seen for himself there was evil there, but how Holm thought and what he was capable of could be very different from when he was George's age.

Was it carelessness on Holm's part that he was seen in public with Playfair? Or was that a very calculated distraction?

Hutton rose. One hand clamped on the chair back, the whites of his knuckles visible to George. He half-dropped his papers onto the table, then shuffled them about with one hand.

"Err, good evening Royal Society...um, honoured Royal Society members..." Hutton spoke to his notes, but his voice was naturally loud enough to be heard. "I'm honoured to... wait, where is it...um, present the second, second half of my paper..."

Playfair folded his arms. A more amateur disrupter would have jeered "get on with it," but Playfair wouldn't waste his cruel barbs so early in the proceedings.

Stammering, Hutton found his way into the meat of his paper. George tuned the words out. He didn't need to understand, and it would take his whole concentration to follow whatever points Hutton was trying to make.

Black and Cullen described Holm as a man who got his hands dirty, but all George had seen of him was a man who used proxies: Playfair, his own wife, Lord Grangemore.

Black had identified most of the men he confronted at Grangemore, and none of them would dare show their face today. But why would Holm use an obvious proxy like that?

What if the man didn't know he was a proxy for Holm? Or didn't know all of what was Holm intended? Black would be able to spot something amiss—but his attention was focussed on Hutton. Smith was observing the audience while Black kept all attention on Hutton. Indeed, Hutton was glancing at Black every few seconds, causing him to lose his place in the speech. Cullen would have an eye out too, but there were more people here than they'd predicted.

Starting at the far left corner, George swept the room, scrutinising every audience member in turn. Most looked bored or impatient. It was unlikely they understood Hutton's argument about latent heat and chemical reactions.

Holm wouldn't have asked a man to kill Hutton—everybody in the room was known to each other, and these weren't hired assassins. It could be like Brunonians' plan to detonate a concealed bomb in the faculty senate, where the proxy wouldn't know what they were triggering by their actions. It could be something innocuous, like shoving Hutton or slipping something into his pocket.

Did anyone in this room look nervous? No, that was a stupid exercise. The few supporters of Hutton were nervous. Rather, was there anyone who looked more nervous than would be expected?

Playfair cleared his throat. It was done in an innocuous-enough manner, no particular malice or emphasis within the sound, but a third of the room snapped their heads in his direction, and Hutton trailed off mid-word. Playfair acted as if he'd done nothing untoward, and refolded his arms. Smith scowled at him.

Playfair was an obvious distraction. Every movement of his face remained under scrutiny.

Playfair was sitting to the left of George, so he turned his attention to the far right of the room and the clump of men closest to Hutton.

Who—or what—was out of place?

The most senior Royal Society members were seated nearest the main table. Their wealthy guests also took prime locations in the room. It was the gossip chasers and students who had to stand or take seats at the back.

Except there at the end of the second row sat a man who clearly wasn't a wealthy Royal Society patron. He was a recent physician graduate—George might remember his name if he put the time to thinking about it—who came to the occasional Society meeting that looked interesting and when the weather was nice.

He had his hands wedged between his thighs, was glancing around the room.

He's barely looking at Hutton or Playfair.

Although he was still tripping over words, Hutton made a few defiant glances at his audience, particularly in the direction of Playfair. Black seemed a little more relaxed, and there might even have been a slight smile on his face. While none of them knew what Playfair would say during the discussion period—and it was likely an aggressive attack—Hutton was more used to debating ideas back and forth than delivering speeches, so he'd probably put in a stronger performance.

George was convinced by now. The nervous gentleman was up to something, and he was closed enough to Hutton to be a threat. Should George warn Black? He'd cross the room as soon as Hutton finished his speech, and judging by the relief dripping off him, it was likely to happen within minutes.

Hutton rushed out his conclusion, thank yous, and sat down so quickly the less-attentive audience members took a second to realise the paper was at its end. The applause was sparing, though even Playfair performed along, but Hutton's friends were grimacing to each other and adjusting in their seats.

As soon as the applause died, George was in position to strike.

"I must say, sir," George began loudly, leaning against the

chair back. "That is a very interesting position to take on the matter. I wonder what could have prompted such a choice?"

There was an audible gasp from someone in the front row. The recent graduate—probably called Kenneth—bristled.

"What did you say?"

"That I consider your position a refreshingly bold one and have great admiration for you expressing it."

A few men swivelled in their seats to get a better look.

"I don't care for your insinuations," Kenneth muttered, aware how many eyes were now on him.

Kenneth was overreacting because of his nerves. He should have ignored George's boorishness, but instead he was engaging. George couldn't see what Smith and Black were doing.

"Do you wish to expound further on your remarks?" George continued. "I would hate to think I was misunderstanding you."

Kenneth swallowed. His eyes appeared to bulge. He hadn't planned for anyone to scrutinise him this closely, and he was deciding under pressure about how to deal with this threat.

"Don't let him touch you, George!"

George jumped at the loud voice in his head. It took him a second to recognise the voice as Cullen's.

"Joe thinks he's holding a poisoned sigil," Cullen added. Sure enough, there was something in Kenneth's fist, which he'd managed to hide by stuffing his hands under his legs.

"Have I misunderstood you?" George asked again, a little more quietly.

Kenneth gulped, blinked, and huffed.

"I don't understand what this is about," he finally muttered. "Please leave me alone."

"I'd like to thank Dr Hutton and the audience for this lively discussion," the secretary interrupted, banging on the podium. "Please join me in thanking Dr Hutton for his fine paper."

George looked up, trying not to lose Kenneth without staring him down. It was then he realised: Black and Smith were already halfway out of the room with Hutton. The three men disappeared down the stairs before anyone had a chance to stop them.

Given Hutton's trembling disposition, no one seemed surprised he'd leave the meeting at the earliest moment. So the guests milled around in an amiable mood to debate the merits of Hutton's theory themselves.

Cullen extracted George from the throng and led him by the elbow to one side. To onlookers, it might appear he was doing so for the purpose of admonishment.

"Good work, lad." Cullen glanced at the door, but it didn't seem anyone was sneaking after Black and the others. Kenneth remained in his chair, not important enough for anyone to check on after his confrontation with George. "Your sharp mind saves the day again."

George was too surprised and pleased to respond. His mind felt like uncombed wool at the best of times.

"It's not the end of it, obviously," Cullen continued. "But getting James' paper read and shared undermines Holm." He fiddled with his coat buttons. "Best be circulating the room. I'll check no one tries to sneak after James or Adam."

By the time he glanced back, Kenneth had wandered off.

George tried to locate him, his solitary vigil was noticed.

"Are you alright, George?"

Playfair.

What was that man still doing here?

George blinked in momentary confusion: unsure whether to ignore his foe and locate Kenneth, or unleash his pent-up emotions on an obvious target. It was dawning on him how close Hutton had come to grievous injury at the hand of a dark chymist.

"Don't ignore me, George." Playfair's voice sharpened, cutting through George's distraction. Sighing, he turned and glared.

"I'm tired of your boorish manners, sir. You are the kind who confuses rudeness for wit."

Playfair looked around in exasperation, resting one hand on the chair back, and the other on his hip.

"I didn't say a word to Dr Hutton, as you well know. Given the state of him I thought it a mercy."

"Well," snarled George, "it might be better than poisoning the eminent philosopher, but that's not a great compliment."

Playfair physically staggered. "I beg your pardon? What deranged nonsense is this?"

"Holm's friend was going to use a dark chymistry sigil on Dr Hutton. To what exact purpose I cannot fathom, but it wouldn't cure his stomach aches or gout, I'm sure of it."

He assumed Playfair better acquainted with the dark chymists and their weaponry than himself.

"That's not Reverend Holm's intention at all. Anyone with intact wits can see that." Playfair raised his voice.

"The Reverend Holm arranged for Hutton to be kidnapped, and threatened his friends. Murder sounds very much within that devil's intentions."

"That's not how it was at all..." Playfair said, but his voice was almost a whisper.

It's funny how we can deceive ourselves better than we can deceive others, George thought. He concentrated on his breathing for a moment. Playfair thought him an out-of-control madman; if he wanted to be taken seriously, he had to prove his sanity.

"I acted in such a belligerent manner to create a distraction and protect Dr Hutton," he said in as close to a conversational tone as he could muster. "Either you knew Kenneth was an associate of Holm or you didn't...but it isn't of great concern to me now."

Playfair looked stricken.

"I only saw them talking once, and it was such a brief exchange I thought they might not be acquainted at all. Before we get too distracted, I actually wanted to ask Dr Hutton more about the granite rock formations."

"I doubt he'll want to speak with you," George sniffed. "This business has been deeply distressing for him. You've caused him enough anguish."

"Oh come on, George!" Playfair exclaimed. Then he sighed. "Fine, I want to talk with him about the granite veins because if he's describing them correctly then it strengthens his argument considerably. And before you start up again, can I try to assure you my intentions are not as scurrilous and murderous as you imagine? Holm isn't paying me; he hasn't locked up my wife or maimed my children; in fact, the last time I spoke to him was March."

"You've not seen him since March?" George didn't want to be distracted, but his curiosity was too great to ignore everything Playfair was trying to tell him.

"No!" Playfair wiped his forehead. "I'm more convinced than ever that there's merit in Hutton's theory, but I need more proof than his mess of a paper. If he can't explain the theory to me in person, maybe Dr Black can try instead?"

"You'll not do any more work for Holm?" George couldn't imagine Hutton letting Playfair into his home for a cosy afternoon discussing rocks, not while Holm menaced him, but he hadn't the energy for the kind of protracted argument Playfair excelled at. He was only becoming aware of how tired he felt.

"If the Reverend Holm approaches me again, you'll be the first to know," Playfair insisted.

"Well, tell Dr Cullen or Black yourself. I'll shortly be in London."

"To study with Dr Hunter? Good luck with that." Playfair looked over his shoulder.

"Thanks, I won't detain you any longer." George bowed and hurried away before Playfair could respond.

Maybe it was a mistake trusting Playfair, but it turned out he wasn't as big a pawn in Holm's game as they'd assumed. Let Black and the others deal with him: George was done for the evening.

36

Once Hutton and Smith were out of the building, Black slipped into the shadows and took off in the opposite direction. He rushed uphill in as fast a walk as possible, hoping he wouldn't draw attention to himself. He'd have to hope Adam could protect Hutton if they were intercepted, but he suspected there wouldn't be an attack tonight.

How could they have missed what Holm was really up to? The signs were there all along?

Black second-guessed where he was going with every close he passed. The Bennetts had rented rooms in Carrubber's Close, had they not? That *was* what George told him.

So why was he sure he was getting the Bennett's address muddled with someone else?

He should have brought George with him, but his priority was getting Hutton away from the rest of the Royal Society.

Slowing his walk, Black crept along the side of the Close walls, craning at the apartment windows above. A few windows had the warm glow of oil lamps in the windows, but most were shuttered, with barely discernible cracks of light coming through. He paused, closing his eyes to concentrate on the landscape of noises around him. There was the usual babble of noise on the edge of hearing: dogs whining, babies squawking, tipsy laughter. No recognisable sounds.

Click.

Oh great, thought Black as he slowly raised his hands. Not this again.

"That's right, Joseph. Please refrain from doing anything foolish...."

"...Such as moving."

Liam Grangemore stepped from the shadows, a flintlock pointed at Black's chest. The noise of the safety catch Black heard had come from behind him, putting him in the unenviable position of being aimed at my two angry nobles.

In the dim light reflected from the lands, Sir Liam's face was swollen and gleaming like an apple. One eye was still swollen shut.

"Let's step someplace more private." The voice behind him continued. It sounded like Viscount Matbury, though his voice rasped painfully. Striking a man in the throat with a silver platter would do that.

"I'm here to save your lives," Black said as quickly but as firmly as he could. The nobles were motioning him further back into the close, away from the turnpike door. Too deep into the close and he wouldn't even be able to see when someone entered the building.

"Oh, I think we're going to enjoy ourselves tonight, Joseph," chuckled the Viscount. Malice seeped off every syllable.

"Malcolm Holm has betrayed you all." Black lowered his voice, each word uttered with forceful calmness. "If any of your friends are still in the Bennett's room when your lackey returns from the Royal Society gathering, they will be dead men."

He could gamble his luck and try to knock Grangemore

and Matbury out before they had a chance to shoot him. But it was better they remained conscious. If he failed to halt what was set to transpire, and the only witnesses were unconscious...well, they might reach an erroneous conclusion concerning his attempted intervention.

"On the contrary," said Grangemore, forcing Black down the close with a threatening wave of his pistol. "Reverend Holm needs our support at next week's Town Council meeting, when we will sort out the election business and present a number of his petitions reining the university back under our control."

"No," Black said. "He doesn't need your support. Not after tonight's grisly demonstration, with you as its unwitting sacrifice. After that, he'll be able to terrify the Town Council and the rest of Edinburgh into doing what he wants."

The trouble with these nobles was they accepted Holm as part of their clique, but never afford him equal respect. Holm was their attack dog; a pawn that they moved to further their own ends. He didn't originate from noble stock, nor did he seem to crave their wealth and status. The disparity meant they never got a handle on what the man *really* wanted.

Despite that, Holm had played the dark chymist's games with the most enthusiasm.

Strike without trace. Leave inexplicable carnage in their wake.

Without dark chymistry and its sigils, how could Holm achieve that terror?

For someone who claimed to hate the corruption of modern society, he was surprisingly adaptable to new ways...

He continued. "The only reason Holm has spared you til now is because he needed a stooge to attack Dr Hutton at the Royal Society tonight, and it's easiest for him to get rid of you all at once."

"Well, of course you'd say this, Joseph. You have an understandable, pressing motivation to tell scary lies." He could hear the sneer in Matbury's voice. "You have good reason to be scared. On the other hand, we have good reason not to fear Malcolm Holm."

It was possible Matbury and Grangemore hadn't decided what they wanted to do with Black. Shooting the most eminent chemist in Britain was a drastic measure, and they perhaps were hesitating about whether to kill him quickly—the safest option—or extract the violent revenge they craved first.

"Dr James Graham was recently in town, demonstrating both the wonders of earth-bathing...and of electricity." Grangemore should be aware of this: his son left Graham's pamphlets in his lodgings. "Holm encountered him while visiting John Brown in the Tolbooth, and the ensuing conversation gave him an idea about how to deal with you."

No longer focussing on the men, Black scanned the tenement buildings again. Talking had kicked his mind back into action, and now it was obvious how he'd identify the building in question.

"So now there's copper wire running into your window from the neighbouring apartment," Black said. "Which happens to belong to Professor Grenville. Or did you not notice that?"

"As if we're falling for your distractions, Dr Black," Grangemore scoffed. "Do you think we're so stupid we'd not take care of Holm once we elected our man to the Town Council?"

"Holm wants power," Black said, quietly. "He just doesn't want to share it with you."

There was no use saying more. These men weren't interested in listening, and Black had heard enough to know nothing could compel them to believe him right now. Distracting Black and manipulating the Town Council vote was where the interests of the nobles and Holm diverged. The nobles thought they held the upper hand; they planned to kill Holm now his purpose was almost served, which Holm may nor may not already have deduced.

* * *

Black took a steading breath. At least his conscience was clean.

Holm's set-up was obvious. As soon as the Society aggravator entered the apartment, Holm would discharge his electrical apparatus from the adjoining rooms. The copper wires running out the window would be attached to objects inside the Bennett's quarters—the table or carpets. Black didn't know how much electricity would be needed to cause fatal electrocution...but thanks to Graham, Holm certainly would.

A flitter in the close at the very edge of his peripheral vision caught his attention. It was hard to make sense of the disturbance, but someone probably passed under a lamplight into the Bennett's turnpike. They certainly weren't approaching him. Holm would be readying himself to attack. Could Black afford to wait for the screaming?

Matbury still hung behind Black, out of his line of vision. Reputedly, the man had duelled in his youth, and he was certainly eager to fire a shot. His warnings weren't getting through: Black estimated he had a few minutes before the men ran out of patience and shot him anyway.

Think.

His options: distraction, attack from a surprise direction, or gamble he could move faster than them both.

Think.

Was there *anything* he could use as an improvised weapon?

Ah...

Black's fingers nudged into his coat pocket, grasping the tip of his handkerchief between thumb and forefinger. He tugged it loose under the concealment of his long coat sleeves, hoping no coins would fall out, scrunching it into his fist as he went.

He wasn't sure how well this would work. But as he clenched the wad of cotton in his fist, hoping his sweaty palms wouldn't dampen the cloth too much, he expelled a slow stream of phlogiston. The natural dispensation of phlogiston involved a flick of muscles in the fingers or wrist to ignite the flammable plasma, but this method allowed unignited phlogiston to seep into the surroundings, with perhaps a second of grace before it caught fire of its own accord...

Black flicked his balled-up handkerchief at Grangemore senior just as that occurred. The concentrated phlogiston hadn't time to diffuse into the air, so it consumed the cloth almost-white fire. Even as he flicked, Black was stepping backwards and turning towards Matbury.

A blast of immobilising aether sent Matbury crashing to the ground before he could discharge his flintlock. Grangemore exclaimed and flinched, distracted for a crucial second by the fire coming towards him. As predicted, he shot towards the projectile rather than his captive, whose head snapped round and focussed on him a second later.

There was barely a heartbeat between Black's three strikes. He stood in the now-silent close, breathing in the acrid scent of gunpowder.

He picked up the pistols, lest they reappear at his back when the men regained consciousness. It would take a minute to recalibrate: Black felt like he was the one struck, since he was missing half his vital energy from discharging phlogiston and aether in such quick fire strikes. Holding on to the wall, he staggered back towards the Bennett's building.

He was reaching for the turnpike door leading to Grenville's apartment when the cries started. A smell of ozone washed over him.

He could see the thick twisted knot of copper wires hung below the adjacent window, leading into a neighbouring, darkened room. They trembled. Black thought he could hear a buzz on the edge of hearing.

Ducking against the wall for cover, Black ran towards the adjacent turnpike. He wouldn't be able to break the twisted knot of copper wires from below, and any attempt to dislodge them put himself at risk of fatal electrocution. He had to kill Holm and disable his contraption.

He didn't dare give himself enough time to think. His opponent would seize every hesitation and use it against him. Black knew he risked a bullet or blade in the chest as soon as he entered the room, but he couldn't bring himself to walk away from the carnage and leave the nobles to a painful death. He thought he would still hear animal screams, so maybe he still had a chance.

He fumbled up the turnpike, aware each breath and footfall produced an ungainly amount of noise. If the door was locked or even jammed, he'd not have the strength to force it open. But it yielded to the lightest touch, almost pitching him over, as if the building itself wanted Black to step inside.

He took in the furniture shoved against the far wall, a couple of candle stubs on the sideboard almost extinguished. In the corner stood the electrical apparatus, a mess of wires and cylinders. The smell of ozone was thick, with a hint of ashy smoke and hot metal.

He didn't know what to make of this. The central contraption looked like a modified spinning apparatus: a man-sized wooden wheel with a foot pedal, linked to a row of Leyden jars and metal cylinders a metre long. The wooden wheel was spinning furiously, and the jars were flickering and crackling with light.

Grabbing a wooden chair, Black thrust it leg-first into the spinning wheel, leaping back as he did so. He felt a snap of static discharge through his body, but aside from the strange feeling of a crackling rush through his body, nothing else happened. The spinning wheel splintered and the glow in the jars flickered off, plunging the room into desolate darkness.

It was too dark to take in every detail, but Black looked around the room as best he could for signs of a smudged sigil. Could Holm have leapt out the window? Climbed up the chimney? The Malcolm Holm in his memory was a lean youth, quick and silent on his feet. It took a lot for Black to remember that Holm was about as old as him now.

But Holm wasn't here. And despite the toll of the years, part of Black's reckless charge into the room was motivated by the fact he hadn't expected him to be.

From the window, Black watched as a man staggered into the close from Bennett's apartment. "Murder!" he gasped, trying to raise his hoarse voice loud enough for other close residents to hear and care about. "Murder!"

37

Sunlight was lowering down the walls of the Crags. Behind them, Edinburgh murmured to life.

"How are you feeling, Dr Hutton?" Black asked.

Hutton gave a thin smile. He looked like he hadn't slept a wink last night. "Have been better, Joseph. Glad I won't have to repeat that again anytime soon."

"I received a reply from the young Earl of Hopetoun," Black said, scanning the trail. "He says he'd love to host you at his hunting lodge near Blair Atholl. He recalls the conversations you had with his father about the pink granite and metasentiment veins in Glen Tilt, so I imagine he'll want to show you in person."

"Excellent," declared Hutton. "That's what we need, Joseph. It's easy to sit in that stuffy library and argue over theories and phrasing, but let's see Playfair try to argue with an outcrop of granite!"

"I suspect Playfair won't offer much resistance," Black said, an amused expression on his face. "He departed from the Royal Society last night in a rather thoughtful mood."

Black had caught George up on events following the

meeting on their way to the Crags. George thought the chemistry professor remarkably bright, given the ghastly circumstances. The rumours about who was killed and who had survived Holm's attack were still shifting. Neither Black nor Cullen were involved in tending to the survivors.

There was no sign of Professor Grenville. He'd not attended the Royal Society Meeting, nor could anyone recall seeing him after George followed him down the Canongate. Cullen promised to keep an eye on the Natural History classroom, but reported the miror shards lay unswept on the floor.

"While it's not improbable that Holm silenced Grenville, it's not improbable either that he slipped away from Edinburgh of his own accord," Black noted. "Grenville doesn't have family in Edinburgh; he's been widowed some time."

George stepped aside to allow Hutton to approach an otherwise unremarkable stone wedged between a man-sized boulder and the Crags cliff. Shaking the scrub bush aside, Hutton rocked the small stone into the clearing. Underneath it lay a tightly wrapped bundle of leather.

It took several minutes for Hutton to unwrap a comic number of leather layers, revealing a handful of papers about a fifth the size of the initial bundle.

"Good, looks like they're still dry." Hutton's tight scratchy handwriting covered the papers, smudged against what appeared to be diagrams of rock formations. "This one is from the Southern Pentlands," Hutton said, seeing him stare.

Black looked amused. "I wondered where you'd hid the papers, and whether they'd be in a location I could guess. I suppose I might have eventually found your papers hidden under that stone...albeit after a couple years."

"Clever, wasn't it?" Hutton beamed. "I suppose I should make some copies now. Not that I think anybody will want to claim credit..."

An out-of-place shadow at the edge of his vision caught

George's eye, and he was filled with a sudden sense of wrongness.

"Joseph!" George pushed Black to the side, knowing he was only reacting, not understanding. As he moved, he felt something smack his biceps, filling his mind with pain. He and Black stumbled against the cliffs, the thrown knife clattering at their feet.

"Bright and alert, George, I see," Holm commented, not moving from where he stood. A second knife was already in his hand. Under his robes poked a pistol barrel aimed at Hutton.

Black turned around and tried to strike at Holm, but he'd fallen awkwardly against the rock face. His leg gave out as he tried to rise.

George was too far away to charge Holm. Instead, he forced himself under Black's arm and helped his former professor steady himself against the cliff face. Black's dark eyes were nothing more than pinpricks.

The second George focussed on Black, he detected another flash of movement from Holm. This time, Black grabbed George's neck and forced him down. The knife ricocheted off the cliff and cut into George's shoulder. A gasp from Black told George his arm was sliced.

Holm either had a third knife to hand, or he was about to shoot. Hutton was frozen in shock, an easy target.

George wasn't going to wait for Black.

Clenching his shoulder muscles, George thrust out his hand. He'd felt the phlogiston stir within him a second before Holm's knife grazed him.

He felt the warmth of the phlogiston and aether rush out of his heart and down his arm. It was like a second sunrise in their cove. Holm didn't have time to react: the yellow-white light struck him squarely in the chest. He folded like a discarded cloak.

The sight of their attacker falling snapped Hutton back. He jogged over to the prone figure and crouched beside him.

Black and George cautiously approached, Black massaging his wrist and examining the daggers.

"Did the knives catch you, George? We'll need to get the wounds washed as soon as we get home." Black didn't even look at the body of Holm.

George didn't know how he was supposed to feel. He felt triumphant, which was surely the wrong emotion to feel after killing a man. When he was stationed in New York, he barely felt anything after the battles—he'd looked into the eyes of men and knew they intended to kill him, unless he pulled the trigger first. That moment with Holm hadn't happened, but he was sure that's what he intended.

Black walked with a slight limp, but was moving fast towards the main path that circled the Crags. George wondered if Black was angry at him for killing Holm when it was something Black intended to do. His years at Edinburgh told him he shouldn't ask Black right now.

They'd almost rounded the corner when Black stopped. George nearly stepped on his heels, and realised they were standing in front of Kitty Holm, who was blocking their way on the path.

"Mrs Holm..." Black began. He sounded like he was going to order her to stand aside.

But George saw by the strangeness of her expression she already knew that if Black, George and Hutton were leaving the cove, it meant her husband wouldn't.

Too late, George saw a flash of metal shoot from Kitty Holm's sleeve towards Black. He hadn't the time to cry out before Black was jerking his right side in on itself.

Kitty was already running away. George had seconds before the billowing cloak disappeared around the curve of the

Crags. He held out his hand, feeling the phlogiston rise from his chest....

...Then he swore and flicked his hand towards the cliff face. The edge of Kitty's cloak curled around the corner and was gone. George couldn't bring himself to strike a fleeing woman.

He turned to Black, who was still standing, but clutching his side with a queasy look on his face. Hutton was already at his friend's side, peeling away Black's hand. George caught only a glimpse of the crimson palm.

"...I don't think it's a mortal injury," Black said, his eyes fixed on the middle distance. Hutton held onto his shoulder, and George saw his former professor sway. "Mrs Holm attempted to stab and run simultaneously."

George tugged his cravat loose and forced the bundle into Black's side, hoping to stem whatever bloody mess was forming.

"Let's get you down the hill, Joseph," Hutton coaxed. "You still need medical attention."

Black grumbled, but began to tramp forwards.

"George, my boy, run ahead and see if you can find a sedan chair—we'll manage from here."

George wished Hutton wasn't correct. He met Black's eyes and saw the spark of agreement.

"She didn't cut too deep, George," Black insisted, though his voice sounded fainter than it had a moment ago. "Go."

Pulling his coat tight, George ran.

EPILOGUE

When George entered Black's study, he found his former chemistry professor seated, stripped to the waist, with Cullen hovering about him. A silvery metal wire ran down the outside of Black's right arm to his knuckles, secured with leather straps at his elbow and wrist. Another wire looped around his shoulder, with leather straps and cloth holding the wires in place as they spread out from his sternum.

"How does it feel now?" Cullen asked, looking up from the straps he was fiddling with.

Black slowly flexed his arm, then turned his hand over.

"It moves well, William," he admitted. Approaching, George saw the forearm wire was actually a fine metal chain that twisted from Black's elbow to the pulse point on his wrist.

"You want to test it, Joe?" Cullen stepped back, to let Black rise to his feet.

As Black headed over to the open bay window, George saw the bandages on Black's ribs from where Kitty Holm stabbed him were still in place, though Black moved without any impediment. Black's torso was covered in ancient scars and burns; many no more than pink or yellow lines, but some appeared severe enough to alter the contours of his body.

The men had made discrete enquiries for weeks, but it appeared the widow of Malcolm Holm hadn't returned to her sister's apartment, and no one could confirm her whereabouts. She could hide for a short time in Edinburgh, but as soon as she left the city, she'd vanish.

Once in front of the window, Black raised his hand and pointed it out into his rear yard.

There was a faint zip noise as a burst of red light shot down the wire. It struck the building behind Black's, boring a hole into its side with a miniature explosion of brick dust.

"Heavens..." George whispered.

While George stood stunned, Black was already shrugging on his white undershirt, with Cullen rushing to assist.

"You felt nothing, Joe? The platina didn't overheat?"

"No, the metal doesn't even feel warm," Black said, scratching his cuff over the thin gauntlet encasing his right hand. "It'll take some time to calibrate the power, though."

"Her Highness will crow for months once she hears about this," Cullen murmured. Then he looked up and laughed. "You too, Dr Stephens—you share some of the credit."

"Only by my own folly," George replied, looking at Black to gauge his reaction.

Black moved on to donning his waistcoat. "Accidents and follies drive progress, George."

"You and Mrs Stephens are ready to depart?" Now Black was dressed, Cullen could turn his attention to George.

"Yes," George said. "The London coach departs upon the hour from the Pleasance."

"Goodness, not long at all," Cullen bustled over from Black to appraise George. "It's a shame you didn't have time to try one of these on for yourself."

"I imagine it will be awhile before these supports are

brought to a tolerable degree of perfection," Black commented, a faint hint of amusement playing about him. "You can try them out when you next visit us."

There would be a next time, George reminded himself. There had to be.

"You'll enjoy Hunter's anatomical courses immensely," Cullen insisted, pressing his hands around George's. "Trust me, your education will progress in leaps and bounds. Any practice in Britain will be an option for you with that kind of training."

"I'm sure of it," agreed George, finally feeling as confident about his prospects as he sounded.

"Mrs Stephens will be anxious if you delay further," Black remarked. "You best reunite with her. I'm so glad you were able to call upon us before you departed. Dr Hutton sends his regards for your fruitful course of study."

Hutton's most recent letter arrived a few days ago, stating he'd arrived at his destination with Playfair and they'd embark on a geological as soon as the rain abated. Their exact location in the Scottish Highlands was not disclosed—a sensible precaution given the inflamed passions still burning and the unaccounted for presence of Kitty Holm—though George suspected the countryside Hopetoun estates would be an obvious starting point. The pair weren't expected to return until the end of summer.

"Send a letter once you've arrived in London, if not sooner," Cullen said. "Pass on my kindest wishes to Dr Hunter."

"Of course..." George felt his throat catch. "Goodbye for now, then."

"Until the next time, Dr Stephens," Black agreed, with his usual smile.

* * *

Once seated in the stagecoach, Phoebe's hand wound its way into George's.

George didn't know what to say, so he squeezed his wife's hand back as the stagecoach jolted into motion. He wanted to look out the window, to take in every last moment of Edinburgh rolling by. Though he told himself it wouldn't be forever, there was a finality to today; his life cleaved at the end of his studies.

Phoebe leaned his head against his shoulder, and together they watched Edinburgh recede to a speck on the horizon.

* * *

Another voice came into Black's head, a proculopathic greeting from afar. He rose his hand to quiet Cullen.

"We have a visitor," he said. Cullen nodded and paused his adjustment of the leather straps. A second later, footfalls came within earshot and Black's door was tapped upon.

"Thomas?" Cullen asked, as a familiar shaggy head came into view. "I didn't realise you were visiting us from Dublin."

"Eh, not quite," Thomas admitted. "Good to see ye, doctors, it's a long tale." He did not appear surprised at the mechanical contraption on Black's arm.

Black motioned him all the way into the room.

"If you sent a letter ahead of your arrival, I must apologise, because it hasn't reached us yet."

Thomas shook his head. "I'm afraid I didn't have time to write, and I was worried about any message falling into the wrong hands."

"Is something up with Dr Brown?"

"Nay," Thomas protested. "He's much the same since I started observing him."

Cullen folded his arms. Both he and Black could—in their

own separate ways—detect the contours of what Thomas' new problem might be, and neither liked what was forming.

Thomas bowed his head, gathering his thoughts before he was forced to lay them out.

"It's something my wife uncovered, y'see."

"The incomparable Mrs Fulhame herself?" Black asked, a smile lightening his face. "I always enjoy her insights."

"Well, we were experimenting with phlogiston, ye see, and then Elizabeth went to check one of her books and...well..." He gestured to Black's arm brace. "Yer going to need every advantage that affords ye, Dr Black..."

HISTORICAL NOTE

Some of this actually happened. Unfortunately.

On the 7th March 1785, Joseph Black surprised the Edinburgh scientific community by presenting the first half of a geological paper to the Royal Society on behalf of James Hutton. We don't know why Hutton did not present the paper himself: could it have been nerves? An unexpected illness? The historical record is silent. Fortunately, as you now know, by the time of the next meeting in April Hutton was able to present the concluding half of his paper. That was my jumping-off point into the life of James Hutton and the accompanying What Ifs?

The Man Who Found Time by Jack Repcheck is a phenomenal biography of Hutton and distillation of the Enlightenment forces that shaped him. A more concise, pop science, treatment of Hutton's theories can be found in *A Short History of Nearly Everything* by Bill Bryson. The chapter on Hutton I consider one of the funniest pieces of science writing I've come across, and it probably sparked my interest in the eccentric geologist when I first read it in my teens. As a novelist, I think about this line from Bryson a lot: "Encouraged by his friends to expand his theory, in the touching hope that he might somehow stumble onto clarity in a more expansive format, Hutton spent the next ten years preparing his magnum opus." Isn't that what all authors hope for?

The other real historical figure who inserts himself into the story is Dr James Graham: arguably, the world's first sex therapist. *Doctor of Love: James Graham and His Celestial Bed* by Lydia Syson recounts his trans-Atlantic medical career and subsequent evolution into celebrity and quack theories. Electrical demonstrations were a popular form of entertainment at the time. He's a man very much of the Georgian era.

Panmure House and St Cecilia's Hall are still in operation today, in much the same capacities they occupied in the eighteenth century. While Adam's Smith home is not preserved as a historical site, I was fortunate to look inside during an annual Edinburgh Open Doors Day. Hutton is memorialised by 'Hutton's Section' at the edge of Salisbury Crags where he studied rock formations, and a memorial garden in Pleasance where his house once stood.

If you head out of Edinburgh and past Haddington one weekend (like I did) you won't find "Grangemore estate"...but you might come across Amsfield Walled Garden, once the largest walled garden in Georgian century Britain, now maintained by volunteers. The accompanying Amsfield House was demolished in 1928 and is now the site of a golf course.

Eat the rich, indeed.

AFTERWORD

Thank you so much for reading *The Chronicles of Earth*. With so many awesome books out there, I'm grateful you chose to pick up mine.

If you enjoyed reading this story, please consider leaving a review on Amazon or Goodreads, even if it's just a sentence to say you liked it. Indie authors like myself depend on your honest reviews to help us find our audience.

The George and the professors will return in book four, *A Codex of Metal*.

The story of how Drs Black and Cullen rid Edinburgh of the dark chymists can be found in my standalone novel *Dark City Rising*.

Acknowledgments

My first thanks goes to you, the reader. Thank you for buying, borrowing, reading, reviewing or sharing *The Edinburgh Doctrines* series with the wider world. An author is nothing without readers, and I'm grateful to have you.

Early chapters of this novel were shared on Critique Circle: thank you to everyone who reviewed and took the time to offer their valuable insight.

As with previous books, the hosts and fellow participants of Shut Up and Write! and Writers HQ, for giving me a space for writing/editing sprints.

Thanks to the staff at the National Library of Scotland, whose collections I drew upon regularly when researching these novels, and whose materials continue to shape more books to come.

Lastly, a final thank you to my family, for reading my books (you aren't obligated to!) and saying nice things about them afterwards.

ABOUT THE AUTHOR

CL Jarvis holds a PhD in chemistry and worked as a science journalist, healthcare copywriter, and medical writer before sitting down to write her first novel. She's held together by cat hair and double espressos, and lives in Philadelphia, USA.

You can learn more about her at: www.clairejarvis.com.

facebook.com/cljarvisauthor

instagram.com/cljarvisauthor